About the Author

Ryan Lailvaux was born in South Africa and lived across the world before settling in the United Kingdom. He grew up with a love for reading, especially anything that involved dinosaurs or monsters. After achieving a first-class honours bachelor's degree and a master's degree, he pursued a career in information technology. From short stories to screenplays, travel blogs to political articles, he would still find time to write. Now he works in technology by day, writing novels by night. In his spare time, Ryan enjoys playing video games, exploring new countries, improving his chess rating, getting lost in Sci-Fi films and is a proud Leeds United fan.

Ghosts of the Danube is his second novel.

GHOSTS OF THE DANUBE

RYAN LAILVAUX

For Dad, my hero

Acknowledgements

I wouldn't have been able to finish the novel if it wasn't for the belief my friends had in me. In particular, I would like to thank Debra Gray, Nathan Kamphuis and Jennifer Blondo for being beta readers and helping me sharpen the writing and the message.

Also, I would like to thank my family for the support they have shown me through the years. My brother for designing the cover and always being available to listen to my strange ideas. My sister for making me believe in myself when doubt crept in. My Mom for being our rock and for her unconditional love. And my Dad, who instilled in me the courage to imagine the impossible.

Hope is a waking dream.

Aristotle

DONNY

ONE

On his eighteenth birthday, Donny's first act would be to steal a boat.

The full moon outlined a selection of possible vessels to choose from. Their bodies dipped and bobbed on either side of the dock, as they pulled against their ropes in a feeble attempt to escape. Gentle waves rushed underneath and headed to the shore. Wooden planks creaked under Donny's feet as he shifted his weight again.

A cool breeze rolled in off the void. Donny turned his back to the darkness and pulled his hoodie tighter around his ears. Streetlights illuminated modest buildings scattered at unusual distances above the shoreline. The collected solar power of the lights burned as the inhabitants slept.

A silhouette emerged from one of the street corners. The low electrical purr of the town competed with the echoing footsteps. The figure was dressed entirely in black, and Donny lost him temporarily in the shadows of the beach before a young man reappeared on the dock, with a mischievous yet warm grin.

'Late as always,' Donny said.

'I have a good excuse this time,' Edwin said. 'My housemates were still awake watching old vids. I had to wait until the coast was clear before I could sneak out. For all they know I'm still in my room. The perfect alibi.'

1

'That's not exactly an alibi but I'm sure we're covered. Fortunately, my Dad goes to bed quite early these days.'

Edwin's handsome features attracted young female admirers, while at the same time endeared him to their mothers. He stood slightly taller than Donny and carried himself with effortless confidence. Even with crooked teeth and unkempt dark hair, Edwin's appearance had a natural charm.

'Happy birthday, you rascal,' Edwin said as he shook Donny by the shoulder.

'We can celebrate when we get back. If we get back.'

'Look on the bright side. If we die, at least you made it to adulthood.'

The pair walked towards the end of the pier. The pungent aroma of fish mixed with the sea's salty spray stung his nostrils. Strewn nets still contained dead sea life from previous expeditions.

They approached the largest of the fleet. It stood at twenty feet tall on the water's surface, balancing on narrow edges with a hollow opening underneath. A lifeless Union Jack ensign hung at the top of a mast, hoping to catch a gust of wind once again.

They were going to steal it. Donny believed the correct term for seizing a ship was commandeer. To be honest, they weren't breaking the law. Laws didn't exist anymore.

'You sure you can handle the controls?' asked Edwin.

'It's quite straightforward. I spent the whole summer on this boat, carrying out repairs and fixing the equipment. The captain showed me how to operate it too. It runs mostly on autopilot, so the only difficulty will be manoeuvring it out into the open waters. I'll teach you once it's safe.'

'You make it sound so easy.'

'I'm going to start the engine and carry out the on-board checks. I'll give you a signal and then you'll need to untie these ropes.'

'Gotcha captain,' Edwin said with a mock salute. 'I'll keep watch until then.'

Donny glanced back towards the town before he stepped across the drop and onto the main deck. His sense of gravity adjusted as the floor matched the measure of the ocean swell. He forced his knees upwards as he ascended the stairs. The glass door opened without protest and he stepped into the familiar setting of the control room. Dull emergency lighting illuminated the ignition on the panel.

He produced keys from the pocket of his hoodie, the spare set the captain had entrusted to him. He turned the main lights dial to its lowest setting before he revved the engine.

The panel lit up like those Las Vegas slot machines he saw in the archived television shows. All the readings were positive. The yacht was a hydrogen-powered model, and the engine showed as fully charged.

'All right, let's go,' Donny said as he stepped back outside. He watched Edwin scuttle between the metal cleats like a crab as he untied the ropes. The last one came undone and Edwin took a running jump and landed with a low thud on the deck below. The boat sensed it had been freed from its land-dwelling prison and rocked freely in the water.

Donny returned to the controls. He put the vehicle into a silent crawling speed and guided it out from between the other ships. A few moments later, they were free. He increased the velocity and he rocked back as the boat came alive with a powerful hum. The autopilot engaged once he had entered the coordinates.

Behind them, the island blended into insignificance between the vastness of the sea and sky.

'What a gnarly view,' Edwin said. Donny sat next to him on the floor. Edwin kept on trying out strange new words, testing if they would be accepted by his friends. Thousands of pre-war films were stored in the archives, and the pair watched them on repeat. Edwin stole pieces of dialogue from vids he found ridiculous. He would use a new word or phrase ironically at first until it became a normal staple of his vocabulary. The word gnarly, was the new flavour of the month.

'Very gnarly,' Donny humoured him.

They sat in silence for a while, watching the island shrink away on the horizon. The openness of the water gave no protection against the elements and the icy winds cut at their exposed skin and extremities. Donny shifted uncomfortably.

'Having second thoughts?' Edwin asked.

'No, it's not that. I can't believe we're heading back to the mainland for the first time in five years. When I try to remember my childhood, it doesn't feel like I lived it. Like those memories belong to someone else. I hate to imagine that we were the last generation to experience such wonders.'

The afterglow of the island vanished, and they were now alone in the darkness.

Edwin lay on his back and Donny copied. Their bodies rolled over each wave as the ambient drone of the engine filled their ears. A swathe of stars blanketed the heavens. Donny tried to find patterns, but the expanse overwhelmed him. He wondered how many of these burning systems harboured life.

'No clouds,' Donny remarked.

'Nope.'

'Shame. Rain would've been helpful.'

'We'll be okay,' Edwin said as he tapped his fingers on the deck. 'I don't mean only us. I mean everybody. People are stubborn creatures. This isn't the end. And if today is a success, it'll be a whole new beginning.'

An hour passed before an alert sounded from the control deck. Donny checked the navigation system and he could see an outline approaching the flashing triangle. He switched to manual control and cut power to the engines. The boat slowed until it gave command back to the current. The anchor deployed, and Donny turned off the remaining power and removed the key. He descended back to the main deck where Edwin detached the landing raft from underneath the yacht. It splashed into the gentle waters below.

'You ready?' asked Edwin.

'Ready,' Donny said.

They fastened their backpacks and walked towards the edge. Edwin stepped down the metal ladder before hopping into the raft. Donny followed.

It was high tide on the beach's pebble covered surface, so it reduced the distance they had to pull the raft to the tree lines. They found a suitable spot and dropped it. Donny removed a ghillie blanket from his backpack, the fake foliage soft on his hands. He unfolded it and threw it over the dull mustard rubber of the raft, and it blended in with its surroundings.

'I have the map up on my holopad,' Edwin said.

'Great. Shame there is no GPS available or this would be a hell of a lot easier. It's a three-mile walk to the plant. We can follow this country lane about halfway and then cut through the fields. There isn't much cover, but the moon is bright so hopefully we won't need to use our flashlights in the open. I have placed a homing beacon in the raft, are you able to connect to it?'

Edwin handed Donny the holopad and played with the settings on his watch. 'I don't see it. No, wait, there it is.'

'If we get split up, we can meet up back here. Otherwise, head to the coast. It'll be sunrise in a few hours so the boat will be visible in the sea. So, let's make it back before anyone else spots it.'

'Gotcha, chief.'

An unspoken silence bloomed as they entered the woods. Their boots crunched on the crispy undergrowth. The tree trunks were frail, like century old mummified bodies. Bark crumbled at the slightest touch. The higher branches managed to keep a hold of their leaves and the barrier blocked out the moonlight. Donny set the flashlight on his watch to a low dim. They navigated through the dark at a steady pace. The trees and upgrown roots fell away to reveal a clearing. Donny couldn't see the grass, but he knew it would be burnt and dead, like back on the island.

A wall served as a border between the field and a lane. They jumped over it and headed west. The road had crumbled, their feet wavered over the cracks and potholes. The faded white lines of the lane illuminated ahead, pretending to be the breadcrumbs from fairy tales. Donny walked confidently in the middle of the lane; he wasn't expecting to run into any oncoming traffic. He knew they didn't like to travel by night.

Further down the road they walked around an abandoned car. The rusted body left forsaken and unused. Donny stole a glance through the window, half expecting to see a dead body, but it was empty. He felt a whole aeon of time slip away from him and his thoughts drifted, wondering if there were any charging stations still operational in Britain.

He remembered his Dad driving him to school. He had a basic four-door electric saloon, in the standard red, the common colour amongst most car owners. A new air freshener always dangled from the rear-view mirror, the smells ranging from ocean mist to forest sanctuary. Donny always preferred riding in his Dad's car rather than the school buses. If he had a bad day, his Dad would rummage through the shopping bags in the boot and produce Donny's favourite chocolate bar if it hadn't melted yet. He also allowed him to have full rein of the music selection. The line was drawn however, at the new studio machine music that Donny had discovered.

Those had been happier times.

The tarmac turned into pebbles and a derelict cottage lay at the end. It reminded him of homes in haunted documentaries. The map showed that they needed to leave the premises and head north.

The fields ahead rolled over and under the horizon. With no cover, they knew they would be exposed. They couldn't use their devices, so they kept a fast pace.

They finally came across an enormous building. It was the length of five football pitches and flat. The solar panels on its roof, glistened in the ineffective lunar rays. The building felt out of place in the plains below. It would be a more fitting image if it were a secret base located in a crater of the moon.

'Wow,' Donny managed to utter. 'Our whole island could fit inside this basin.'

'I'm starting to doubt the strength of our scavenger party. We better run if we're going to cover enough ground and search the entire place.'

The structure offered no protection. There were no gates and no fences. A gaping hole on the side of the building invited them inside. Donny flicked a switch on his watch and a beam shot into the darkness. He formed a fist and focused the light in front of him. It immobilised the eyes of an animal, possibly a fox. It broke from its trance and ran out of sight. He swung the light around the huge hanger. Endless rows of steel shelves. Some had been knocked over and its contents scattered across the floor.

Dust particles lingered in the beam.

'No one seems to be home,' Donny said. 'It's not the safest option, but we should split up. If we don't, we might never find a battery, and this will all have been for nothing.'

'I'm sure we'll find hundreds,' smiled Edwin as he adjusted the intensity of his flashlight. 'We might even have to take a second trip to stock up.'

'Not likely. This place has been ransacked a few times over. And everything else might've deteriorated beyond use. Let's take a floor each. Shout if you see something.'

'Or if you see someone,' Edwin whispered stepping into the darkness.

Donny systematically scanned each shelf. They contained raw materials, building tools and other workshop essentials. Nothing they didn't have back home. The heavier machinery lay dormant in the open spaces. Their panels had been removed and they had been gutted like fish. His shoulders arched over and the enthusiasm that oozed from him earlier at the dock, now evaporated in the musky mausoleum. If scavengers had taken the bare bones, the vital organs would've also been lifted. He hoped they were only scavengers, passing through. An icy chill formed in bumps across his skin at the thought of one of *their* settlements being close by.

They don't like the darkness, he reassured himself.

Donny thought back to how this all began. He found himself bored most days on the island. Most of the inhabitants watched vids. Donny preferred to read, and he read anything. Science fiction, horror and fantasy. Any story that offered an escape and a sense of adventure. He also loved history. He read every available book in the archive about it. When he ran out of intriguing titles, he skimmed over pre-war articles. Besides the climate emergency, most of the pieces seemed trivial. People seemed to enjoy worrying. The complacent occupants of the early 21st century didn't know how good they had it.

One morning before work, a headline caught his eye. *New plant to open in countryside*. A factory to produce gigawatt batteries. The date read six months before the first missile fired. When he discovered the location, he almost knocked his breakfast off the table, and he rushed to Edwin's house. Once he calmed down enough to explain to his half-asleep friend the significance of the article, they both agreed they had to cross the sea.

After an hour, the battery life on his watch flashed half empty. His back ached as it made the case for him to give up. He stepped up from some debris and stretched. Oil slicked across his forehead as he wiped away the sweat.

Edwin's flashlight wobbled as he ambled towards him. 'How did you get on?'

'No luck. There is nothing here.'

'I'm really sorry. I know you had your heart set on this. It was worth it though, eh? We'd be the last people from the island to have visited the mainland. We'll be written into folklore and they will sing songs about us,' Edwin grinned. 'Your grandchildren will be sitting around you, their little jaws dropping as you recall our tale. Maybe throw in a dragon or troll for good measure.'

Donny didn't reply. He stared at his boots. He kicked a loose bolt across the floor, and it pinged against a machine.

'Hey mate, cheer up. I want to show you something.'

He trailed behind Edwin up the stairs and across one of the walkways. They entered an office in the heart of the factory. Donny's flashlight showed luxurious décor and company branding. A large display case of trophies and crystal prizes collected dust. It might've belonged to a manager or director. Edwin opened one of the drawers in the lone desk and pulled out two bottles of an amber liquid.

'I didn't take them as I thought our backpacks would be stuffed with batteries but hey, you're now going to have one gnarly birthday party.'

Edwin loaded the bottles into side pouches of his backpack. Even though he knew that Edwin meant well, Donny's mind remained stormy. Only a few days earlier had he uncovered a glimmer of hope. A chance of a new start. Where his life mattered. To be able to add to the progress of humanity. Not stuck in some stupid fishing village. He pitied his grandchildren and the future generations.

A cabinet caught his attention. He walked towards it and shone his light through the glass. A weak line ran up the wall behind. He shoved the cabinet and the carpet gave little resistance. He examined the line closer now. It expanded easily when he stuck his fingers in, and a panel slid away.

'No way,' Donny said under his breath.

A hidden room.

Their flashlights revealed a tiny compartment. Old bank currency notes poured out of a safe and littered the floor. Edwin bent over and picked out an object from the safe and studied it in his hand. 'Wow, would you get a load of this? An old school revolver. It even has four bullets in the chamber.'

Donny ventured further in as Edwin posed with his new toy. A metal case lay next to the safe. His fingers played with the latch for a few moments and he felt the mechanism move and give way. He stared inside.

Batteries. At least a dozen. Their silver bodies brightened up the box like a pirate's chest full of magical treasures.

'Oh my God,' Edwin said. 'You found them.'

Donny let out a cry of joy and put his arm around Edwin.

'I can't remember the last time I saw you this happy,' Edwin laughed. 'Let's get out of here.'

The night still held some heat as they stepped back out into the carpark. The indigo sky broke into a few lighter shades; a hint of a new dawn.

'We're still on schedule,' Donny said as he adjusted the straps of his bag. The weight of the batteries rested on the lower part of his back. The metallic coldness tingled through his hoodie. 'We should make it back before sunrise.'

'Damn it, Donny. You are the most annoying guy I know. Everything seems to work out for you. You've found the missing piece of our project. We have two bottles of whiskey. And to top it all off, you have the best human being in the world as a friend. If I were a betting man...' Edwin's voice trailed into silence.

'Edwin?' Donny followed his gaze. He didn't understand what caused Edwin's face to fall flat so quickly. He studied the horizon until he found the answer. The ominous outline of a figure who stood at the top of the hill.

'Shit, is it one of them?' Donny whispered. His blood turned into an icy slush that ran from his heart through his entire body.

'I don't know. Whoever it is, we're in trouble.'

'You think he's seen us?'

'Maybe, maybe not. Though he will when we cross the carpark and it's going to be light soon. Here, give me your bag.'

'What are you doing?'

'Shut up and give it to me now.'

Donny shook off the straps. He knew better to argue with his friend when his voice lost its warmth. Edwin snatched it from his grasp and knelt, unzipping both backpacks. He transferred three of his batteries to Donny's bag.

'I'm going to run across the field,' Edwin said, his tone cold. 'I'll get their attention and if they're in the mood for a pursuit, they'll come after me. I have a loaded gun, I'll be fine.' He handed Donny his bag and continued. 'I want you to go back the way we came. Wait for me near the raft in the forest. I'll meet up with you when it's safe. Run as fast as you can and don't look back.'

'What if --'

'Go. Now.'

Donny's legs performed without command, as his boots pounded the concrete. He passed the stationary vehicles as he burst out into the field. The extra batteries cut against his spine, but he ignored the pain and pressed on.

After he climbed up the far bank, he stole a glance over his shoulder across the plain. No sign of Edwin or the other being.

Donny refused to turn on his flashlight as he hurried through the forest. His vision had grown accustomed to the dark and he could make out the freakish forms of the trees.

The cottage reappeared before him. Donny gave himself a minute to take in extra breaths of air before he continued. He followed the road at a half jog, his lungs burning in protest.

The familiar scene of the abandoned saloon in the middle of the road brought a little comfort. The shore grew closer. The watch had plenty of battery life left and he switched on the tracker. A light flashed on a rotating map on the interface.

The beacon.

• • • • •

Donny collapsed next to the camouflaged boat. His heart pumped wildly, and his vision seared at the borders. The gentle rush of water on the pebbles brought him back to the world.

He sat up and stared out to the sea. He couldn't see the yacht but felt its presence.

Time lost all meaning as he waited for his friend.

Donny found a spot between two trees with the covered raft behind his back to keep himself hidden. He checked his watch regularly. Five minutes. Ten minutes. Thirty minutes. Edwin hadn't arrived yet. Donny exhaled. He listened out for gun shots, but none came.

The yacht materialised from its point out in the calm waters. It wouldn't be long until the boat would be visible from miles down the coast. They would find him, and he would be forced to make a decision. Whether to wait for Edwin or use the raft to and leave him behind.

ANA

TWO

Ana walked up onto the porch and knocked on the door.

The sun edged to its zenith and Ana felt relief to be in the shade of the house. She wore khaki shorts and a yellow pastel jersey. A cool breeze blew against her legs. The air around her crackled in a humid haze as crickets chattered furiously amongst themselves. A bead of sweat ran down her temple and she swiped it away with her free hand. Her other hand in a cotton glove, remained hidden under the clipboard.

Ana sensed someone approaching the door. She inhaled sharply and steadied herself. With her back straight, chin held high and a warm smile on her face, she was ready.

The door creaked back, and an elderly woman peered out. Her dishevelled grey hair dangled in knots, as if it hadn't been washed in weeks. Her eyes squinted as they adjusted to the brightness.

'Yes?' said the woman with an edge of caution in her throat.

'Hello Mrs. Munteanu. How are you today?'

'I'm fine. What do you want?' the lady snapped.

Ana tried her best to keep her composure and continued to smile.

'I wanted to remind you that the election is this evening. It'll take place in the town hall from sundown, where there will be refreshments and speeches from both candidates. My name is Ana and I'm Mihai's daughter. My father has many exciting plans for our community --'

'I know your father well enough,' said the old lady. 'And I'm perfectly capable of making up my own mind. I don't need *you* to tell me what's good for me.'

The door slammed in Ana's face before her brain could formulate a response. She walked back into the light and her skin tingled, more from embarrassment than from the UV rays. Her dirt-covered trainers bounded down the road. The heat radiated off the crumpled tarmac like a fire. Houses with blood red roofs littered either side of the rolling brown hills in the distance.

Ana could imagine more enjoyable ways to spend her last summer vacation before the final year of school, yet for as long as she could remember, this had been her dream.

She added another cross to the sheet of residents on her clipboard. Only a few hours remained until the vote and she hadn't even gotten halfway through the list. Some of the lonelier residents would keep her standing on their doorsteps for minutes on end when they complained about the problems they faced. She promised them her father would investigate the issues once he had won, but they continued to grumble away until she had to excuse herself. Then there were voters like Mrs. Munteanu who would refuse to speak to her.

She needed help.

Hazel lived right next to her house. This made it convenient for whenever she needed someone to vent to and equally, Ana took the role of being a shoulder to cry on in return.

A portly woman with frizzy hair strained over a washboard in the back-garden. Her hands acted furiously with the fabric, running it against the steel blades of the board into the frothy waters. Her expression softened when she saw Ana approach her.

'Hi sweetheart,' said the woman as she wrung the water out of the material. 'Looking for Hazel?'

'Yes ma'am,' Ana said.

'She'll be where she always is. Fast asleep in bed.' The woman shook the wet fabric and threw it over a clothesline to add to the collection of clothes with faded colours. 'I can't believe that child of mine. A beautiful summer's day and she chooses to sleep it away. I know it can sap your energy but there are still chores to be done. But I know I'll end up doing them all anyway.' She clipped the garment to its place on the line.

'Do you think I could borrow her for a couple of hours?'

'If you can manage to wake her up, you are welcome to her.'

Ana found Hazel's room shrouded in darkness, as an extra pair of sheets had been draped over the curtains to block out the intrusion of any natural light. A staleness of sweat and perfume hung in the air. Hazel lay in the centre of a single bed with a thin sheet entangled around her stagnant body.

Ana marched across the room; her feet kicked clothes strewn across the floor. Most people owned only a few items of clothing, but Hazel managed to have an entire wardrobe's worth. Ana yanked away the sheet and pulled open the curtains. Hazel moaned and turned away from the window.

'Wake up sleepy head,' Ana said as she settled on the bed next to her.

'It's so early,' Hazel argued.

'Your definition of early is different than the rest of us. It's way past midday. Aren't you hungry?'

16

Hazel ignored the question and rose from the bed like a zombie that had caught the scent of humans. She stomped to the en-suite and leaned over a bucket and threw water into her face. She groaned with each splash.

'You do realise its summer vacation, right? Our last summer vacation before the selection.'

'Exactly,' Ana said. 'You shouldn't waste it in bed. Let's get you ready.'

Hazel walked back into the bedroom and sat in front of her dressing table. Her fingers ran across an assortment of combs before settling on one. She forced the comb through the thick locks in her dark forest of hair. Ana studied her friend's flawless complexion. Despite her unhealthy eating and peculiar sleeping habits, her skin glowed.

'You have something more exciting in mind?' Hazel asked.

'Can't a girl spend time with her best friend without having an ulterior motive?'

'You're always planning something, Ana. And you know, I'll always help.'

'Well, now that you've offered, I do need some help talking to our neighbours about Papa.'

'There it is. You know I don't know anything about politics. I'll probably say something offensive and lose your Dad votes. There are a lot of people here who annoy me and there is nothing I enjoy more than teasing them.'

Ana laughed. 'You're smarter than you give yourself credit for. Plus, you're charming. So charming. Everyone worships you. You could throw the whole harvest into the river and everyone would still love you.'

'Whatever, bitch,' Hazel spun around on the stool and studied her friend with a mischievous twinkle in her eye. 'What are you doing this for?'

'For Papa,' Ana said. 'He'll be a great leader. Our community will get better with him in charge.'

'Spare me. What's the real reason?'

Ana opened the windows and a fresh breeze brushed over her. She savoured any moment to take refuge from the heat.

'You know me too well, Haze. I don't know. I think *I* could be a great leader of this community one day. There are so many ideas I have, if only I had the platform to put them into action. This place is so close to becoming a paradise. It only needs a little push. People have always doubted me. I want to prove them wrong.'

'I believe you can do it. You're always ten minutes early to class. You tutor me on nearly every subject and still find the time to ace the exams. You're the teacher's pet. Hell, you've been class president since we were young. I love the socks off you. Yet sometimes you disappear into that head of yours and people don't see you for who you are. There are going to be obstacles in your way, but you need to believe in yourself to get past them. You need to show them what Ana stands for. Once you believe in yourself, there is no stopping you, girl.'

'You're right,' Ana sighed. 'I just need to convince the adults. One year to go and I'll get the best results and my dream will come true during the selection.'

'You bet your ass it will,' Hazel said as she returned to grooming herself. 'Just don't forget about us little people when you make it, babe.'

Ana lay on the bed and examined the dried stains on the ceiling. It had been a long time since the storms ravaged the town. How desperately their town needed those rains again for the crops. She thanked God that they lived in walking distance from a generous water source.

She replayed the conversation back in her head. How Hazel cherished her. How her teacher adored her. How her

18

parents loved her, unconditionally of course. The grown-ups in the village on the other hand, had more cautionary feelings. Some were disgusted by her. Some probably even feared her. How could they form opinions on Ana without even knowing her? It kept her up at night.

A book came to mind. She couldn't remember the title but believed it was written by Luigi Pirandello. Ana could speak, read and write in three languages; English, Romanian and Italian. The library acted as her sanctuary. Thousands of books in her trilingual languages to be devoured until the candle wax would melt away.

The older generation didn't care for the library. They didn't like the concept of having to read from dead trees. The texture of the worn pages against their fingers when they had to physically turn every page. Back in their day, a single holopad could contain any book imaginable from human history. Ana thought it a foolish notion. A stubbornness of old age. The inability to adapt. Their loss was her gain. She declared herself the caretaker of the marvellous characters, perilous adventures and mystic fables.

The book she thought of played around with the concept that there are hundreds of versions of yourself. Everyone perceives Ana differently. From her family members, to her classmates, to the old couple she delivered firewood to in the winters. She wondered if she behaved in a unique manner in each social situation. These counterfeited Anas existed in the minds of others. She wanted them to acknowledge the real Ana.

But who was the real Ana?

Clouds intermeshed to provide a blanket of safety when the pair left the house. Hazel had transformed. Her brown doe eyes were wide with excitement as she bounded ahead. Her short floral dress radiated brightly against the tanned skin. Ana smiled as she quickened her pace. She swore her friend only had two settings. Comatose teenager or energetic shrew.

Hazel grabbed Ana's gloveless right-hand and swung it in the air as they followed the dirt path.

'Who is our first victim?' asked Hazel.

'This isn't a game,' Ana said. 'We need to produce more support for Papa ahead of tonight. This will help him out in two ways. First, if more voters are enthusiastic about Papa, they will tell their friends. People tend to lean towards their friends' judgement if they don't have a strong opinion themselves. Then secondly, the momentum will carry towards the rally. They will care more about the vision he will lay out. They will cheer. They will hang on his every word.'

'I know it's not a game,' Hazel said. 'It doesn't mean we can't have fun with it. And after we do all that...then what?'

'Then we win.'

Ana consulted the papers on her clipboard as they waited at the end of a driveway. A corroded Dacia lay stagnant in front of the garage. A repugnant smell hung in the air. The resident hadn't taken their food waste to the compost yet.

'OK, this is where Mr Răducanu lives. He is fifty-seven. Former salesperson but now works in the kitchens. The notes say a vocal supporter of military aggression in the war. That could come in handy.'

'We shouldn't plan it so much. Life never turns out the way you expect it.'

Ana knocked on the door and Hazel shot her a mischievous glance. *She better behave herself*, thought Ana.

The door swung open to reveal a tall man wearing faded khakis and an unbuttoned Hawaiian shirt. Dark bags were etched deeply under his eyes. Eyes which ran up and down the girls, studying them as he rubbed his side.

'Yeah?' he asked hoarsely.

'Good afternoon Mr Rǎducanu, I hope you're doing well,' Ana greeted him with a natural smile on her face. 'My name is Ana, and this is my friend Hazel. We're going around reminding our neighbours it's the election this evening. Do you have a moment to hear about my father, Mihai?'

Mr Rǎducanu folded his arms and leaned against the door frame. Hazel captured his attention, so Ana wasn't sure if he had listened to a word she had said.

After a pause he replied. 'Sure.'

'Well, my Father enlisted in the army as soon as he became of age. He longed to serve and protect his country. The first to call for military action when the bombs dropped on Paris. He continues to use his extraordinary intuition in the --'

'Let me stop you there, girl. That is all good and well that Mihai has one of the best military records around but is it relevant today? What about the meat shortages? The animals we hunt for food are migrating north. What plans does he have for that?'

Ana stuttered but before her mouth could form a response, Hazel stepped forward.

'I understand, sir,' Hazel said. 'These are trying times for everyone. It's not just going to take one person to get through these problems. It's going to take all of us, working towards a common goal. Though for a ship to reach its destination, it needs a captain who has the influence to steer us through choppy waters.'

'Go on,' Mr Rǎducanu said as his gaze darted between Hazel's breasts and her unfaltering stare.

'Mr Rǎducanu, you are a strong and capable man,' Hazel said as she placed a hand on his bicep. 'So, is it safe

21

for me to presume that you would like this town to have strong leadership? Who would you rather have in charge? Some geek with no experience? Or someone, like Mihai, who is courageous enough to make those tough calls. For example, setting up hunting parties to track animal migration patterns, even if it means they have to be away days at a time.'

'Well, if you put it like that, it's a no brainer,' grinned Mr Răducanu as his body untensed. 'Now that I think about it, I like Mihai, I honestly do. He is a great man to talk to, he makes you feel like you are part of his family. On the other hand, the doc looks book smart. Seems to have a few ideas bouncing around in his skull.'

'Sure, he's a doctor,' sighed Hazel. 'Yet he's not like you or Mihai. He's not even from Europe. He doesn't understand the land and the people as Mihai does. Mihai has passion that will bring us all together and lead us to a brighter future.'

Mr Răducanu laughed. 'We could've used someone with your persuasive talents back in the good ol' days.'

'Oh, you flatter me,' Hazel said in a kittenish manner. 'I'm going to put you down as a supporter. Will we see you there this evening?'

'Sure, Mihai can count on my vote. You have a good day now, ladies.'

Ana made a note on her sheet against his name. The ticks on the pages were beginning to outnumber the crosses and question marks. Her father might have a chance to win.

'It's great to hear people say they will support Papa, but that guy was a sleazeball.'

'Sleazeball and predictable,' Hazel said. 'You just have to tell them what they want to hear. It's too easy sometimes. Also, if you want a life in public services, these are the type of people you'll have to deal with.'

Ana rolled her eyes. 'I know, I know.'

Hazel looked over her shoulder and studied the sheet.

'If we are going to finish this list in time, we might need to split up,' Ana said. 'You have proven yourself a worthy ally in the fight for democracy and justice, young Hazel. Do you accept this mission without bias or ulterior motive?'

'I do my queen,' Hazel said as she gave her friend a fake curtsy. She rose and snatched one of the sheets from Ana's hand. 'My only wish is that I'm allowed to come over for frequent dinners with your family once you move into the manor.'

'I'm sure I can arrange that,' Ana said. 'Good luck.'

'We have this in the bag.'

The positive encouragement from Hazel reinvigorated Ana as she walked from door to door with a spring in her step. She found most residents were taking advantage of their rare day off work for the election celebrations, using it as a chance to take refuge from the heat. There were more positive responses, but it would still be too close to call. She had given Hazel the house numbers on the west part of town, known as the flat side. She hoped this would conserve Hazel's energy and eagerness.

Ana headed in the direction of the houses on the hillside. A shortcut would be to cross the village square.

The square was a shadow of its former glory. The pots once displayed flowers of every colour of the rainbow, now only contained dirt. The once bright signs of soft drinks had faded to a dull tint. Boarded up shop fronts littered the view. Impractical goods such as televisions and computers were no longer manufactured, making most of the stores irrelevant. A giant oak tree swayed as a showpiece in the centre of the square. The usually lush green of the leaves had prematurely turned to a mustard yellow.

The oldest store of the square belonged to a lady who died of pneumonia a couple of years ago. A sweet shop. It became her and Hazel's usual hangout spot. During the summer holidays, they would loiter on the bench in the front. They swapped stories of drama and snapped selfies on their holophones. She remembered one time that idiot Foghorn stuck an ice cream cone in Hazel's hair. Foghorn towered over Ana, but she still sent him flying into a hedge.

The memory of Ana's favourite liquorice wet her dry mouth. She wished the sweet shop was still open.

Ana walked by the shop and turned a corner at the bakery. A pain fired through her side as she smacked into someone and her clipboard and pencils clattered on the ground. Someone snorted in amusement.

Long legs ran up an awkward frame. A young woman with vibrant auburn hair. Round wire glasses augmented eyes that pierced as deep as the sea.

'Victoria?'

'Watch where you're going, hoser,' said Victoria.

Ana swayed back to her feet. She noticed Victoria carried two large plastic containers brimming with colourful desserts.

'I'm sorry, I was in my own world,' Ana shrunk into herself.

'Well if it isn't my fellow activist. How is the door knocking going?' Victoria spoke with a smugness permanently etched into her features. She spoke again before Ana could reply. 'If this summer has taught me anything, it's how gruelling a campaign trail can be. All that schmoozing and listening to people complain about anything and everything. This gutter is broken. My eighty-year-old mother doesn't have enough medicine. Blah blah blah. Am I right?'

'It's not trivial. I actually want to help people,' Ana said.

'Oh, me too, sweetie. But to win, you must be confident, approachable and give reassurances you can get the job done. Sadly, you have none of these qualities. Lucky for you, this contest is between our dads, otherwise you would've had to concede a long time ago. Don't get your hopes up tonight. I would hate to see you crushed.'

'Can I go now?'

'Wait. Are you heading to the neighbourhood near the stables? I wouldn't bother. I've been there this morning and had some delightful chats. They loved my baking by the way. And after a sweet snack I suggested the best way to enjoy their day off was with a nap. Who is crazy like us to be walking around in this sweltering heat? It would be so rude if you were to knock on their doors and wake them up.'

'Bribing voters is against the rules,' Ana protested as she pointed to Victoria's cupcakes. 'Not that I would expect anything less from you. I heard you always tried to cheat in school.'

'There is nothing wrong with treating your neighbours. Has the society fallen apart so much that we can't show kindness any longer?'

'You know what Victoria? I can see right through your façade. Papa has everyone's best interests at heart. He's going to make this town the way it used to be again. When everyone enjoyed themselves, and we didn't have to worry about where our next meal came from. Where we felt safe. Where we looked forward to the sunrise. With God's guidance, Papa will bring a joyful richness back to our lives.'

Victoria balanced the containers in one hand as she pushed her glasses back up her face. 'How many times did you practice your little speech in the mirror? It almost sounds authentic. Anyway, my cupcakes and my attention are beginning to melt away. Though I seriously wish you and your note taking the best of luck.'

Humiliation flushed over Ana. She picked up her clipboard and stomped past her.

Victoria called after her. 'The worst fate that could fall upon us, is having someone like you living in the mayor's manor. Someone who isn't even *human*.'

DONNY

THREE

A whistle jolted Donny from a dreamless sleep. How long had he been out? The sun teased its arrival. A mixture of golden blue streaks formed on the horizon. The yacht swayed in the calm sea. In clear view for anyone to see.

The whistling grew louder as crunching stones resonated down the shore. He leaned out slightly from his hiding spot and saw a young man on the pebble beach. The man munched on an apple on his casual stroll.

'Made it,' Edwin said as he lobbed the apple core deep into the woods.

Donny jumped up and hugged him. His clothes were damp, with his hair slicked back.

'I'm alright,' Edwin said.

'I was worried. Did they follow you?'

'Yeah they did. I think it was one of them.'

Donny considered the idea and shook his head. 'How could you be sure?'

'It was how it moved. I led them in the opposite direction of the boat. I circled to the coast and headed back. I found a river and swam over it. Once I reached the other side I hid and watched to see if they had trailed behind. I couldn't see its face, but it approached the river, studied it for a minute, before it turned around and went back the way it came.'

'They don't like the water.' After a short pause, Donny continued. 'That cut it close. If we had left the factory a little bit later, it would've found us.'

'But it didn't,' Edwin said. 'Let's go home.'

• • • • •

Donny slid the window of his bedroom upwards. He slung the backpack off his shoulder and lowered it gently to his bedroom floor.

The house was on the outskirts of the community and his bedroom faced the cliffs. Grateful for the privacy, Donny peeled off the drenched clothes from his skin. The sun shone brightly by the time they had made it back to the island. No chance of taking the yacht back to the dock without being seen. They anchored it on the east side of the island, where the cliffs blocked off any visibility. Donny became soaked when he fell into the surf trying to get to shore. He recalled the taste of saltwater with pride thinking about how he had managed to keep the bag at a safe distance above his head when the rest of him went under the waves.

The clothes and shoes he wore on the trip could dry in the sun without anyone spotting them.

Donny climbed through the window and landed softly on the carpet. The room was basic in nature. A single bed with white sheets and desk in the corner took up much of the space. A poster with splashed neon effects and people in eccentric clothing provided the only bright colours. Korean characters ran along the foot of the poster. He searched his cupboard for a towel and dried off his naked body. He threw on an old t-shirt and some boxers.

The batteries were still dry in the safety of the backpack. He sighed happily, and his fingers ran across the cool metallic surface. Edwin wanted to head to the lab straight away to test them, but Donny convinced him they needed some sleep first. He checked his watch. Three or four hours would be doable before his Dad would knock on his door.

His brain was so wired from the trip that he only managed to get two hours before his Dad knocked.

'Breakfast is ready.'

His father waited for him in the kitchen, working away at the stove. A faded bathrobe covered his tight clothes. Since moving to the island, they had never known hunger. War day rations had been replaced with a plentiful seafood diet.

'Sit down, sit down,' said his Dad as he banged a pan on the stovetop.

Donny rubbed his face as he slouched on a chair at the kitchen table. He could smell the sea water on his skin over the scent coming from the freshly made food. He'd rather be with Edwin in the labs.

'Happy birthday, champ,' his Dad said as he lay down a plate in front of Donny. Steam rose off from the pancakes. A sweet, sharp smell caught his nose.

'Maple syrup?' Donny jumped from his chair.

'Spot on.'

'How did you get this?'

'I had to do some trades with the lads at the docks. Don't worry, I know pancakes are your favourite. I wanted today to be special.'

Donny stuffed a layer of pancakes into his mouth and chomped on it purposely. When the sweet syrup touched his tongue, nostalgia swept over him. His Dad watched him from across the table. He ate another mouthful and another, until he scoffed every morsel of the plate.

'Quicker than usual,' his Dad laughed. 'Sadly, there is no more left.'

Donny wiped the sticky liquid from his mouth on the back of his hand and darted around the counter to give his father a huge hug.

'Listen. I got you something,' his Dad said as he squeezed his son in a tight embrace. 'It's nothing much, but I think you would enjoy it.' His father lifted a rectangular shape wrapped in a thin cloth from his lap. He placed it in front of Donny. 'Your Grandfather bought it for me for one of my birthdays. I've read it so many times since.'

Donny unwrapped the cloth and stared at it. *Catcher in the Rye by J. D. Salinger*. An old book. Made from paper. The cover had lost its gloss, and the corners were soft and bent. He thumbed through the worn brown sheets.

'It helped a lot when I was younger. It's hard to find your place in the world sometimes. Especially how the world is these days. I hope it helps you too.'

'I don't think I have this book on my holopad library,' Donny said.

'Sorry, I know you prefer to read on your holopad.' His father's face dropped.

'No, it's awesome,' Donny smiled. 'I'll pretend I'm back in the olden days reading the words from the remains of dead trees.'

Donny's Dad let out a roar of laughter. 'There is nothing wrong with good ol' fashioned books. I always believed it made reading a story more magical. I wandered around bookstores, searching for an eye-catching cover. I would breathe in that new smell when I flipped through the freshly printed pages. Delicious.'

'I can't wait to read it,' Donny said. 'Wish I could stay for longer, but I promised Edwin I would meet him at the lab.'

'Alright, alright,' said his father as a look of disapproval flashed quickly over his face. A moment passed. 'Please don't work too late. It's your birthday after all. Also, take these slices of cake with you. Sorry there's no icing, so it might be a bit bland.'

'I'm sure it'll taste great.'

Donny returned to his room and placed the wrapped cake and book in his bag. He could share it with Edwin. He threw on his favourite t-shirt and jeans. The temperature in the labs could be unpleasant so he borrowed his Dad's hoodie. His other clothes were currently drying outside his window.

Donny breathed in the sea air as he blinked in the harsh sunlight. He didn't feel tired. An exciting day lay ahead of him. He walked his usual route around the perimeter of the island to reach the lab. The hustle and bustle of the markets could be heard through the spaces of the houses. Simple lives of contented folk who were happy to have a normal life away from what was left of society. From the cliff, Donny could observe Britain in the distance from over the sea.

Only a few hours ago, Donny had been running for his life on the mainland.

Hurried footsteps on the dried grass came up behind him. A young boy with a dark bowl haircut and serious raven eyes on an oval face stared up at him. He took exaggerated steps to match his pace.

'Can I carry your bag?' asked the boy.

'It's a bit heavy today,' Donny said. 'Maybe next week.'

'Okay,' said the boy.

They walked in silence across the field for a couple of minutes. Solar panels twinkled in the sunlight nearby. The boy accompanied Donny on his walks to the lab. It had become a ritual. The boy probably waited eagerly at a window and would rush out to meet him when he went by.

Donny considered telling the boy it was his birthday, but it might only make him feel bad for not knowing.

'What do you have planned for home studies today?' Donny asked.

'Geography,' said the boy.

'Geography? The best subject at school by far. What in geography are you learning about?'

'Volcanos. Well not just volcanos. Plate tectonics and magma. Where the magma comes from. All the parts of the planet basically. The crust. The lithosphere. The outer core. The inner core. Sorry. Also, the mantle. Do you know how hot it gets in the inner core?'

'No, tell me. How hot does it get?' asked Donny.

'5,500 degrees Celsius.'

'Wow, really? That's interesting.'

'Yeah, it's seriously hot. Way hotter than staying outdoors for the whole day.'

They left the outskirts of the town and headed uphill. A lighthouse loomed in the distance.

'Are you enjoying learning about volcanos?'

'I prefer learning about space, but I guess learning about lava is fun too.'

'Space is a great topic as well,' Donny agreed.

Donny and the boy reached the top of the path. Situated near the cape, the lighthouse rose from the sea and towered over the rest of the island. From the vantage point, Donny could see the hundreds of houses and the harbour where the boats were leaving on fishing expeditions.

The monstrous lighthouse towered over them. Red and white stripes ran up the cylinder building up to the lantern room. The lamp in the room had been deactivated since they moved to the island, to avoid attracting unwanted attention.

'I want to work with you here one day,' said the boy.

'You have to be smart to work here,' Donny said. 'So, make sure you study hard. Knowledge is the most important commodity in life. If you take your studies seriously, you can be whatever you want. Okay?'

'Okay,' said the boy. He turned around and ran down the hill.

Donny swiped his ID card and the entrance doors slid back with a swish. The cement chamber was empty except for an elevator shaft and a vacant desk. The admin usually checked him in and called for the elevator. He couldn't wait all day for her to get back, so he leant behind the desk and pressed the button. The security screens for each floor were switched off.

The freight elevator doors opened, and Donny walked inside. The numbers ran from floor five to basement level two. He thumbed the B2 button and the doors closed him in. The elevator sunk down into the ground.

The lighthouse acted as the technological hub of the village. The engineering rooms occupied the above-surface floors. Designated for new fishing and agricultural equipment, in order to find more efficient ways to turn the sea water into drinking water and to improve the renewable energy intake to distribute across the island. The basement levels were the high security floors. Basement level one stored the weapons. Basement level two had been assigned for experimental machinery.

Edwin had his finger twirled in the receptionist's hair as the elevator doors opened to the basement. Her smile vanished, and she straightened up. 'Of course, you're right. This is no good. I'll get someone to look at the leak straight away.'

'Thank you, Claire,' Edwin coughed and cleared his throat. 'This leak has been such a nuisance. What would I do without you?'

She nodded politely at Donny as she passed him on her way into the elevator. The two young men watched her until the doors closed.

'So, how long have you been sleeping with her?' Donny asked.

'Hey man, that would be highly unethical. Why do you always think the worst of me?'

'Two weeks?'

'Three,' Edwin grinned. 'I thought it would be best to keep it under wraps since we work together. Also, I asked her nicely to keep the surveillance cameras off today for our special experiment.'

'I hope you treat her better than your last girlfriend. You do realise there is a limited pool of women who are on the island? Your reputation might make you a bachelor for life.'

'Nothing wrong with that,' Edwin grinned. 'Anyway, today is the day we make our world a bigger place.'

The basement floor had tech gadgets and tools scattered across the floors and workbenches. Dismantled hoverbikes. Drone scouts. An old satellite. Florescent lights glowed harshly from the ceiling.

A threatening presence lay at the end of the room. A monstrous, metallic form. Cables and pipes stretched away from a capsule that lay suspended upright in the centre of a huge mechanism. It could've been the artificial heart of one those giant robots in the old Japanese animes. A smooth charcoal-coloured door covered the front of the capsule. A clear window stood at face height with a dark control panel screen beneath.

The machine lay lifeless.

Donny lay his backpack near the front of the capsule. The patch of perspiration on the back of his t-shirt turned icy in the cool air of the underground room. He shivered as he studied the motionless light bulbs and the metallic veins.

Donny bent over and unzipped the bag. He picked up the cake slices wrapped in cloth and handed them to Edwin. 'Here, take a slice. My Dad baked it for me.'

'Too gnarly,' Edwin said.

The birthday present lay on top of the batteries. Donny examined the cover of *Catcher in the Rye* briefly before he slid it into one of the backpack's front pouches. He proceeded to unload the batteries onto the rock ground. The batteries were cool and heavy in his hand, and they made a satisfying thud when he placed them on the floor. When added up with Edwin's pile, there were twelve gigawatt batteries in total. They could now power numerous trips. The magnitude of possibilities made his emotions swell like a violent current.

Edwin rested a hand on his shoulder. 'It has come down to this moment. Let's fire her up.'

Donny moved to the machine. He unfastened the safety latch on the side and the flap swung open. A hexagonal shape with silver plating became exposed. The same shape as the batteries. Edwin moved next to him; a battery ready in his hands. The battery slid effortlessly into the hole and Donny secured the panel back into place.

Edwin hurried to the opposite side of the capsule. A blood-red button lay under a glass case with yellow warning stickers. He opened the case and looked expectantly at Donny.

Donny nodded.

Edwin pushed his palm against the button and stepped backwards. Nothing happened at first. After a few seconds, a slow, unmistakable hum filled the room. Neon lights flicked in sequence until a running surge of power boomed. The aftermath of echoes diminished in the chamber.

The pair cautiously edged back towards the machine. It whined and buzzed like a sleeping futuristic creature. Donny glanced at the pad on the door, now painted with a beautiful user interface. He read it out loud. 'Middlesex Industries present the Lightspeed Capsule. Condition, operational. Ten charges remaining. Please enter destination code.'

'We did it,' Edwin exclaimed. 'You crazy bastard, we did it!'

Donny burst into laughter. A manic laughter. His dream for the last five years had been realised. Edwin put him in a headlock and ruffled his hair. A peculiar sight for the two youngest and most talented engineers on the island.

Once they had calmed themselves, they opened the door of the capsule. Maroon fitted cushions ran up at the back of the pod at a slight incline so the passenger could lean back before the trip. Overhead, menacing claws and laser bulbs fitted in its ceiling. Donny shuddered at the actual process of the machine. In the inner part of the door was a matching holopad like the one on the outside.

Edwin stepped in and lay in the capsule. 'Very snug. It looks like you can operate it from inside as well. Its best if I enter the coordinates. Who knows where you would end up sending me on our first run?'

'Who said you're going first?' Donny demanded.

'I'm only joking,' Edwin said as he stepped out of the pod. He walked towards a yellowing booklet on one of the benches. It contained city names with numbers underneath. 'Want to tell me again your arguments for why we should choose Seoul?'

'Are you sure?' Donny asked as he closed the capsule door shut.

'Tell me before I change my mind. Though if you do it in that monotone voice you use when explaining things, I'll send you to the moon.'

Donny cleared his throat and licked his lips, 'Seoul is the obvious choice if you think about it. First, South Korea is the most advanced country when it came to technology innovation. We would protect it at all costs. The Americans have their largest overseas base located outside of the city. Plenty of ground troops. Fighter jets. Anti-aircraft missiles. Imagine the firepower. Finally, the Demilitarized Zone is one of the most protected borders on the planet. No way they could ever get past that. If Earth had to choose a capital city, it would be Seoul. I'm telling you, that is where we are making our final stand.'

'I hope you're right,' Edwin smiled. 'Tomorrow we can do some tests and send notes to some of the major city locations. See if we get any responses. I know you have your heart set on Seoul, but we must be realistic. Most of the capsules are either out of commission or don't have a battery. Even worse, they could be underwater, in radiation areas, buried, or even behind enemy lines. We have to check which capsules are active and if any, which have humans on the other side.'

'I understand,' Donny said. 'Though why do we have to wait until tomorrow to start testing? Why can't we start now?'

'Mate, it's your birthday and we have booked our ticket off this stupid piece of rock. It's a night for celebrations. The portal will still be here tomorrow.' Edwin walked back to the device and powered it down.

'I suppose you're right.'

Donny placed the unused batteries back into his backpack. He wrapped up the remaining piece of cake and placed them at the top, obscuring the batteries from view.

His long-awaited adventure would have to wait at least one more day.

· · · · ·

A fire crackled under the cloudless night sky. The ambience of waves whispered as the tide dug into the island under the cliff edge. A perpetual peacefulness had fallen on the land.

Edwin poked the fire with a stick and embers flew into the dark. Claire the receptionist giggled and threw her arms around him. Shadows danced on their faces.

Donny watched Edwin from the opposite stone of the fire. A young woman sat close to him. Slightly taller than him with a curvy body. A purple ribbon tied her hair up, a loose curl fell to one side of her chubby cheeks. A citrus perfume mixed with the woody smoke hung in the air. She stole a glance of Donny every few seconds. Their silence was offset with the laughter from Edwin and Claire.

'Take this,' Edwin said as he handed Donny a bottle. 'It's one of those secret bottles of whiskey we found. Your first-ever drink.'

'What about last month when we became drunk on that disgusting homemade peatreek whiskey?'

'Touché, but this is your first official drink as an adult. Happy birthday.'

The three companions stared at Donny expectantly. He raised the bottle half-heartedly in the air and sipped it. Everyone cheered and clapped as he choked on the liquid. It burnt his throat on the way down.

Donny rubbed his face. He had managed to get a few more hours of sleep that afternoon, but the adrenaline from the trip to the mainland and powering the Lightspeed Capsule had run out and he entered the stages of a massive comedown.

Donny took another swig of the whiskey and handed it to the young woman. She chugged a few gulps and placed the bottle near their feet. Edwin and Claire were kissing so his eyes dropped to the ground to give them privacy.

A hand rested on his knee.

'I hope you're having a nice birthday,' said the young woman. Donny studied her face properly for the first time. In the flickering light he noticed something strange. Her teeth. They were covered in something. Blood? No, it was lipstick. Her face was heavily plastered in make-up and some of the lipstick ran onto her teeth.

'It's been good,' Donny finally managed to say. 'I don't think I'll ever forget it.'

'Oh? I can help with that.' Her hand rubbed up and down the top of Donny's thigh. 'Edwin tells me you don't have much experience. With women.'

Donny gulped. 'No, I mean yes. I mean, I have experience, just not doing *that*.'

The young woman snorted. 'That's okay, pet. We can go as slow or as fast as you like.' She closed her eyes and pouted her lips that were caked with lipstick.

A voice carried in the night.

'Donny? Donny, where are you?' The voice urgent and annoyed.

'Dad?' Donny shouted back in surprise.

A shadow walked up to the fireplace. 'There you are. I have been looking everywhere for you,' said his father. The flames mirrored in his eyes.

'What's wrong?' asked Donny.

'You're in trouble. I've had that unruly captain shout at me because you stole the most expensive ship in the fleet so you and your friends could go out for a joyride last night.'

'It's no big deal,' Edwin said. 'We brought it home safely. Not a scratch on her.'

'I'm not talking to you,' his words cold and cutting. Edwin closed his mouth and looked away.

'You're overreacting,' Donny said.

'Overreacting?' his father shouted. 'You took a boat out into the open sea without telling anybody. When no one else was awake. What if something happened to you? You could've died.'

'But we didn't, if you --'

'This is not a discussion,' his Dad snapped. 'Home, right now.'

Donny exhaled loudly and jumped from his spot. He didn't see the faces of the others as he left but he knew they were embarrassed. His father shoved him in the back. He walked back towards the town, his breathing forced and agitated. How could he live this down?

They walked back in silence.

As they entered the house, Donny's father closed the door behind him with an angry restraint. 'Straight to your room, young man. You need a break from Edwin and the laboratory. They're a bad influence on you.'

'You cannot stop me from going, I'm an adult now.'

'As long as you live under my roof, you will obey my rules,' said his father.

'Rules. That's all its ever been since we lost Mum. You and your rules. You've always been controlling my life. But soon. Soon, I'll be off this stupid island, and living a better life.'

'This island has been good to us,' shouted his father as he followed him through the house. 'You want to be back out there? With those monsters hunting us down. I don't think you do. We have a good life here. You know what your problem is? You always have your head in the clouds.'

'I'm not a kid anymore,' shot back Donny. 'I can't wait to leave here.' He slammed his bedroom door in his father's face and locked it. He paced his room and kicked a plush toy from his childhood across the room. He closed his eyes and focused on his breathing.

Donny knew he had to get away from this place. No future waited for him here.

• • • • •

On the perimeter of nightmares, Donny's mind struggled before a beckoning in the distance of the nocturnal land that called for him. He heard taps beyond his realm. At first the taps were slow, millennia apart and then microseconds together. Taps on the glass of time.

Donny groaned as the tapping persisted with more urgency. His body slipped out of the bed and he pulled up the blinds. Edwin stood outside.

'Edwin? What is it?'

'We need to leave right now.' Edwin had his serious face on.

Dazed and still not sure if had left the dreamworld, Donny's hands patted around the floor, searching for his clothes. He changed quickly as commanded. He hopped around, sliding on his shoes. 'Is it the lab? Did something happen?'

'Quick, I need to show you something.'

Donny climbed out the window and followed Edwin up the base of the hill. Here at the top they could see the entire vista of their secure home. Most of it was bathed in darkness apart from a red glow from the other side of the island. An inferno danced on the harbour jetties; the ships engulfed in flames. Though a crack had formed, and hell had broken through

'They're on the island.'

Donny's blood froze. His sweat icy, chilled by the ocean breeze. *How did they find them?* Donny thought.

They were so far away from civilisation. How did they cross the sea?

'I need to get my Dad,' Donny said.

An explosion of noise crashed from afar. The unmistakable sound of gun blasts from his childhood rang in his ears. Another explosion, a house at the bottom of the hill. The smell of burning brick and wood sped toward him. Another explosion.

In the interval of gun fire, houses were erupting flames, like a domino effect. Donny's eyes desperately tried to pick out his home in the confused cries and ash. He located it just as it disintegrated into a ball of fire and smog.

Donny took a step into a sprint, but powerful arms wrapped around him and held him in place.

'Let me go,' Donny screamed and struggled with all his strength.

Edwin slapped Donny across the head so hard he fell to his knees. 'There is nothing you can do for your Dad now. He's gone, I'm sorry. It's only us now. Okay? Do you understand?' Another explosion detonated as a stem of blackened smoke rose from the town. 'Follow me, be quick and we might get out of this alive.' Edwin dragged Donny along as they raced along the cliff edge. More laser shots flashed across the town. Cries dying out against detonations.

'How are we going to escape?' Donny yelled out.

'The lighthouse. It's our only option.'

They hurried up the hill to the sleeping giant striped in red. Unharmed from the chaos. Donny watched the village as Edwin fumbled with his ID card. No one had followed them. He thought of the young boy and if he was okay.

They entered the building and Edwin scowled at Donny for reaching for the light switches. Edwin turned on his flashlight and called for the elevator. The humming matched Donny's heartbeat. The doors opened and they darted in, Edwin pushed for basement level two.

'We won't have much time. Here, take this,' Edwin said as he gave Donny the revolver they found at the factory. Donny stuffed the gun into the pocket of his hoodie without question. 'Once they destroy the dock and the inner town, they'll be searching the buildings on the outskirts. I want you to power up the Capsule and get the coordinates for Seoul ready.'

'I knew you were going to say that,' Donny said. 'We haven't even tested it yet. It could turn us into a genetic gloop.'

'As I see it, our only choices are either using the pod, or swimming miles back to the mainland.' The doors opened to the lab. 'I'm going back up to B1 to break into the weapon cache. It'll set the alarms off but we're heading into the unknown. We could end up teleporting to a place with more hostiles. Get that portal running.'

The elevator doors closed, and Donny was alone in the laboratory.

He shook out of his daydream state and rushed across the room knocking over a case of screwdrivers. He reached the pod and smashed the red button with his palm. The machine hummed into life, the lights flickering on in the same pattern as before. A familiar message appeared on the screen. *Please enter destination code.*

Donny's eyes scanned over the room. Where did Edwin put the booklet? He opened and slammed drawers, pushed off schematics and checked the waste bins. The booklet couldn't be found. Edwin probably had it with him. He noticed his backpack in the corner. It still had pieces of cake on top of the batteries. He pushed the thoughts of his father out of his mind. There would be time to grieve later. Donny's thoughts raced. We would need these batteries if the pod on the other side didn't have any spare. And who knows when they would eat again?

Donny positioned the backpack at the front of his torso. It would allow him to lay back in the pod for teleportation. He fastened the straps behind him as he heard the elevator creep back down the shaft. The doors opened.

Three beings in armoured suits entered. Masks covered their faces, laser rifles poised in their hands.

Donny dashed towards the pod as a blast exploded on the wall behind his head. He groped for the handle and squeezed into the capsule. The door closed and locked in front of him.

Muffled shouts from outside seeped through the glass.

The holopad on the front of the door powered on.

Please enter destination code.

Donny didn't know the code for Seoul. He didn't know the code for any city.

Figures appeared at the window. Shadows loomed behind the glass as Donny's breath quickened.

He punched in random numbers and hit enter.

Invalid number. Please enter destination code.

Donny tried another number.

Invalid number. Please enter destination code.

The handle of the pod shook. He tried again.

Preparing for destination. Standby.

An electric bolt ran through every bone, nerve and cell in Donny's body.

The world turned white.

ANA

FOUR

The dying sunlight filtered through the leaves, finding refuge from the dusk sky. The foliage of the forest acted as a defensive wall. Trees climbed up the hills until they ran into the ancient cliffs. Clouds lay provocatively at the top, teasing a release of a downpour.

Ana watched the branches as they swayed in the wind. The trunks creaked on their dry trunks in synchronised movements as if it were some ancient rain dance. She stood motionless, being absorbed into the scene as a lonely spectator.

The town was secluded from the rest of the world. The wild river played as a natural border towards the south and the partition of mountains served as a barrier to the north. They were secluded and safe. Beyond the mountains were the remnants of the pre-war civilizations of Earth. Ana would spend hours at the edge wondering about what still existed beyond the boundaries. What terrors they could be.

Her hand snapped her out of the trance. A cotton glove concealed it from the villagers, though they knew what was hidden beneath. Ana studied the hand. The fingers twitched in an unnatural rhythm.

'Not again,' she cursed under her breath.

In her prayers she asked God why did it happen to her? Why couldn't she be like her friends? She knew existence equalled pain. She knew she had to suffer for her sins, but why did she receive a greater burden than the others?

The fingers continued to spasm.

Her other hand grasped the fingers and they resisted against her grip. After a minute the tremors ceased, and her hands remained still. Ana stretched out her gloved hand and studied it. Each finger moved individually to her command. She had full control again.

Someone grabbed her shoulder and she jumped.

'I didn't mean to startle you,' said the boy. His eyes were a serious blue, which turned even sterner when he wore his denim shirt. His blonde hair was short and neat, the way he always kept it. She could feel his presence. Powerful and safe. She surrendered to his touch and slid her arms around his waist.

'Liam,' she said as she nuzzled her head against his chest. 'I'm glad to see you.'

'What's wrong?' he asked. His arms were wrapped securely around her body. She lost herself in the warm embrace and his scent. The day's heat faded with each passing minute, and she longed to keep the cold away.

'It's nothing. I guess I'm a bit anxious about the vote.'

Liam laughed. A boisterous laugh that carried through the woods. 'Are you kidding me? He's going to walk it. There is no reason to worry.'

'Really?'

'Of course,' he said. 'This is your Dad we're talking about. I don't think he has lost at anything in his life. Also, he has you. You worked your butt off this summer running his campaign. The dream team.'

'I hope I didn't ruin his chances. People might vote against him because I'm his daughter and --'

He pulled back and stared at her with a quizzical expression. 'Whoa, hey. Where is all this coming from?'

She shrugged.

'Is this about school starting soon? I know there is a lot of pressure with the selections. Even *I* feel unnerved about

it. And you know me, I'm always as cool as a cucumber.'
He flashed her one of his signature smiles. In a former life
he could've easily been a model or a teenage heartthrob in
the movies.

'Maybe it's been on my mind a lot recently. I've been
trying to ignore the significance the next year will have on
our lives. I hate that there is only one top spot.'

'What has changed? You've come top of the class for
the last three years. It'll be the same again this year.
You'll be on the council; I'll get the defences
apprenticeship. We'll run this place together one day.'

Ana smiled as he kissed her forehead.

She shook the doubt from her mind. 'Come on, I bet
they've saved us the best seats.'

They walked back towards the town, his strong arm
around her shoulders. Liam would flirt with her in front of
their friends. He would hold her hand in front of their
families. Despite how old they were, he'd even pass her
notes of affection in the classroom.

An old man with thinning hair held up a long, polished
branch with a light at the top, towards a metal cage. The
cage burst into life with the flame. The lamplighter had
created a path of illumination leading down the road. A
trickle of people left their homes and followed the lights
towards the town hall.

When they arrived, there were already people seated. A
quiet murmur vibrated in the air. In the last few weeks, the
town became consumed in uncertainty by the passing of
the former leader. An unexpected death that left a huge
void in the stability of the community. The vote tonight
would change all of that.

The town hall had fallen apart by the time they
relocated here after the war. The carpenters did the odd
patch up job when someone complained but they spent
most of the time repairing houses, the church or helping

on the farms. The floorboards were worn and creaked when stepped on. The walls were stained and peeling. An assortment of plastic chairs had been laid out in preparation for the event. Ana hoped hers wouldn't wobble back and forth through the proceedings.

'I'm going to catch up with the lads. Save me a seat?'

'Of course,' Ana said.

She watched him head off to the side of the room where his friends were standing. He playfully punched one of the boys in the stomach and he lurched back in protest.

Ana located her mother on the chair closest to the stage. She appeared to be in a heated debate with Hazel's mother. They always seemed to be in an argument over some trivial matter. Who had the greenest garden? Who made the best sarmale? Hazel sat next to them looking hopelessly bored. She would have to save her.

'Nervous about losing?' asked a familiar voice from behind her. Victoria towered over her. She wore a maroon shirt over her slender body that complimented her auburn hair. Her style fresh, and it became evident she had bathed since she had last saw her earlier in the day. Ana cursed herself. Why didn't she save some water to wash herself before tonight? The campaign distracted her from even changing into a new set of clothes.

'No,' Ana said. 'Rather the opposite. I'm confident of Papa's chances. Hazel and I compared notes at the end, and it looks like most of the town prefer my father over yours.' This wasn't entirely true; the figures were too close to call.

'I know you're lying because when I speak to people, they show much more favour for my Dad. Let's face it, Mihai is reckless and an old war hack like the old leader. Dinosaurs like him belong in a museum along with the old tech. My Dad is dependable and what this town needs.'

'You're wrong about him,' Ana said. 'He'll be a great leader of this town for a generation. I'll be by his side through the ups and downs. Then one day, I'll be able to take his place.'

Victoria snorted and pushed her glasses up her nose. 'You? Don't make me laugh. We would perish before the first harvest.'

A prime example of the obstacles that Hazel spoke of. To make an impact on the council, she would need to learn on how to influence people. Especially those who weren't her biggest fans, like Victoria.

'I know the final year of the selection process is tough,' Ana said changing the direction of the conversation. 'I can see it can crack the smartest of kids. It's inspiring seeing those from the grades above me making it into the top five and getting the best roles in the community. I hope to achieve what you did.'

For a few seconds, Victoria didn't know what to say. She seemed stunned by Ana's genuineness. 'Yes, you're right. The selection process is demanding. Not everyone has what it takes.'

'Do you have any tips you could give me? The final year starts next week.'

'You want my advice?'

'Yeah, who best to ask than someone who excelled at the process?'

A moment passed before Victoria spoke. 'Well, this is only because I feel sorry for you. As you know, the selection process is about getting the younger residents ready for their new life here. Obviously, the most talented need to be put into positions that would best serve the community. You know the examinations are an important part of it. They test your aptitude but don't get too fixated on only the tests. I know you're a book worm. Don't expect to study for the whole year and assume you'll get a place on the council.'

'Why not? What else is there?'

'You have to understand, the council decides the roles for us. The exam results are more like guidelines. Half of their decision is based on you as a person. How you present yourself in the village. You need to network your ass off and stay out of trouble.'

'Alright, thank you.'

Victoria folded her arms and stared at Ana. 'It's not like *you* would stand a chance anyway.'

Ana felt the blood rush to her face as Victoria walked away. *Why did Victoria always need to put her down?* Ana thought as she fought against the roots of anxiety spreading out in her chest.

The hall had almost reached full capacity, so Ana made her way through the crowds and found a free seat next to her mother. Hazel shot her a dark expression from the end of the row. Ana mouthed *sorry* to her friend.

'There you are pumpkin,' said Ana's mother. Her mother was a naturally beautiful woman who always dressed impeccably whatever the occasion. The journey and joys of life had blessed her with crow feet wrinkles and slightly pulled down jowls. This made her overcompensate with more makeup, which made her appear older. 'Don't you look lovely tonight?'

'I feel gross,' Ana said. 'At least I think I've convinced enough people to consider voting for Papa.'

'Nonsense, you look precious. Our family comes as a package. Remember to smile and sit up straight. They won't just be watching your father; they'll be judging us as well.'

Ana rolled her eyes and turned in her chair. The lanterns burned brightly but they weren't strong enough to brighten the entire room. She scanned the hall and was pleased to see that everyone was present for the vote. This only happened on Sunday's for church. If it was on a Sunday that is. She hadn't seen a new calendar since the war, and they relied on someone keeping track of the dates. She wondered if she would celebrate her eighteenth birthday on the correct day.

The stage in front had a simple set up. One podium, with two empty chairs on each side. A skinny bald man shuffled through some papers on the podium stand.

'Please take your seats,' said the bald man. The weak tone didn't carry across the hall. He could've done with a microphone.

The news eventually spread through the crowd and the people slowly searched for free seats. Liam dropped in the space next to Ana and gave her a nod. Ana left her hands resting in her lap. Liam would normally hold her hand, but not when he sat or walked on her left side. Never her left hand.

The bald man cleared his throat and attempted to speak louder. 'Good evening. My name is Timotei, and I'm the spokesperson for the council. Yes, if you could find a seat and settle down please. For those in the back, there are plenty of single seats dotted around here at the front.'

Timotei waited for the audience to relax before he spoke again. 'Thank you for attending this evening. This will be a historic event for our community. The first democratic vote following the passing of our dear leader. The council has been in many meetings since and decided the best course of action would be to let the residents decide who they want to lead us through these turbulent times. Amongst us we created a shortlist of the best candidates from the council members and narrowed it down to two. May I welcome to the stage, William and Mihai.'

Polite applause echoed in the hall as two men walked up the stairs to the stage. They waved at the crowd before they sat in their seats.

'The council have decided on the following rules for tonight's proceedings,' Timotei began. 'Each candidate will have a time limit of ten minutes for a speech. After both men have spoken, we'll be taking questions from the audience. This will have a time cap of forty minutes. Please make sure your questions are applicable to both candidates and are short and concise. Everyone is here to listen to William and Mihai, so no waffling on about your own lives. I'm looking at you Mr Stroescu.'

An elderly man with a walking stick, who sat on the aisle, waved away the hearty laughter that surrounded him. Timotei continued. 'Earlier this evening we flipped a coin. William won the toss and decided to go first. So, please welcome Dr William Lafave.'

A tall, slender man rose from his seat. His long legs carried him to the podium in two easy steps, and he gripped the edges of it tightly. The man wore a suit, the first suit Ana had seen in years. He stared above everyone's heads as if he was squinting at something in the distance. A solemn and hard expression on his face.

'Good evening,' he cleared his throat. 'My name is Dr William Lafave, and I'm running to be the next leader of the community. First, it would be proper if I told you about myself. I was born and raised in Canada. Before anyone asks, no, I don't like ice hockey.' This drew a few gracious chuckles from the crowd. 'Actually, I'm a keen tennis player, and even won a few youth tournaments. Though, don't get me wrong, my studies were always my priority and its where I excelled. I graduated top of my class at McMaster University Medical School. I then spent a couple of years volunteering in deprived areas of Sub-Saharan Africa. When I returned to Canada, I continued my training and became one of the most sought out surgeons in the country.'

'The best moment though was when I married a beautiful woman and together, we brought up a wonderful daughter. I wanted a quieter life. I accepted a post in Romania and for a long time, my young family had the perfect life. Then the bombs dropped, and everything changed. We all lost people we loved and did what we could to survive. Though if my darling wife saw what a terrific community we have built, she would be proud.' Murmurs of agreement carried across the crowd. Ana had vague memories of Victoria's mother being well liked in the village. 'But I'm proud most of all, of how exceptional our daughter has turned out. I have complete faith that she will follow in my footsteps and be an excellent doctor for you all. Victoria, please stand.'

Victoria bounced up from the other side of the hall. She soaked in the attention and waved shyly at the crowd who clapped for her. Ana rolled her eyes at the staged performance. Maybe she was jealous. Would her own father publicly shower her in such praise?

'I know what you're thinking, why do I deserve to be leader? I have a vital quality that not many men have. I never faulter under pressure. I'll always remain calm when in charge. I'm also intelligent, forward thinking and if you ask my patients, I have a sympathetic bedside manner. Everyone would be welcome in my home.'

'The life built here is a marvellous achievement. I want to help maintain the great success and keep the peace. Thank you.'

Applause rebounded against the bare walls. *A solid speech*, Ana thought. It would take something special from her father to win the crowd back. Her mother poked her in the side. 'Stop slouching and clap.' She had to act like the perfect daughter. Supportive of her father but magnanimous towards his opponent. Ana gently slapped her thigh with her right hand in modest support.

'Thank you, William,' Timotei said. 'Please hold your questions until the end. Next, I would like to call to the stage, Mihai.'

A burst of joy raptured through Ana's body as her father walked up to the podium. Marks in his face showed his wisdom and experience, and his hair was a shimmer of silver. Heavily tanned skin from his days outside contrasted against his dull shirt. He didn't speak until a hush fell upon the audience. His steely eyes surveyed everyone seated before him.

'The fires that ravaged across our old city remain with me until this day. How our former houses transformed from homes to crumbling rubble. Whenever the sun scorches my skin, I remember the heat of those flames.'

Ana looked at her mother, but she had become transfixed by his words. Ana had not heard his speech until now, only the murmurings from the closed door of his study each evening.

'I stood by our great leader's side on top of the hill, we debated on how we should act. He was always thinking about what came next, not dwelling in the past. God rest his soul. As Moses led the Israelites from slavery, our great leader led us away from our doomed fate. Away from the demons who now rule our world. He marched us across our own Red Sea with slim odds. Without him, we would never have made it to this piece of paradise. We escaped our desert and he delivered us to the promised land. We have our great leader to thank for that.'

His smile vanished and his voice projected with a newfound force. 'However, not once did the doctor thank our great leader, for everything he has done for us.' He gestured back to William. 'I sat and listened to your speech and no one here denies you are a well-educated man with a lovely family. I'm proud to call you a friend. Yet, you only focus on what you can offer these people. I'm more interested on what we can achieve *together*.'

Liam shouted in approval. Villagers leaned forward in their seats while some whispered excitedly. The energy in the room had shifted.

'If we are the last human society that remains, we will be the hope to those who wander the planet, searching for somewhere safe. We have been blessed with the mountains that provide us protection. We have been blessed with the Danube that offers us nourishment. And we have our faith that will get us through the worst of times.'

'As the head of the security forces, I've kept this town unscathed for five years. From bandits to wild animals, you have remained safe. And those monsters out there. They haven't dared come near us. This is the land of my ancestors. Here, in our great leader's stead, I will protect you, I will feed you, and I will bring you the prosperity you deserve.'

'My name is Mihai and together, we can achieve remarkable things.'

The hall erupted into cheers. Ana jumped to her feet with Liam and her mother. They applauded devotedly. Tears gathered at the edge of Ana's eyes. She had never been prouder to be Mihai's daughter.

The question and answer segment followed after Timotei had gotten control of the crowd. It wasn't as eventful as the speeches, with residents repeating the same concerns they all heard a few minutes before.

'That concludes the question section of this debate,' Timotei said waving away more raised hands. 'Next, I would like to call each of you to cast your vote. You will be given a marked marble when you enter the room to my right. You will be allowed to go in one at a time and drop your marble in the pot with the name of who you would like to win, William or Mihai. Once everyone has voted, we'll tally up the votes and announce our next leader. It's beautiful to watch democracy in action.'

When her turn came, Ana placed a marble in the jar marked with Mihai's name clearly written on it and returned to the room. Nothing left for her family to do now but wait. She recalled the charisma he displayed, saving it in a special place of her psyche hoping that one day she could tap into the energy. He appeared so natural on stage. Would she be able to emulate his command of the language so gracefully? Ana joined her friends near the stage.

'Your Dad was so awesome,' Hazel said.

'Thanks Haze. I hope we did enough.'

Liam laughed. 'My girl, the eternal pessimist. Don't worry babe, Mihai will win for sure.'

'Could you imagine if William won?' Hazel started. 'Victoria as the princess of town. I couldn't handle it. Imagine seeing that smug face each day? Is it possible for her to become even more smug? I would honestly start a mutiny.'

'I'm in,' Liam said.

'Once we kick the witch and her father out, we would instate Ana. Leader for life.'

'Long live Queen Ana,' Liam said.

Ana shook her head. 'You guys are too much.'

Her friends continued their conversation of the fictitious timeline and snickered hysterically as Ana escaped into herself. The anxiety of the result ate away at the pit of her stomach. From over her shoulder she spotted Victoria with Dr Lafave. Despite the dim lights she witnessed Victoria's smile disappear when she caught Ana's gaze. Only Ana had the ability to spoil Victoria's mood.

'Oh my God,' Hazel said. 'It's the council. Looks like they have finished counting.'

The stage quickly filled with the members of the council, all dressed in their smartest attire. Timotei retook his place at the podium with William and Mihai stood at each side. Ana studied her father's face. He looked confident but he always did. Did he know if he had won or lost?

'We have the result,' Timotei squeaked. 'Before I announce it, I would like to thank both men for running, either would've made excellent heads of this council and town. Thank you to everyone here tonight who participated in this town's first democratic vote. We have heard your voices and you have decided.'

'I'm proud to present to you, your new leader. Mihai.'

Ana's heart soared in triumph. They had done it.

Hazel and Liam jumped up and down next to her. They were dancing and saying words, but she could not understand them.

Mihai stood at the podium, a nonchalant grin on his face as though he did not have a care in the world. He waved his hand down, commanding a silence. 'I don't want to say too much. I believe in action, not in the emptiness of words. I would like to pay a tribute to the great leader, whose guidance has made me the man I am today. And thanks to my wife and daughter. I love you both.'

Ana bounded up the stairs and threw her arms around her father. 'You did it, Papa,' Ana said as she squeezed him tight.

Mihai stroked her head. 'This is our victory, Ana. We will make this town a better place.'

· · · · ·

The final few stragglers left the town hall. Many wanted to stay behind to congratulate Mihai on his victory. The majority spoke to him at great lengths, some who wanted to offload their worries and others who wanted to get closer to the source of power.

Ana's friends had gone home except for Liam. Only the council members remained to speak further business with Mihai. Some young men volunteered to stay behind to stack away the chairs and sweep the floor.

Many members of the security force were posted at the doors and windows. They dressed in the old camouflage uniforms of the Romanian army. Most of the recruits had served in the war and naturally stepped up to be the town's guardians. Their roles ranged from protecting the gates, patrolling the woods, breaking up drunken fights and protecting the leader. Something Ana would now have to get used to.

'Aren't you tired, pumpkin?' Ana's mother asked. 'You should go home and get some rest.'

'No Mama, I'm fine.'

Ana didn't think she would be able to sleep. Adrenaline pumped in her veins from the evening's events. Her life would change tomorrow. She would move into the leader's manor. She would watch and learn from her father as he took on his new role. Her dream life was about to begin.

The windows illuminated with a flash of bright light before a huge crack of thunder boomed through the hall.

The walls trembled and some of the stacked chairs fell over. Ana felt the vibrations from the ground move up through her. She swore she could hear the moans of a mechanical giant in the distance.

A moment later everything became still and silent.

'Was that an earthquake?' asked Liam, his face pale.

'No,' Mihai said. 'Something much worse. Soldiers, on me.' He signalled to the security forces who followed him out of the main doors.

Ana turned to follow them, but Liam grabbed her by the arm.

'Ana stay here,' he said. 'It might not be safe.'

'This is my town. I need to go find out what's happening.'

Ana ran out into the summer night. A warm and humid evening made beads of sweat run down the back of her neck. She jogged towards the troop of men who were moving across the village. People emerged from their homes to find out what had happened. The troops shouted instructions for them to remain inside and lock the doors.

Ana followed them to the outskirts where the old barn was located. No one used the barn. It stored the old, pre-war tech no one was allowed to use anymore. The great leader had been strict on what devices could be kept and most gadgets had been confiscated when he had taken over.

A nearby lantern exposed the worn tiles of an unremarkable barn. They lay above faded walls made of timber. A collection of chopped wood lay neatly on racks to the side. The tree with the thick trunk thrust out of the ground as if it were escaping hell, its claw-like branches clinging to the roof of the barn.

Mist poured from the cracks in the walls.

'Someone open that door now,' Mihai commanded.

One of the soldiers fumbled with a ring of keys on his belt. Ana moved closer, silently standing behind the men. Mihai spotted her and shouted to stay back but Ana remained still watching with fascination.

The padlock clicked open and fell to the floor with a thud.

The man ran back to the line of soldiers who raised their rifles pointing at the door, now ajar.

'Hold your fire,' Mihai said, his hand stretched out. He stepped toward the barn and raised his voice to a near shout. 'If there is anyone in there, come out peacefully with your hands raised. I have a dozen rifles pointed at your location so don't try anything foolish.'

A pause and the barn door slowly opened. Ana gasped at the sight of a boy, perhaps in his late teens, standing there unnerved with his hands raised. He had chestnut hair, which looked like it had been electrified. Sunken blue eyes sparkled in the low light. His full lips remained expressionless.

'Who are you?' Mihai asked.

'Please don't shoot, I'm a human' the boy said calmly, his hands still raised. 'My island was attacked.'

Before the boy could continue the heavens burst open and heavy rain pelted the world. The droplets thudded against the soldier's guns and the barn roof.

Ana lifted her face to the sky, letting the rain run down her, her clothes quickly absorbing the water. She looked back and watched her father approach the new visitor. The storm made it too difficult to hear, but she swore she heard the word *miracle* escape her father's mouth between the raindrops.

DONNY

FIVE

Donny sat on the edge of a firm mattress suspended on wheels. It reminded him of the beds in medical dramas he watched on his holopad. He wore a flimsy gown with nothing underneath. He didn't know where his clothes were. Bottles of clear liquids and multi-coloured pills occupied the shelves with no sense of order.

A man in a camouflaged uniform blocked the doorway, a menacing black assault rifle in his hands.

A fuzzy haze clouded Donny's mind. He tried to calculate how many hours he had slept in recent days, but his brain couldn't comprehend the equations. The nap he took on the British coast seemed like it happened to someone else.

A knock came from the door. Two men entered and stood before Donny, examining him with wary eyes. They couldn't have been more different in appearance. A tall, lanky man with a slim face and ginger hair wore a dull lab coat. His companion was the man who had escorted Donny to the medical room. A stocky man with leathery outdoorsman skin. His silver mane was combed neatly with acceptance of his aging days. Both had their arms crossed with their eyes glued on Donny.

'I did the test on his blood,' the lanky man said, a North American twang to his voice. 'He is human.'

'I already knew that,' the man with the silver hair snapped. 'You can tell by interacting with him. You didn't spend much time on the battlefield during the war, did you William?'

William's face soured. 'Enough to still have nightmares, Mihai. I would like to carry out some more exams. I need to test his reflexes. Check his heartbeat and blood pressure for irregularities --'

'Silence,' Mihai said. 'Can't you see this young man has been through enough trauma? You'll only be happy once you start cutting him up.'

Donny squirmed on the spot.

'Don't worry, that won't happen on my watch,' Mihai said. 'What happened, son? You said your people were attacked?'

Donny remained silent as his eyes dropped to the floor.

'Of course not, it's too soon. You can talk about it when you're ready. Could you at least tell us your name?'

'Donny. My name is Donny.'

'Pleased to meet you, Donny. My name is Mihai, the newly elected leader of this community. This is your home now for as long as you want. I've spoken to one of my old friends. He has a large house and no family, so he has plenty of room. You can stay with him until we figure out what happened.'

'Thank you.'

· · · · ·

Rain gently tapped the windowpane behind his head, urging him to wake up. Donny opened his eyes to unfamiliar wooden beams that ran along the ceiling. This wasn't his bedroom.

He found his clothes neatly folded on an oddly shaped chair made of red and golden fabric. He dressed quickly and peaked out from a crack in the door. Worn out floorboards groaned under his weight as he explored the house. He had stepped back in time. The soviet-esque designed tablecloth contrasted against the bright rug the table rested on. A beautifully carved bureau sat nested in the corner with tableware and ceramic ornaments of creepy cartoon characters hiding behind the glass.

A door behind Donny creaked open.

A giant of a man ducked under the doorframe and entered the house shaking off the rain from his hat. He struck Donny as a friendly version of Frankenstein's monster. Dull eyes were separated by a huge nose. A grotesque scar ran down the side of his cheek.

'Ah, you finally awake now,' the man spoke in a broken English. He stomped by Donny and lay a basket on the table. When he pulled back the cover, a beautiful sweet smell made Donny's stomach grumble. He couldn't remember the last time he had eaten. 'I brought us lunch, so we eat now.'

Donny cautiously slid into a seat as the tall man fetched plates from the bureau. He laid the plates down on the table and rummaged through the basket.

'Where am I?' Donny asked. His question cracked from the dry cave of his mouth.

'Ah, yes.' The man left the room and returned with a plastic jug of water. He poured them a glass each before he searched through the basket again.

Donny remembered fragments of the previous night. Mihai said he had a place for him at an old friend's house. A friend who had no family. Donny wondered if a man so frightening looking ever had a wife or children.

'My name is Gheorghe,' the man volunteered. 'Last night, Mihai knock on door. He knock on door until I answer. He says, new boy in village. I must look after him. He important boy. You stay in Mama's old room. You safe here.' He placed a loaf of bread on Donny's plate. Instead of a rectangle, it had an oval shape, like a shell or a bug.

'Thank you for the bread,' Donny said. His hunger overpowered the surrealness of the situation. He needed to block out the harrowing memories that attempted to claw into fruition so he could get through the day. 'Could I have a knife please?'

'No knife. Use hands.'

Donny picked up the bread. It felt like a warm rock in his grip. He tapped the shell against the plate, and it thudded like a metal. Gheorghe ripped the loaf in half with his giant hands and devoured the innards. Donny flipped the loaf over and examined the bottom. His fingers ran along the bumpy soft coating and he ripped it free.

Fluffy white bread steamed inside the granite exoskeleton. He pulled out a piece as soft as candy floss and stuck it in his mouth. The texture was delicate and the taste sweet. He continued to eat.

'You must eat crust too,' Gheorghe said. 'It make you strong man.'

'Alright, sorry.'

'Not many strict rules,' Gheorghe said as he stuffed another piece in his mouth. 'I have food two times a day. Morning and night-time. If you not here, I eat without you. That your room. No lock for door. You come, go, don't go far from village. You do what you want but keep house tidy. And no girls.'

'Understood,' Donny said.

• • • • •

The rain had ceased by the time Donny ventured out into the new town. His parents had taken him on a holiday to Prague a decade ago. The houses they passed on the way from the airport reminded him of the current

64

surroundings. They were all blessed with colourful patterns and mosaics. He managed to walk around the entire enclosure in under twenty minutes. On his second loop he stopped at the barn.

The barn looked less menacing during the day. Once he regained consciousness in the pod, he could hear shouts from outside. He didn't know what country he ended up in and couldn't risk the gigawatt batteries falling into enemy hands. He hid the backpack as he heard them approach the door.

Donny needed to get back in the barn. The batteries and pod were waiting for him.

The guard stationed posed to be the only problem.

Like the other soldiers, he wore a faded camouflage suit and carried a gun. He tested the waters and he walked by at a close distance, but the guard shouted him away in an Eastern European language and tapped on the side of the rifle.

That wasn't successful, Donny thought. He would need to scout the barn regularly to check if they always posted a sentry. Maybe they only posted a guard since he arrived in the pod. They would need to relieve him at some point and Donny would be ready to sneak in. He would need a key to the padlock, which might prove difficult to obtain if only the soldiers carried them.

Donny's mind drifted to Edwin. Was he alive? Did he manage to get to the pod? Did he end up in Seoul? So many questions he would never know the answers to unless his path crossed again with his friend. The only way to find out would be to get to Seoul, and the only way to Seoul lay inside the barn.

He continued to explore a different area of the village until he came across an open field. The ground become soft from the rains, and the grass had a yellow tinge to it. A group of people rushed after a ball around between two naked football goals. He watched them as they hoofed the ball up the field and chased it down until possession changed to the other team, forcing them to head back in the opposite direction. The players were mostly men around his age. Spots of congealing mud hardened on their bare calves.

'You lost?' someone shouted at him.

Donny followed the noise to a girl who sat on a stone wall at the edge of the pitch. Red-hot hair danced over a scarlet cardigan. She uncrossed her arms to push her wired glasses up a tiny nose to inspect him.

'Excuse me?'

'Are you lost?' she asked again becoming frustrated. 'You see, you might know my Dad. He was doing some tests on a lost boy they found last night. No idea where he came from. Sound familiar?'

Donny stood awkwardly, not knowing what to say.

'Don't just stand there. Come sit down.' He obeyed and sat next to her. The stone felt cold but not damp. They watched the football for a bit longer before she spoke again.

'Are you dumb and mute?'

'No, I'm not,' Donny said defensively.

The ball hit the post of one of the goal frames and some of the teenagers groaned in anguish.

'I didn't mean to be rude. Sometimes people tell me I have no filter and say whatever comes into my head. I heard you are staying at old man Gheorghe's house. He isn't much of a talker either, you're both going to get on like a house on fire. I wish I could be a fly on the wall for those riveting conversations.'

Donny laughed. 'It did get pretty intense when we were eating bread.'

'I can only imagine. Any highlights I should be aware of?' She spoke fast but clear in an American accent.

66

'Well, he did ban me from having girls over.'

Her nose crinkled and she snorted. 'A wise move on his part. You have lady killer written all over you.'

Donny flushed and tried to change the subject. 'Where are we anyway?'

'Um, we're on a soccer pitch,' she said.

'No, I mean what country are we in?'

'Oh my God, has no one told you anything?'

'Nothing,' Donny said. 'I arrived here, had some weird medical examinations. You said your Dad was the doctor? He didn't tell me much. Then I slept for ages. Had some lunch with Gheorghe but his English wasn't good, and he left shortly after that. And, I've been wandering around ever since.'

'Wow,' she said loudly. 'I can't believe how relaxed we've become in this place. The first stranger who waltzes into our village and no one blinks an eye. You sure you're not some kind of cannibal? Don't bite me.'

'I promise you, I won't.'

'Never make a promise you can't keep,' she winked at him.

Donny laughed nervously and blushed. A strange feeling came over him. One he never felt before. 'So, where are we?' Donny said changing the subject.

'Oh shit, yeah sorry. This is Romania. Whatever is left of Romania anyway.'

Romania. That explained the houses and the Eastern European accents. Someone sprinted by with the ball at his feet, mud being kicked up behind him.

'Why do you and your Dad sound American then?'

Her lips opened and closed as she wanted to say a hundred words at the same time but couldn't manage to get anything out at all.

'First of all, buster, I'm Canadian. Also, just because you never left your isolated corner of the world doesn't mean there aren't other people out there who weren't scared to migrate. We moved before the war. They posted my Dad here. The best part of my childhood. Well, until…you know.'

'I know,' he said understanding exactly what she meant. Nothing was the same after Paris. 'So, what is your name?'

'I'm Victoria and your fine self?'

'Donny.'

'The pleasure is all mine.' Victoria studied him in a blatant manner. He supposed it was the first time she had seen a new face in years. He must've been a curiosity to her. An air of dorkiness struck him about her presentation, but she came across as confident.

'Wait,' he said. 'Your Dad's name is William, like the king, right?'

'Yes.'

'And your name is Victoria.'

She folded her arms. 'I know what you're about to say so you can shut up. Yes, my family is obsessed with the royals. For your information, I like my name. It's classy and daring.'

'Hey, I didn't say it wasn't a good name. I think it's cool.'

'Thank you,' she said.

'I wonder what ever happened to the royal family.'

'My theory is they moved to an underground bunker somewhere in the English countryside. Those Buckingham Palace guards in their funny hats, waiting behind the reinforced doors in case anyone found them.'

'That's the best theory I've heard.'

'You're from England, right? What's it like living there after the war? I've never been. I wish I did before it all happened.'

'Well, I couldn't tell you much about the mainland --'

Donny couldn't dodge the blur that darted at him. A lightning bolt of pain shot from his ankle to his brain as someone collided into him. His fingertips scraped into sharp edges of the wall to prevent himself from falling backwards.

'Sorry about that mate,' said a boy who lifted his shoe from Donny's leg. His tight t-shirt and shorts showed off an athletic build with a cocksure smile to go with it. His sandy hair was suited to a head prefect or a rugby captain. Donny winced grabbing his ankle.

'Liam, you're such a dickhead,' said Victoria.

Liam chuckled as he ran back to the pitch. 'Simply an accident; I'm not accustomed to such slippery conditions.'

Before Victoria could ask him how he felt, Donny darted up behind Liam and threw his weight into him. Liam stumbled a few strides forward before falling into a puddle of mud. He threw back a look of disbelief while his teammates burst out in laughter. Liam picked himself up and stared at his mud-covered outfit and his confusion smouldered into fury. He squared up to Donny, standing a few inches taller.

'You have a death wish?' Liam's anger flared as he grabbed Donny by the front of his t-shirt.

Donny held his gaze, not saying anything. His hands clenched into firm fists by his sides.

'What's going on here?' a voice boomed.

Donny brushed Liam off to spot Mihai at the edge of the field. His presence wavered over Donny's emotions like an unseen phantom. Victoria and the football teams quickly dispersed. Mihai approached the two young men stood frozen in place.

'Liam, are you treating our new guest with respect?'

'Of course, sir,' Liam said. 'I was wishing him a pleasant stay in our town.'

'I see,' Mihai said. 'Go get yourself cleaned up; you are in a state. I'm sure you can find better ways to be productive than diving into mud baths. Also, I expect to see you soon for dinner at the manor.'

'Yes, sir. I'm very much looking forward to it.' Liam turned and ran away in the opposite direction. Mihai stared at Donny with those steely eyes, but he could detect a faint smile.

Mihai nodded in a direction and Donny hobbled after him. Fire rushed from his ankle each time he put weight on it.

'I should've come to find you earlier to check on how you're settling in. You chose a busy day to arrive. I've been pulled between endless meetings and moving into the mayor's mansion. I can't imagine what is going through your head right now. How are you holding up?'

'I'm not too bad,' Donny said.

'What of your parents? Where are they?'

'My Mum died during the war. My Dad…he didn't make it when the island was attacked. I don't know what happened to my friend Edwin. Maybe he made it out. I'm not sure.'

'I'm sorry to hear this. God willing, maybe your friend Edwin will find his way to us one day.'

They walked further into the village. The soldiers saluted Mihai as he passed them. Donny wondered what type of man the leader had been to demand such respect from hardened-looking men. A scruffy dog trotted up to Donny, sniffing his legs before it scurried away.

'I want to let you know that you have a home here if you would like to stay. Gheorghe is a good man and will look after you until you get settled. This is a safe place. A simple life with hard work, but you will have a roof over your head and food in your belly. Even if you wished to leave, we don't know of any other human settlements. To

70

be honest, we thought we were the last ones left. Until you showed up.'

'I know this isn't ideal for you to hear, but you must forget about that life. God has given you a second chance right here with us. Also, I must warn you not to trek over the mountains. The woods on the other side are absolutely out of bounds. It's too dangerous and crawling with those monsters. I was an officer during the war, so I've seen these beings in action. They are ruthless and unforgiving. They have no soul. Therefore, they have no compassion for life. If you choose to stay, I want you to forget about the island and focus on the future. Do I make myself crystal clear?'

Donny's shoulders slumped. 'I understand.' He realised he would have to play along with this society and whatever quirky rules they had until he earned their trust. Once he became part of the scenery, he could sneak into the barn and find a way to Seoul. He needed to get there at all costs. 'I would like to stay.'

Mihai turned towards him and placed a giant paw of a hand on his shoulder. 'I'm glad to hear this. Tell me Donny, are you a religious man?'

'My parents were Anglican, but we didn't practice.'

'That is a shame,' Mihai said. He looked visibly upset by this revelation. 'Well we don't have a specific religion we follow. The members of our flock are from all walks of life. We had a priest, but he sadly died a couple of years ago. I apologise for bringing up death again. I suppose it's something we cannot escape in this new world. Yet the Lord will look after those who are bold and kind-hearted. I do a sermon each Sunday at the church. Nothing fancy at all. I read a bible passage, deliver some positive messages, and sing a few hymns. It builds up our morale and it would be the perfect chance to introduce you to everyone. Please attend tomorrow with Gheorghe.'

'Sure, I'll be there.'

•••••

Donny followed Gheorghe into the church. Wooden pews ran down immaculate black and white tiles. Statues of saints with their arms outstretched, lined against the walls. A golden altar rested at the end of the runway with a colourful mosaic of biblical characters with halos as the backdrop, illuminated by old light fittings now containing dozens of candles.

Gheorghe knelt and blessed himself before he entered a bench near the back. Gheorghe towered over him even more when seated. Donny picked up a hymn book and flipped through the pages while the other residents filtered in and found their seats. Some shot him accusing glances as to say, what are you doing here? Yet most of them whispered to their neighbours, while others knelt in the pews to pray.

A door slammed from the opposite side of the church and Mihai walked to the front of the altar. A white gown trimmed with gold and blood orange crosses covered his clothes. His presence alone made everyone stand.

Mihai waved his hands down. 'Please, be seated.' His voice carried to Donny's ears clearly across the occupied benches with no difficulty.

'For this service, I would like to share with you one of my favourite stories. *The Parable of the Workers in the Vineyard.* It starts off by saying there once was a landowner who left early in the morning to hire workers for his vineyard. He agreed to pay them a denarius for the day and sent them into his fields. A denarius being the standard wage in those times for a day's labour.'

'Later in the morning he found some labourers in the marketplace lying about doing nothing. He told them if

72

they worked in his vineyard for remainder of the day, he would pay them whatever was fair. So, they walked off to work. He returned at midday when the sun reached its highest point. He found more people with nothing to do. He hired them as well.'

Mihai moved around the stage, more animated now. Telling the story with his hands, not only his words, like a conductor willing music to life with a baton. 'Later in the afternoon he found that he still had fields to be worked on. He returned to the marketplace and found more men standing around and he asked them, "Why have you been standing here all day long doing nothing?". One of the men replied to him simply, "Because no one has hired us." He hired those men as well.'

'When night fell, the owner told the foreman to call the workers from the fields to pay them. Those who worked in the afternoon and at midday, all received a denarius. Just like those who had worked the entire day. When the first hired workers discovered this, they complained. "Those who were hired last worked only for one hour, and you have made them equal to us who have borne the burden of the work and the heat of the day." The owner simply shook his head and said to them, "I am not being unfair to you. Didn't you agree to work for a denarius? I want to give the one who was hired last the same as I gave you. Don't I have the right to do what I want with my own money? Or are you envious because I am generous?"'

'So, the last will be first, and the first will be last.'

Mihai stood still for a moment, letting the story wash over his congregation, seeping into their minds so they could ponder its meaning before he spoke again. 'Today is a special day. We welcome the newest member to our flock. Donny, could you join me up here?'

Heads turned in unison to face Donny who sat blinking until he understood that he had been summoned. He exited the pew and made his way to the front of the church. Hushed murmurs followed him as he took to the stage.

'This is Donny. This brave, young man barely escaped his fishing village with his life. I would class it as a miracle that he found us here, where we can protect him. Some of you might ask why someone who has joined us so late, deserves all the benefits the town has to offer? Why a stranger who hasn't contributed to the creation of this society deserves to reap the rewards? Who didn't suffer? But I will tell you now, like the vineyard owner told his workers, God's grace is not something to be earned by the number of hours you put in. It is given to those who have God in their hearts.'

Mihai grabbed Donny and pointed to the ceiling. 'This boy brought the rains with him. A sign. A sign he has destiny written in his future. He will bring prosperity and in return, the last will be first, and the first will be last.'

Mihai gestured Donny to follow him to a marble basin filled with water. Donny's jaw dropped to observe it being stored in such a way. Back on the island, water was considered a valuable commodity created by their filtering machine. They would never be careless enough to leave such a large amount in the open like this.

'Donny, before these people today, do you accept to be part of our family? Serving and protecting it as if it were your own?'

'Yes.'

'Louder,' Mihai boomed. 'So everyone can hear you.'

Donny shifted uncomfortably and looked down. 'Yes, I accept,' he said louder this time.

Mihai smiled and stepped closer to the marble basin. 'Donny, I now baptize you in the name of the Father, the Son, and the Holy Ghost, for the forgiveness of your sins, and the gift of the river.'

Before Donny could react, Mihai lunged at him, grabbing him by his hair.

Donny's head plunged into the water. It flooded his nose and plugged his senses. He struggled trying to break from the grasp, but it hurt to resist against Mihai's gorilla-sized forearms. He choked on water that rushed into his lungs. A second felt like an hour and he regretted taking every breath that proceeded this moment for granted.

Mihai released him.

Donny fell to the floor, spluttering the liquid from his lungs. His throat burned and his vision blinked in and out of focus. He could see faces of the villagers staring at him, their lips moving in unison. Saying a prayer.

'Welcome to the Order of the Danube,' Mihai said.

ANA

SIX

Hazel waited for Ana under the shade of the old oak tree in the village square. She wore a lemon tank top and short khaki shorts, her bronzed arms and legs on show. She had an extensive collection of sunglasses and today, she wore an oversized pair that covered a third of her face.

'Who are you trying to impress?' Ana asked as she poked her friend in the side.

'It's the first day of our final year of school,' Hazel said fluffing up her hair. 'This is our last chance to bask in youthfulness. I'm going to make a statement. Hell, I'll make a statement every day if I have to.'

Ana smiled. 'We also need to take the classes seriously you know. This year is going to determine our futures.'

'This is serious too,' Hazel said. 'Don't you want to make the most amazing memories? The books will always be there, but not our youth. It'll slowly disintegrate into the wind like a beautiful dandelion, their puffball seeds drifting towards the sunset.'

'That is perhaps the most poetic thing you've ever said. Save it for essays.'

The pair headed to one of the old barrack buildings. During the war, the soldiers were stationed in dorm rooms before they were posted to battlefields. Since then, the remaining soldiers moved into the town's vacant houses and the rooms had been transformed into schools. Ana loved her classroom. It flooded her with nostalgia. A

76

periodic table, eager artwork, and a blackboard decorated the room. A giant map of the world covered most of a wall. Even though she couldn't visit any of the old countries, she still enjoyed staring at it in a daydreaming daze. All those political borders seemed silly to her now. People fighting over land when they could've enjoyed the abundance of wealth, they took for granted.

One of Ana's best poems hung framed near the door.

The new school system assigned them a dedicated teacher, Mr Ferguson, but he insisted his students call him Jaspar. He sat in the front desk frantically sorting through a lesson plan. Students lounged on their desks while they waited for the class to begin, where the jocks postured, and the nerds dwelled in their teenage awkwardness.

Ana and Hazel had argued on where they wanted to sit. Ana wanted to be at the front so she could hear Jaspar more clearly. Hazel opted for the back row where she could observe her classmates and have her own privacy. As a compromise, they decided on two seats on the side row.

Ana spotted Liam who gave her a nod.

'Settle down, settle down you hooligans,' Jaspar said in his musical tone. His curly hair and beard were both as dark as coal, but his spirit was as bright as a diamond. 'You might remember me from the last few school years. And news flash! You're stuck with me again.' Some students moaned, some giggled.

Ana smiled and adjusted the chalkboard on the desk in front of her. Paper and journals were a luxury and she only recorded the most vital school notes and profound thoughts in them. Class exercises were suitable for her board. She stored a pack of pastel coloured chalk safely in her desk. She used her favourite baby blue chalk piece to draw her name at the top with the date.

Life couldn't get any better for Ana. Her family had moved into the luxury manor when her father became the leader. She had a close group of pals, with a best friend that always had her back. She had also caught the eye of Liam, the most handsome and athletic boy in the village. School and the library, her sanctuaries, were always available. To top it all off, everything had fallen into place for her to secure the final council spot at the end of the academic term.

Ana closed her eyes and let out a blissful sigh.

'Before we raise the curtain on our studies, I have an announcement,' Jaspar said clapping his hands together. 'A new student will be joining us. What a novelty. Please come in, don't be frightened.'

Ana followed her classmates' gaze to find a boy stood at the back door. It was the new boy Papa had baptized at church yesterday. The same one from the barn. She heard her father speak to some of the council members about him. They said he had arrived using some of the pre-war tech they thought had been broken. She wondered where on the classroom map the boy had come from.

'Come there is a desk free at the back,' Jaspar said. 'To the side of the lovely Hazel. Hazel, please don't torment him.'

Hazel smiled. 'You have my word.'

'This is Donny,' Jaspar said with a wild hand gesture. 'He is all the way from the British Isles, and it is our absolute pleasure to have him with us. He has just turned eighteen so he'll be doing the final year with the rest of you so we can evaluate what role will best suit Donny. I won't embarrass you and make you stand up, but please could you indulge us with an interesting fact about yourself.'

The boy stared at the floor, deep in thought. 'This one time when I was climbing up the side of a cliff with my friend Edwin, I grabbed --'

'Boring,' a boy with peculiar shaped eyebrows shouted. The class burst into laughter.

· · · · ·

The rest of the school day passed without incident. Nothing to test Ana's brain but she enjoyed listening to the outlines of each subject and the topics they would cover. Hazel passed her a note on a scrap piece of paper. *This new boy is hella cute. Dibs!*

Ana half expected Jaspar to send them home early since it was the first day and no real work had begun. Instead, her teacher had a mischievous smile hidden under his beard, like he knew a secret no one else did.

'I have a surprise for you all, he said. 'A pop quiz.' The class groaned in unison, but Ana's heartbeat fluttered. She lived for tests and anything that pushed her intellect to its limits.

'It's a short mock exam. It takes questions from all the subjects we study. It covers material from the upcoming year, so I don't expect anyone to get a good score, but it'll give an indication of how hard you'll have to work if you're aiming to impress the council. Please wipe off your boards, you're going to need both sides.'

Ana moved her blue chalk with vigour as she felt she knew most of the questions already. A summer of revision had proved useful. At the end, everyone passed their boards to the front for Jaspar to mark them. The class remained in their seats and chatted waiting until they were dismissed.

'Very interesting,' Jaspar said getting up and stroking his hairy chin. 'None of you did terribly, but lots of effort needed to get you into shape. That means studying all year through and not just when the exams are around the corner. In fact, only two of you managed a grade of a B.'

'Who?' someone asked.

'No shock here. Ana had the highest score of 86. Maybe she should be teaching the class.'

Ana's spirt soared and it threw in some cartwheels for good measure. Liam mouthed the word *swot* at her. She stuck a tongue out at him.

'And in second place with an impressive 80 percent, only our newest student. Well done, Donny.'

Ana spun in her chair to study the new kid. He seemed unmoved by the news, playing with an object in his hand, oblivious to the world around him.

Who is this mystery kid? Ana thought.

• • • • •

Ana stared at herself in her new standing mirror. The dress she wore was her favourite. A deep navy bell dress with large sleeves that made her feel like a superhero. She wore her long blue glove to match it as an accessory.

Ana left her new room and roamed the top floor of the manor. She had only lived there for a few days and still got lost in the labyrinth of hallways, dimly lit by candles on the console tables. The corridor opened to the majestic manor lobby, with beautifully carved bannisters that descended two staircases.

Liam waited at the bottom under the glow of the chandelier. Ana descended the stairs feeling his eyes on her legs and for a moment felt self-conscious. She didn't appreciate being viewed as an object, but tonight was a night for celebration. She would treat herself to a night free of books for a night of glamour.

'Good evening, gorgeous,' Liam said. He was dressed in his sports blazer with his trademark golden hair slicked back. He reminded her of those English gentlemen in the old black and white movies she enjoyed as a child.

'You look pretty dapper yourself,' Ana replied as she fixed his tie.

'Are you going to give me the grand tour?'

'I would show you around, but this place is like a maze. We would only get lost and then get in trouble because they'll think we are up to all sorts.'

Liam grinned. 'Maybe we should get up to all sorts.'

Ana playfully landed her fist on his chin. 'Behave yourself. Dinner is being served shortly.'

'I shall escort you, m'lady.' Liam offered his arm and Ana gratefully accepted wrapping her arm around his and he led her to the dining area.

The room was as massive as the entire ground floor of her last house. A single table appeared to be the only furniture as it engulfed the room with its presence. The stretched table had enough space to fit in two dozen people at least, with Mihai already sitting at the head. Servants rushed in carrying trays of Romanian dishes. Steam rising between the candelabras as they were carefully placed down. The moonlight flooded in through bay windows with velvet drape curtains, creating a scene from an old vampire novel.

'Please, take a seat,' Mihai's voice echoed around the chamber. Ana sat next to her father with her mother opposite and Liam to her other side.

'You look stunning, pumpkin' Ana's mother Rozene remarked.

'Thank you, Mama,' Ana said. 'I know you always tell me I should make more of an effort so for tonight I will humour you. And all this food smells so splendid. I don't know what I want to try first.'

'I haven't seen so much on one table before,' Liam added. 'Thank you for inviting me, sir.'

'No need to thank me. You're already part of the family,' Mihai said. He waved his hand and another servant appeared carrying a bottle. A middle-aged woman Ana recognised. Time had not been kind to her, and wrinkles had made their mark early. Her oily hair was tied back behind her head. She always hovered around the old leader and now she followed her own father's command. She poured a dark blood liquid into a glass. Mihai picked up the glass and swivelled it before inhaling the airy vapours above. He sipped it and nodded slowly.

'Perfect,' he said. 'Liam would you like to try some?'

'Dear, they are still too young,' Ana's mother objected. 'Plus, they have school in the morning.'

'You make a good point,' Mihai said. 'Only for me and my wife then.'

The servant topped up the two glasses and left the room.

Liam reached for the jug and poured himself a glass of water. He lifted his glass into the air. 'Even though I don't have an alcoholic drink, I would like to make a toast. To Mihai, who will lead our corner of the world to great prosperity. To Rozene, who will bring love to her family. And to my beautiful girl, Ana, who will finish top of the class this year.'

'Well said,' Rozene said as she clinked glasses with Liam and her family.

Mihai took a sip and placed down his glass. 'A fine toast indeed, though it's going to take a lot of work and political will if I'm going to improve the conditions for us. To be a successful leader you need to show no hesitation to act. The people might fear me, but they will respect me. In return, I will love them. I believe in the teachings of

Sun Tzu. The best military strategist of his time. Have you heard of him, Liam?'

'Not sure that I have,' Liam said.

'I have Papa,' Ana said quickly. 'His words are so wise.'

Mihai sliced a piece off from his cut of meat and stuffed it into his mouth. He chewed slowly as to savour the taste. His face was an expression of thought, as if he were a general again thinking of the next plan of attack. 'There is one quote of his I always love to repeat to myself. "Regard your soldiers as your children, and they will follow you into the deepest valleys. Look on them as your own beloved sons, and they will stand by you even unto death." You see Liam, I see the soldiers here as my own children. I'll praise them when they do good, and I'll punish them when they do wrong. When they die protecting us, I mourn them as if I lost my own child.'

Mihai paused as he studied Liam. 'You'll make a fine soldier after you finish school. I'll train you up myself and you'll be rising through the ranks in no time. You have the strength and the aptitude. All you need now is the experience.'

'Thank you, sir,' Liam said. 'I'll do whatever it takes. I won't let you down.'

'Liam will do so well for himself when we finish school,' Ana added. 'I also scored the highest in a mock exam today. The two of us will work hard for this community, Papa.'

Mihai swallowed another mouthful of food as he continued to ponder. The candlelight cast his shadow against the far wall, it made his stature even more intimidating. Like a centaur in the mystic worlds.

'You have the right attitude, Liam,' Mihai continued. 'I'll insist you attend future security meetings. I know, we must wait until the council decides the roles for you children based on your exam results. However, I have a lot of say on these matters now and you can rest assured you'll fill one of the vacant soldier spots. It'll be beneficial to get that insight early on before you join them.'

Ana played with the food on her plate while Mihai and Liam continued to talk across her, discussing military strategy of the town. *They always do this*, she thought. *Her father ignored her test result and instead prefers to talk about defence and guns with Liam.*

'What about the new boy?' Mihai asked with an eyebrow raised. 'Do you think he is soldier material?'

Ana perked up at the mention of Donny's name. 'He had the second-best exam result after me,' she said. 'I thought he was from a backward place, but it turns out he is quite smart.'

Mihai stroke his chin. 'Is that so?'

'He strikes me as a big-time nerd,' Liam said. 'He's too scrawny to make it into the army.'

'He looks good to me,' Ana said. 'I mean, I've been studying the entire summer, so my score makes sense. He has come in clueless from what sounds like a warzone and he scored almost as high as I did.'

'It must've been luck,' Liam said. 'I mean he screamed like a girl when I accidentally stood on his foot. He doesn't have what it takes.'

Mihai shrugged. 'We can always wait and see how he performs in the physical section of the exams. If not the army, I have an idea of where I can use him. I have a good feeling about that boy.'

Mihai turned to Rozene as she caught his attention. Her voice was low and soft, so he leaned in to listen while he continued to devour the contents of his plate.

Ana glanced at Liam. He ate noiselessly and stared at his lap. They ate in silence for a while. Ana decided to break the silence. 'Is everything okay?'

'Yeah,' Liam said sharply.

'Was it something I did?'

'No, I'm fine.'

The dinner ran its natural course. It finished when everyone couldn't eat another bite, conversation had reached a pleasant conclusion and the servants had entered to take away the plates.

Liam said his goodbyes to Mihai and Rozene, and Ana walked him to the door.

'Thank you for coming tonight,' Ana said. 'Papa loves you like you were his own son. It meant a lot to him that you could make it to celebrate with the family.'

'Yeah,' he said. 'Mihai is a decent man.'

Ana rubbed her shoulder and tried to catch his distant stare. 'You sure everything is okay?'

'Whatever. See you at school.'

Liam walked out into the darkness. The guard posted at the door glanced back at the commotion. Ana's skin prickled as she closed the door behind her. *What had gotten into Liam?* she thought.

The annoyance tore away at her.

Ana decided to head to bed. She found her bedroom on the first attempt, not ending up at one of the many passageways' dead ends.

Her bedroom was more than she could've asked for. In her previous house, her books were stored in stacks at the back of her closest, here she had a huge bookcase. She spent an entire lunchtime arranging her extensive collection, their spines boastfully displaying her favourite classic titles. A poster bed lay at the centre of the room. Lace fabric between each wooden pillar. Six pillows lay at the end of a huge patterned duvet. It was the type of bed she dreamed of when she was a little girl.

She removed her dress and crossed the wooden floorboards to lay it on the chair next to her dressing table. She studied her body in the mirror. Ribs protruded underneath her bra in an exaggerated fashion. A pang of guilt hit her as she couldn't finish her food tonight. Maybe the feast was a one-off to celebrate Papa's victory. Hunger had become a way of life since the war. Her body had adapted to the scarcity of food.

The thoughts of Liam's coldness crept back into her mind, like a spider crawling along its web to check for prey. She still didn't know what she did to upset him. For a young man who projected such confidence and machismo, the smallest inconvenience would set him off and she had to watch how she behaved around him. She had even worn the dress he liked.

She felt rejected.

If her own boyfriend disliked her, what did others think of her? The time and effort she had spent studying might've been in vain and she would miss out on the council position. She'll end up in the fields like most people. Her life unextraordinary, like everyone else.

The long blue glove. A symbol that she would never be like any of them.

She peeled off the soft fabric and let it drop on the floor.

A twinning of carbon fibre and titanium grew down from the half-way mark of her upper bicep. The orange glow of the candlelight gave fiery life to the darkness of the materials. The forearm was plain and smooth besides the ridges left by the many panels. Padding ran across her palm with a spongier fabric so she wouldn't destroy delicate objects in her grip. Four coal coloured fingers extended with metal pistons stretching on the insides. The thumb looked more like one of those old-fashioned car gear sticks with floppy leather at the bottom of the shaft.

Ana raised her bionic arm in front of her face. She tested each finger individually, marvelling at the abnormal movement of each. The silvery pistons flashed with lightning speed back and forth. The hand rotated in place, before she could even command the action in her head. It wasn't fair. No one around could finish the artificial skin for the arm.

'They will always think I'm different,' Ana whispered into the night. 'I need to prove myself.'

DONNY

SEVEN

A routine had quickly cemented itself in Donny's new life. Gheorghe would wake him early in the morning to carry out chores around the house. Once he finished his tasks, he spent most of the day at school. The classes were easy and came naturally to him. The only time he would pay attention would be in the science classes, but only to absorb a new piece of information he didn't know already. The final period would be dedicated to health education or agriculture, neither of which interested him. Finally, he would eat a warm meal with Gheorghe before bed. And repeat the next day.

The worst part was the gap between school and dinner.

With nothing to do and no friends, Donny would roam the town with no destination and observe the surroundings. The residents would avoid him whenever he walked by. The town and fields snugly fit into the nature-made enclosure of the mountains and river. The boredom and claustrophobia dragged down his emotions as the days blended together. He felt trapped once again. His life had lost its purpose.

Donny made a customary pass by the barn as he did every day after school. He stood still and stared at the guard. A new guard. The two men he usually saw stationed at the barn were old and grumpy. They always shooed Donny away if he moved into their vision. This one was baby faced. It looked like he had stopped growing at the age of seventeen but had since managed to get splashes of salt and pepper in his hair, so it proved difficult to pinpoint his exact age. His posture wasn't as uptight as the others and his shirt hung untucked. Donny decided this one might not be as dedicated to the rules as his comrades.

Donny experimented by walking in a close a proximity of the barn. The young soldier watched him curiously but said nothing.

'Beautiful day, isn't it?' Donny said trying to be as casual as he could.

The guard rubbed the stubble on his chin and stared at the clear skies. 'Are you making a joke? It's another stupid day. All the same.'

Donny immediately liked him. 'You're right. Every day is the damn same. I imagine this is what prison life used to be like. At least the air is clean, and the surroundings are pleasant.'

A long awkward pause followed.

'Aren't you the kid who arrived through the portal?'

'The very same.'

The young soldier studied him and grunted. 'I imagined you to be a tough guy. Instead, you're mildly annoying.'

'That's what my friend always told me.' Donny became aware at the assault rifle the man carried. How intimidating it appeared suspended over his shoulder. The guard followed his gaze and read his mind.

'Don't worry, I wouldn't shoot you. You're harmless. I save them for any raiders or hungry animals that try their luck.'

'What about the androids?' Donny asked.

'I'll be honest with you. We haven't seen many since the war. There were a couple in the first year who stumbled across our town, but we destroyed them quickly and buried their remains deep underground. Our theory is they only stay near the large cities and attack those who appear to be dangerous. We are secluded out here, and our numbers wouldn't be a threat to any of their forces.'

'That was our theory too. Until they attacked us.'

'Are you the only one who survived?'

Donny nodded slowly.

'Shit. I'm sorry.'

'No problem. It hasn't sunk in yet.'

'If there is anything you need, give me a shout. The name's Stefan.' The man had a pointy jaw, covered in a few days of dark stubble. Sunken eyes perched above high cheekbones as if he hadn't slept well for a year.

'Thanks. I'm Donny by the way. Hey, would you mind if I go in?'

'What? Into the barn?'

'Yeah.'

Stefan rubbed his face as he contemplated his request. 'I don't know, it's supposed to be off limits.'

'I won't touch anything,' Donny said.

Stefan sighed as if having an argument would've been too much effort. He unlocked the door with his chain of keys on his belt and pushed the door ajar. As Donny entered, the door immediately slammed shut, leaving him in the stale air touched with the scent of sawdust.

Donny blinked a few times, trying to adjust to the dull light. Batches of old technology stacked up against the walls. Old holopads, computers, terminals, screens, projectors, and medical equipment lay undisturbed in their dirty coatings. As an archaeologist who stumbled into an ancient tomb, he wiped dust from the surfaces to examine the treasures.

The buildings in the town were void of technology. At first, Donny suspected the village didn't have access to a renewable energy source. Maybe they relied on nuclear power or one of the last remaining fossil fuel power plants. The hidden tech suggested the people had tried to wipe away this part of their history. To pretend it never happened.

The Lightspeed Capsule stood silently in the centre of the clutter like a sleeping monster in its cave. Black veins ran on the ground from the mammoth machine. Mechanical units that lay near the pod had been charcoaled to crispy frames, a result from the energy discharge.

Never had he imagined it would be this easy to gain entry back to the pod.

Donny lay his hand on the battery hatch, cool under his touch. He flipped it open to reveal a darkened gigawatt battery in the slot. The capsule device had probably been in standby mode for years. If they hadn't left the battery in the slot, he wouldn't have been able to transport himself here and instead would've been killed by the intruders on his island. He shuddered and pushed the *what if* scenarios out of his head.

The used battery was dropped to the floor throwing a cloud of dust and dirt in the air. Dozens of metallic computer cases lined up along the shelves. Donny searched them, testing the grip of the panels with his fingertips. One finally gave way and the panel fell to the side. Enclosed was Donny's backpack. He pulled the pack out and examined its contents. In a panic, Donny had hidden the bag on the night of his arrival. The gigawatt batteries falling into the wrong hands wasn't something he wanted to live with.

Donny glanced at the door. He half-expected Mihai or the doctor to barge in after he had restored power to the capsule and declare it for themselves. He waited for a minute. The door remained closed and no other noises seemed irregular. All he could hear were the shouts of field workers in the distance.

The gun Edwin had given him appeared at the bag's opening. He stuffed it in the back of his jeans. A piece of cake wrapped in a kitchen towel and the book his Dad had given for his birthday, lay at the top of the batteries. Donny placed them on a shelf nearby and picked out a new battery. The smooth surface felt pleasing against his touch.

His heart pounded with a renewed force when he slid the new battery into the machine. If it worked, it would emit a loud sound. He would have to turn it back off and explain that he knocked something over by accident if Stefan grew suspicious. He needed access to the screen to carry out tests to reach other operational pods. A chance to contact Seoul.

If it failed, he would be stuck here forever.

Donny lifted the glass case and held his breath. He pushed the red button.

He waited but nothing happened. Last time there had been a delay, but an eternity passed, and the machine remained in its slumber like Rip Van Winkle.

The screen lit up.

Middlesex Industries present The Lightspeed Capsule. Condition, malfunctioning. Error WAY0044: Please replace thermal gauge conduit. Ten charges remaining. Destination GUI unavailable.

Donny hit the red button again and the screen turned black. He picked out a screwdriver from the backpack's pouch and dismantled the back of the pod. Once he found the part, he agreed with the warning message. The conduit had been burnt to a crisp and needed replacing. A component would have been easy to source in the lighthouse. Donny examined what his options were like in the barn. There was a slim chance a conduit would be in any of these machines and it could take him days or weeks to dismantle all of them. It would not be today. The sunlight had faded from the windows and Donny wasn't in the right state of mind. He couldn't afford any mistakes of damaging the capsule.

Donny located the empty computer tower where he had stored his backpack. He removed the battery from the capsule device and loaded it into the computer case with the other spare batteries. If anyone were to check the barn, he didn't want to leave any clues of what he planned. He used screws from other cases to screw the panel back into place. No one would find them.

The guard waited for him as he emerged and quickly moved behind Donny to secure the lock in place. He eyed Donny's bag.

'What's in there?'

'It's my backpack,' Donny said as he handed it over. 'I forgot it inside when I first arrived. It only contains a book, a couple t-shirts and some spare underwear. I didn't take anything from the barn.' He was thankful he always carried spare clothes in his backpack. There were no signs of a huge clothing store around and the thought of living here with only one outfit made him shudder.

Stefan lifted the cake pieces wrapped in the kitchen towel, examining it like a grenade ready to explode.

'It's only cake,' Donny said. 'You can keep it. It was from my birthday.'

'Happy birthday,' Stefan said with no hint of sarcasm. He stuffed his face with a slice and devoured it greedily. 'Very good cake. Who made it?' Crumbs flew from his mouth as he mumbled.

Donny pretended he didn't hear the question as he bent down and placed the strewn possessions back in the pack.

'You think I could come back here tomorrow after school?' Donny asked. 'I'd like to do my homework in the barn. I'm finding this place hard to adjust to you see. In the barn, it feels more like my old home. It'll help me study better.'

Stefan wiped his mouth with the back of a camouflaged sleeve. 'If I'm here on shift, no problem. You strike me as a good kid.'

'Thank you,' Donny said. 'So, I have another question,'

'Sure.'

'Why do you think you guys haven't been discovered by the androids yet?'

Stefan's brow creased. 'We are protected by nature here. The mountains are hard to climb. Then the Danube is a monstrous river. Tough for anyone to swim across and they --'

'They don't like water,' Donny finished the sentence.

'Correct,' Stefan nodded. 'The river is its own living force. It means life, but it also means death. Always respect the river. Never go out on it by yourself. I had a crazy Grandmother who told me stories at bedtime. I'm not sure if they were true or if she told them to scare me away from the river. She said the stories were passed on to her from her own Grandmother. This one story scared me shitless. Once during a terrible war, the men were away from the village. They had been conscripted into the army. It didn't matter if they were young or old, if you could grow hair on your face, you could fire a gun. The women stayed behind in the village to look after the children and to work on the fields.'

Stefan paused trying to get the details of the story from his childhood memories. 'One day a wounded soldier entered the village. He told the women the enemy army had wiped out his entire troop and they were marching right towards them. The women became terrorised with fear. They knew the enemy soldiers would defile them and murder their young ones. In the middle of the night, they dragged their children to the river where they drowned them, before drowning themselves. Every evening, if you watch from the banks of the Danube, you can make out their ghosts roaming in the mists.'

Donny blinked as he stared towards the forest.

A look of sadness flashed over Stefan's face before it returned to its neutral position. 'The moral of the story is never go to the river by yourself. And never by night.'

'Thank you,' Donny said. 'I'll keep that in mind.'

Donny wandered back through the village stunned. He grabbed tightly on the straps of his backpack. He wasn't sure what to make of Stefan's story. The pod hadn't transported him to somewhere in Europe but instead to a dark place in his imagination. The characters he had met so far were strange with hidden secrets. The weird looks he would receive walking down the streets. The baptism ceremony he had been subjected to at the church. Something seemed off about the village. As if a thorn had lodged itself in his skin but he couldn't detect where the pain came from.

Victoria caught his eye and she made a beeline straight to him. At least one normal person lived here.

'Hey lost boy,' said Victoria. 'Looks like you've seen a ghost.'

'You can say that again.'

'The other kids still tormenting you?'

'No. I guess I've lived on a tiny island for the last five years so being in a huge town with different customs takes some getting used to. Plus, there is so much land around. It's like the opposite of being claustrophobic.'

'Agoraphobia.'

'What?'

'The fear of the open.'

'Nah, that can't be right. I'm fearless.'

'Really? You do have a death wish if you're trying to pick a fight with Liam. I do feel bad for you though. The class you've been stuck in is full of hosers.'

'It is what it is,' Donny said.

Victoria smiled; her features glowed in the sunshine. She ran her fingers through a stray strand of scarlet hair, brushing it behind her ear. 'Listen, I'm throwing a party tomorrow night. The adults are having their annual bridge tournament, which finishes early in the morning, so I thought I would host something a bit more spectacular. Yeah, some of your stupid classmates will be there but also some cool chill people as well. You should come along.'

'I'm not sure.'

Victoria crossed her arms and frowned. 'What better things do you have to do? Sit in your room and sulk?'

Donny debated the decision in his head. It would be wise not to raise suspicions and go with the flow. Also, it might benefit him to have a break before he repaired the Lightspeed Capsule.

'Sure, I'll go,' he said.

'Awesome. I don't mean to be blunt, but do you have anything else to wear? I swear I've seen you in the same t-shirt for the whole week.'

'Not to worry, I've found my backpack in the barn. I have a few changes of clothes in here.' He patted the bag in modest triumph.

'Good. I didn't want you stinking up the place.'

• • • • •

The medical centre gave off a different mood under the dying rays of dusk. The building had a peculiar design. The formal stiffness of a general practitioner office, with utilitarian windows and grey walls. It had only one story with a wheelchair ramp up to glass sliding doors. Attached to it was a house that had a more homely appearance with a warm wooden exterior. A high thatched roof sat on the top like a hat.

Donny knocked on the door. Animated conversations seeped out from cracks.

Someone opened the door to unleash the noise of the party into the open. Victoria stood there, but gone were her baggy clothes, replaced with a silver dress that floated above her knees. A velvet band wrapped around above her waist and Donny became aware of her figure. Her lips were a ruby red and a light dusting of eye shadow turned her irises into sparling stars under her glasses.

'I hardly recognised you with the new top,' said Victoria as she took him by the arm and led him into the madness of the party.

Donny flushed as his heartbeat increased. 'I could say the same about you.'

'Let me give you the grand tour,' she said pulling on his arm. 'This is the living room where we are hanging out. Probably nothing as fancy as what you have back home, but we know how to have fun without any fancy gadgets. That door over there is the bathroom. Its early so I don't think anyone has passed out in it yet. And the staircase will lead you upstairs, but you'll only find bedrooms. Off limits mister.'

'Understood,' Donny said.

They squeezed past two young men who were having an animated debate. The kitchen felt smooth on the senses. Marble counter tops and pure vinyl linoleum flooring. An assortment of bottles stood in a mess of plastic red cups.

'If there is one thing this town is never short in supply of, its vodka,' said Victoria. 'Can I pour you a cup?'

'Sure, thank you.'

'Did you ever watch those teen movies when you were a kid? We were never allowed to of course, with all the swearing and sex. At sleepovers, me and my friends watched them. Mostly those cheesy chick flicks but sometimes gross comedies too. They always had the best college parties. I guess we should be thankful for what we have. But I always wanted to experience a life like the ones on screen. A life of excitement.'

Victoria handed him a cup, their fingers slightly brushing each other's in the exchange. Their eyes met. Donny couldn't ever remember glimpsing something as overwhelming as the hidden cosmos in her eyes.

Donny sipped the vodka. He coughed instinctively and leaned over. The liquid burnt his throat and clogged his wit.

She laughed. 'Easy sailor, lots of water to cover.'

'This is way stronger than what we had back home.' Donny could always be counted on to ruin a moment

'You'll get used to it. Once you recover there are some chopped carrots over there. Don't you dare say I don't know how to throw a damn good party.'

'I would never dream of saying such a thing,' Donny said.

A huge crash came from the other room.

'What the hell is going on in there?' Victoria yelled as she stomped in the direction of the noise. 'Kyle what did you do?'

'C'mon, Vic. It was an accident,' Donny heard someone say from the other room.

The volume of conversation and laughter returned to normal as Victoria continued to berate some poor boy. Donny picked up a couple of carrot slices and popped them into his mouth. They were cool and crunchy. He washed them down with the bitter vodka.

Donny wandered back into the living room. Candles were perched in unusual spots around the house and gave the place a medieval feel. The flames cast long shadows of the guests against the walls. Victoria stood in the middle of scattered ceramic fragments as a boy apologised profusely while placing the pieces in a pile. The other party goers sipped from their plastic cups and huddled closely to each other. He recognised a few boys from his class on a sofa. Their smiles vanished when they saw him, and they lowered their voices.

Donny ignored the harsh stares and moved to the other side of the room. A bookcase full of medical texts caught his eye. His thirst of knowledge easily attracted him to scientific fields he knew nothing about. He slid one out and squinted at words he didn't recognise. The pages felt glossy as he flipped to a diagram of the human anatomy. The book slid back in easily amongst other mammoth volumes.

A passageway shrouded in darkness led away from the party deep into the unknown. Donny glanced over his shoulder. His classmates were no longer paying him any attention. He placed his drink above the fireplace and picked up the candle by its brass holder. With the light, he could sneak down the hall. He turned and ended at a heavy reinforced door. His hand tried the handle.

The door clicked open and he walked in.

A sterile smell clung to the inside of his nostrils. The surfaces were ridiculously clean compared to the dirty world they lived in.

Even in the dull light he knew he had been here before.

He walked over to the bed where they carried out tests on him when he first arrived. A tray of metallic tools lay to one side. Donny noticed the lack of equipment. No patient monitor, no defibrillators, no anaesthetic machine, no electrosurgical units and no surgical lights. Simple prehistoric tools and cabinets of liquids.

How could these people survive with such basic medical equipment? Donny thought.

He placed the candle on a countertop and examined a tool more closely. A bone saw. The thoughts of this being used in an operation made his stomach heave. How could they trust the human hand to make accurate incisions and cuts over the precision of a computer's laser? The absence of power turned this medical centre into a museum.

'What are you doing in here?'

Donny spun around to find a girl standing in the doorway. She was short in stature with tanned skin and hair as dark as the Romanian night sky. Her stare cold and stern. A long glove covered her left arm.

'Huh?'

'You're not allowed to be in here,' she said in a soft Romanian accent. 'This is the medical centre; it is off limits unless you are sick. Are you sick?'

'No. I don't think so at least.'

'Well, you shouldn't be in here.' She walked over and snatched the saw from his hand and lay it back on the table. Her eyes ran up and down his body as if she was a machine herself scanning him.

'I was only curious. I'm surprised your people use such ancient tools here. No electricity, no proper lighting. I'd be terrified if I had to have an operation.'

'We do just fine, thank you *very* much. Our community has been running successfully for five years without power. If anything, it has brought has closer together.'

Donny raised his hands. 'I didn't mean to cause offence. My name is Donny. I'm the new guy in Grade 12.'

'I know who you are. I sit a row in front of you in class.'

'Oh really? There are a lot of new faces, I'm not sure where I know each one from.'

The girl rolled her eyes. 'Save it. Well you know my father at least.'

'Is your father the doctor? Are you Victoria's sister?'

This only made the girl angrier. 'Victoria? No. I'm not related to Victoria Lafave.'

'You don't seem to like her much. How come you're at her house?'

She flushed. 'I don't need to explain myself to you. She has a nice house and throws the best parties, I guess. My friends are here, so why shouldn't I be?'

'Why are you being defensive?'

'I'm not being defensive. Why are you being annoying?'

Donny laughed. 'I get that a lot.'

'You know the old saying? "If one person tells you you're a horse tell them they're crazy. If three people tell you you're a horse, it's time to buy a saddle."'

He smiled. 'I know the one. So, who is your dad?'

'Mihai. He has taken a real shining to you, you know?'

'He sure fooled me,' Donny said as he sat on the bed. 'He almost drowned me during the church service.'

'Papa is all show. He lives for theatrics, it's part of his charisma. In this world, you are either a sheep or a shepherd. My father is a born leader. The people here love him, and he loves them fiercely in return. And he loves you too.'

'Tell me...' Donny looked at the girl expectantly.

'Ana.'

'Tell me Ana. Are you a sheep or a shepherd?'

Ana's glare softly transformed into a smirk. She strolled closer to him. 'A shepherd, but of course.'

'But of course,' he repeated. For the first time Donny could see her eyes in the dull glow. Donny believed eyes were the gateways into a person's soul. Ana's were so dark they absorbed the entirety of the spectrum. The flame that danced at the top of the candle, sparkled in her eyes.

'Tell me, Donny. How did you get such a high score on the mock test?'

'I don't know, it was easy.'

'Easy? It was easy?! I spent the whole summer studying every possible past paper and I found it difficult.'

'I'm sorry,' Donny said. 'Did you get a bad mark?'

'I got the highest! God, don't you ever pay attention?'

Donny smiled. 'Impressive. I think you and I have different standards of what constitutes as difficult.'

'Maybe I have higher standards than you. I do see you talking to Victoria a lot.'

'Ouch. I'm wounded. Yet this raises more questions. Do you spend a lot of time watching me?'

'Quiet you,' Ana said and kicked one of the legs of the bed. Her lips parted as they were about to say something and closed again.

A guy's voice called for Ana from deep in the house.

'They're probably trying to start up a game. Would you like to join us?'

'I don't know,' Donny said. 'I haven't played party games in a long time.'

She picked up his candle. 'Come on, it'll be good for you. Instead of spending your energy going around criticising everything, you could use it to make friends. I know how it feels to be an outsider. You need to throw yourself headfirst into opportunities, even if they don't seem appealing.'

'Okay,' he said.

They walked back to the living room where the young party attendees had gathered in a circle, either sitting on chairs or on the floor. They all had drinks in hand. The air was charged with adolescent inquisitiveness. Ana manoeuvred through the crowd and sat next to Liam. He wrapped an arm around her shoulders, glaring in Donny's direction. Donny looked away and retrieved his drink. He found a place on the floor near the fireplace.

'Ladies and gentlemen, could I please have your attention.' A tall boy with strange eyebrows stood up waving his arms. 'May I first thank our glorious hostess, Victoria for this rather sophisticated gathering. While the adults have their uptight evening of activities, we're out here having the night of our lives.' The young people in the circle cheered and whooped.

'Now, now, settle down now children. A grown up needs to explain the rules for the event of the evening. The game is "Never have I ever". The rules are quite simple. Someone will go first, and they will say a basic statement describing something they have never done before starting with the phrase "Never have I ever". The more ludicrous, the better. Anyone who has done the action suggested, must drink. Who would like to kick us off?'

A young girl with tanned skin and a mischievous grin, almost fell over from her seated position, grasping on to her cup. Not a drop of drink was spilt. 'I'm going first, I'm going first,' she giggled.

'No one ever thought otherwise, Haze,' Ana said.

The kid with the weird eyebrows raised his hand. 'It has been decided. Hazel will go first, and we'll continue clockwise. Let the games begin.'

Expectant eyes fell on Hazel as she composed herself. 'Never have I ever,' she hushed her voice. 'Said I love you just to get laid.'

A well-built boy who had been responsible for smashing something in Victoria's house sipped his drink. A girl cried out and threw a cushion at him while everyone burst into hysterics.

Once everyone calmed down, the game continued. The questions from then on were tame and Donny sipped his own drink a couple of times. *I bet none of these kids have been used as a Guinea pig in a jet pack experiment only to crash in the sea,* he chuckled to himself.

The memory evaporated as Liam's eyes squinted at Donny. 'Never have I ever had one of my parents murdered by the androids.'

An icy chill ran down Donny's spine. His skin prickled uncomfortably as everyone stared at him.

Liam knew. They all knew.

Donny bolted from the group. His leg caught the side of a sofa and pain soared through his body, but he kept moving towards the door. Commotion stirred behind him. He could hear Victoria shouting and the slaps of high fives.

He broke out into the cool air of the night and sprinted down the path lit by the swaying lanterns. His shoes pounded against the worn tarmac until he made out Gheorghe's house from the shadows.

The deafening echoes of his blood ricocheted around his ears. His fingers trembled as he struck a match to light his candle. It guided him to the bedroom, where he shut the door and let out a heavy sigh.

Donny's mind raced with nostalgic thoughts. He missed the sea breeze that drifted into his bedroom. He missed the young boy who idolised him. He missed working at the lab. He missed Edwin, with his goofy smile and lame jokes. He missed his Dad.

He rolled over on the mattress and reached towards his backpack. He pulled out the book his Dad gave to him on his birthday. His palm brushed over the embroidered title on the cover. *Catcher in the Rye.* Donny flipped open the book and noticed an inscription that lay inside.

Donny,

I know you're growing up so fast, so I wanted to pass on this book to you. It's about a young man finding his place in the world. You will find your place one day, never put unneeded pressure on yourself. Enjoy the journey. Life is short so make the most of every minute, of every hour. I know your Mum watches over you, and how proud she is to see the man you've become. I'm proud of you too. Not a day goes by where you don't bring joy to my life. Keep shooting for the stars.

Love,
Dad

Donny dropped the book and cried. The dam had broken and everything he had been holding inside flooded out of him. He had cried a few times as a child, but nothing like this before. So raw, so unapologetic. His entire body convulsed in agony with each sob, his wail low and desperate. What he would give to see his father again and to tell him that he loved him.

Donny cried until he became exhausted and he could cry no more.

No matter the cost, he would make it to Seoul.

ANA

EIGHT

Ana kicked up dirt from the road. A storm of dust circled above her ankles before falling on her mud caked Converse shoes.

A wild dog emerged cautiously from the nearby bushes. Her coat matted was in rough patches. A scar lay across her snout, a notch of achievement for surviving out in the wilderness. She panted happily trying to cool down from the exposed sky. After scouting for danger, she trotted along the road as if she owned the land. Two smaller figures darted out closely behind her. Puppies with matching patterns on their fuzzy fur. They yapped at each other as they stayed close on their mother's heels.

The litter shrank in size each time Ana noticed them. There had been four puppies the week before. She dared not imagine what fates they had met. The mother and her two young pups turned around a fence and disappeared.

'Are we going to wait out here forever?' Hazel asked impatiently. She leaned against a wall with her darkest shades pushed up against her nose.

'Haze is right,' Foghorn said. He was both the tallest and loudest of all of Ana's friends with noticeably bushy eyebrows. A long hunting rifle hung off his shoulder. 'If we want to leave, we should leave now. I don't see the point of taking him with us. He could be a liability.'

Ana looked up from the markings she made in the dirt. 'Papa told me the new boy ventured off his island and

106

entered their territories. Foghorn, have you been out in the woods without your hunting party? Has anyone? We could do with his experience, who knows what could happen out there. We're taking him.'

A collective murmur of agreement rose from her friends. A noise she had become accustomed to over the past few years. Despite being naturally reserved, she always got her way in such matters. No one came close to Ana's stubbornness. Maybe that's why she clashed heads with Victoria so often.

'Liam,' she said. 'Are you going to knock on Donny's door? You do owe him an apology after what you said.'

Liam folded his arms. 'It's not my fault he can't take a joke.'

'A joke that was funny to the most abhorrent of creatures perhaps. Come on, my love,' Ana grabbed him by the hand and led him up to the porch. 'You can be a bigger man and swallow your pride.'

The door shook on its hinges as Ana pounded on it with a gloved fist. She needed to watch her strength.

A moment later the door swung open and Donny stood there in a t-shirt and boxers. His ruffled hair fell over squinted eyes.

'Morning?' Donny asked hesitantly.

Ana averted her eyes away from Donny's bare legs. After a few moments the silence became unbearable and Ana nudged Liam in his side.

'About what happened the other night,' Liam started. 'I didn't mean it.'

'No harm done,' Donny said in a flat tone.

'And,' Ana said.

'And we were thinking of heading out,' Liam said. 'There is a city a two hour walk north of here. Its deserted and mostly rubble. It'll be fun and maybe we can find some new clothes or whatever floats your boat. You're welcome to join us.'

Donny ran his fingers through his hair as if he was deep in thought. His head moved into a slow shake. 'No thanks,' he said and closed the door.

Ana blinked a few times, not sure what to say.

'Told you he was a weirdo,' Liam said under his breath. The pair turned and walked back down the path to join their friends. 'What a waste of time.'

'Wait a minute,' a voice called behind them. Donny appeared at the door again, still half dressed. 'Does this city have any factories?'

'I guess it does,' Ana said as she exchanged a perplexed expression with Liam.

'Nice one,' Donny exclaimed. 'Let me change and I'll be with you in a bit.'

A few moments later, Donny jogged towards them. He wore cream shorts and a deep navy polo shirt that exposed his hairy arms and legs. A shabby attempt had been made to smarten his hair.

'Sorry I kept you waiting,' Donny said as he slipped into what appeared to be an empty backpack. 'I'm ready to go.'

'Great,' Ana said. 'Let me introduce you to everyone. You already know Liam and --'

Hazel grabbed Donny by the arm and kissed the back of his hand. 'Enchanté,' she said. Donny blushed.

Ana rolled her eyes. 'This is Hazel, my incorrigible friend. Over there is Kyle and Nicole. And this is Brennan. We call him Foghorn.'

Foghorn held the rifle strap tightly with one hand and shook Donny's hand firmly with the other. 'Nice to meet you, newbie. I hope you're settling in alright.'

Donny nodded.

'Right,' Ana said clapping her hands. 'Shall we make a move?'

The group treaded cautiously up the narrow path on the mountain side in single file. Ana's shoes shuffled at short paces so she wouldn't make the mistake of stepping on a feeble piece of ground. She ran the fingertips of her gloved hand along the cliff face. The metal resonated satisfyingly against the hard surface. If she felt herself falling, she could cling onto the side.

At the top of the mountain, a lush vegetation of forest fell before them. The trees ran for miles in every direction as if a celestial being had spent an eon placing them in their perfect locations, in the way an artist lays paint on a canvass. The mixture of olive and khaki shades lathered the branches while blocks of concrete peeked out in the far distance.

The group let out a collective sigh of relief once they had reached the forest floor. Ana didn't mind climbing the mountain and enjoyed spending time on the peak to read or be alone with her thoughts. She knew Liam struggled with his fear of heights. She would calm him down once they had returned home.

The forest floor was cool and shaded from the harsh rays of the sun. Moss and grass grew undisturbed in the umbrellaed shadows. The ground cushioned her shoes as though they walked on a carpet.

Ana couldn't remember the last time she saw such pure greenery. She breathed in the dew edged scent of the wilds.

'Won't the adults know we've gone missing?' Donny asked from behind her.

'No one minds when you leave the town,' Foghorn said. 'We have to leave for all kinds of reasons. To hunt. Gather fruit. Fish. They only care who enters the town.'

'Oh,' Donny said, slightly confused as he had gotten a different impression by what Mihai told him. 'What do the other kids get up to? I've been wondering about the school we go to. There doesn't seem to be many students. Or other classes. Are the younger children in a different school?'

The teenagers exchanged glances.

'Times were uncertain during the war,' Ana said. 'When the council was formed, they decided the children might not be safe here. If I remember correctly the soldiers used the trucks to transport the children who were eleven and younger to a safehold base for children outside of Bucharest. My Father said it was an old orphanage converted to a day care for the children of soldiers who were fighting in the great war. That happened over five years ago. With no petrol, it is too far to reach them safely.'

'I miss my sister,' Hazel said as her voice slightly broke. She composed herself and continued. 'We need to keep praying that one day they will return to us.'

'I see,' Donny said.

Once the conversation had died out Donny approached Ana. 'Hazel seemed upset. Does she believe the orphanage was destroyed?'

Ana sighed. 'There is a terrible stigma surrounding orphanages in Romania. Would you like to hear about it?'

Donny nodded.

'At the end of the last century we were ruled by the communist leader Nicolae Ceaușescu. He wanted Romania to be a global superpower, so in order to fulfil his dream he believed a population surge would equal an economic growth. He forced families to have many children and taxed those who were childless. Many of those families couldn't afford to look after their kids so they sent them to orphanages. They became overcrowded and when the economy crashed, many of the orphanages had no electricity or heat. Disease and infections riddled the children. By the year 1989, there were 100,000 children in orphanages. Hazel and many of the parents in the village are worried that this orphanage my Father speaks of is like the ones of old.'

'I see,' Donny said again.

The group continued their march through the woods. They stayed close together, not letting anyone wander too far from sight. The chatter of birds made up the background ambience. When someone spoke, they kept it in a low voice. Except for Foghorn who had to be told frequently to be quiet.

They took a break. A few of the boys in the group were arguing over a map Kyle had taken from the library. From the top of a ridge, the route appeared to be in a straight direction. After an hour of walking through the trees, their bearings had been distorted. They finally came to an agreement and they proceeded.

Nicole, who was usually a timid and quiet girl, coughed gently before asking a question. 'What if we run into one of *them*?'

'There is nothing to worry about,' Ana reassured her. 'All the scouting parties who have patrolled this forest have seen no signs of android activity. This region is deserted except for the animals.'

'Big scary animals that will eat us,' Foghorn said.

'And also roaming bandits that will capture us and turn us into their slaves,' Liam added as the colour drained from Nicole's face.

They laughed and Ana shot the pair a dark look.

'We'll be safe,' Donny said to Nicole walking up beside her. 'If any bandits do show up, they'll take one look at Liam and Foghorn, decide there is not a single braincell between them and continue their search for intelligent life.'

The teenagers burst into laughter while Ana did her best to suppress a smile.

Foghorn slapped Donny on the back. 'You're alright, newbie.'

Ana imagined the trees would clear as they reached the city. Instead, a concrete wall emerged through the trunks as if someone had built a random office block in the middle of the wilderness. Another building soon appeared shortly after and the grassy under footing transformed into crumbling rubble.

They walked out into an old road. Young trees grew out of the tarmac, lining up the street like a freshly created orchard. The grey buildings, with missing windows and soulless paint, acted as an artificial pot for the plant life.

Nature had taken back the city.

After searching the area, they found an old shopping centre. Liam and Kyle found a fallen trash bin and threw it against one of the large display windows. The glass shattered into shards as a decrepit mannequin fell over. The glass cracked under Ana's weight as she followed her friends into the building. Donny stood motionless outside on the road.

'Aren't you coming in?' Ana asked him.

'I'm going to explore other parts of the city,' he said.

'Meet us back here when you're done. Be safe, okay?'

Donny smiled. 'I will. See you later, crocodile.'

'That's not how…that doesn't even rhyme.' Ana shook her head and walked through the store's window.

She blinked as her vision adjusted to the dwindling light that crept into the building. The others hollered and laughed as they ran down the shopping aisles. She stepped over clothes strewn over the floor like an old sweatshop. She ventured deeper in.

Dull fabrics hung from creepy mannequins without heads. Mounds of dust particles exploded in the air when Ana pushed the t-shirts down the bannisters, the hangers screeching on the metal poles. She remembered the shopping centre being crowded during the pre-war days. She guessed when they evacuated the city, material items such as the latest summer fashion wasn't on top of the looter's lists.

The back of store was damp and smelt of mould. Liam sat on a dirty bench as he struggled with a boot, unable to pull it onto his foot.

'Where is your *friend*?' he asked.

'He wanted to explore some of the other buildings,' Ana said ignoring the blatant dig. She inspected his new footwear. 'Oh good. You said you needed a new pair.'

Liam pulled the boot off and tossed it to the side. 'There's not much choice here.'

She stroked the back of his head. 'That's okay. If you see a pair you like, we can check the stockroom to find one in your size. If nothing takes your fancy, I'm sure there is a dedicated shoe store somewhere in the city.'

Liam patted her leg. 'Thanks babe.'

The unmistakable sound of metal shirking against metal caught Ana's ear as she saw a curtain being pulled back from the changing room area. Hazel strutted towards them as if she were a model from the old-fashioned catwalk era. Hazel wore a skin-tight red dress that hugged her body. Ana imagined it was what adults wore when they danced at the night clubs. The notion of night clubs was as foreign to her as castles in fairy tales.

Hazel pouted. 'How do I look, bitches?'

Liam whistled.

'Foarte frumos,' Ana said in Romanian. 'Very beautiful.'

113

Another figure slid from the other side in his socks. Kyle wore a gym tank top vest with the word *beast* in italics across the front. His lean muscular arms flexed in different positions as he roared.

'Don't mean to steal your thunder, Haze. I can't help it when the gun show is on display'. Kyle grinned and pumped his arm, his slender bicep bulging.

'You need some more protein in your diet, mate,' Liam said.

'You what?'

Ana jumped back as Kyle tackled Liam off the bench. The pair wrestled on the ground, with grumbles and laughter. Liam held him down before Kyle broke free and pinned Liam's arm behind his back.

'You better be careful, Liam,' Kyle said. 'The beast is back in town. Ana tell him how buff I look in my top.'

'Get off me you idiot,' Liam grunted.

Hazel tugged her by the right hand and led her away from the fight. 'Come on, I want to find a dress for you too. We will finally be the badass queens that we know we are.'

Ana rolled her eyes and grinned. She felt like the popular teacher while her pupils fought for her attention.

'See here,' Kyle said behind her back. 'Ana likes me more than you now.'

'Is there anything you are dying to wear?' Hazel asked.

'I'm not sure,' Ana said honestly. 'All I want to find is a new toothbrush.'

'Don't be silly,' Hazel smiled. 'I've found this cute lil' number for you. It's a bit short but what daddy doesn't know won't hurt him.'

'Guys, you better come see this.' Foghorn's voice froze them in their tracks. It carried across the store, a serious and panicked tone coated his speech.

The group met him at the bottom of the stairs. Foghorn paced on one of the steps further up, not saying a word. The rifle was no longer on his shoulder as he held it tightly in his hands. Even in the shadows, Ana could tell the colour had drained from Foghorn's face. She couldn't remember the last time he had been lost for words.

'Spit it out,' Hazel said as she stuffed the red dress in her backpack. 'We still have a lot of shopping to do.'

'There is...something on the third floor,' Foghorn said.

'Is it a big summer sale?' Hazel asked. 'I'm sure the whole store has the same deal going on. It's called everything is free.'

'Don't joke,' he said. 'This is important, Haze. I think the girls should wait downstairs.'

Ana exhaled sharply. 'Even though we appreciate your outdated chivalry, it'll be safer if we stick together. Show us what you've found.'

The group ascended the stairs, following closely behind Foghorn with the tip of his rifle pointing forwards. Ana held her breath as they passed through the darkened areas in the stairwell. They stepped out onto the third floor and the light from the windows found its way to her skin again. A repugnant smell assaulted Ana's senses. She had to breathe in through her mouth to avoid losing her breakfast.

Death hung in the air.

It took a moment for Ana to understand what she observed. Three men lay on the floor. Or what was left of them. Their hands were bound behind their backs and gaping holes had been buried in their skulls. Most of their unprotected flesh and been eaten away, exposing the bone and rotting flesh. They lay in their own congealed blood.

Nicole shrieked in horror. Hazel grabbed onto her and led her back to the stairs.

'Who could have done this?' Liam asked.

'By their clothes, they look like raiders,' Foghorn said. 'All have a single laser blast to the head. They were executed.'

'It happened recently,' Ana added. 'Maybe a few days ago. The wolves found them like this.' The war had been five years ago but the bodies in front of her brought back disturbing memories of death and destruction. She shuddered refusing the memories to resurface. 'We need to go back. Whoever did this, could still be here.'

Ana led her friends back into the scorching sunlight. The deserted street showed no signs of life. The dry leaves crackled under their feet. A figure darted out of a building in the distance and Foghorn raised his rifle. Ana lay her gloved hand of the rifle and pushed it down.

'It's Donny,' Ana said.

'Maybe he was involved in what happened to those men in the shop,' Liam said. 'Maybe he shot them.'

'We know he arrived in that pod thingy,' Kyle said. 'You know, the old tech.'

'Thanks for that, Einstein,' Liam said. 'Who knows where he came from? We don't know anything about him. Maybe he teleported from somewhere close. A spy from the enemy. Was he even interrogated properly?'

'Exactly,' Hazel agreed. 'He could even be working with *them*.'

'Enough,' Ana snapped. 'I'll go fetch Donny. The rest of you head back into the woods and start making your way home. We'll catch up.'

Liam looked hurt. 'You can't go by yourself, it's not safe.'

'What would be dangerous is if all of us moved deeper into the city. I'll be faster by myself. See you guys in a few minutes.'

Ana headed towards the centre of the forested metropolis. After a couple of minutes, she came to the entrance of an old factory. The doors were wide open on rusted hinges. Ana stopped herself from calling out for Donny to avoid being heard.

She ventured in, passing a reception desk, before reaching the shop floor. Metallic tools and computers lay around her, a glimpse into the past.

Ana gasped as a hand tapped her on the shoulder.

'Don't worry, it's only me,' Donny said.

'There you are,' she sighed feeling relief entering her body. 'It's time for us to leave.'

'I assumed you would be hours still. There's so much good loot here. I wouldn't mind exploring for a bit longer.'

'It's not safe. Please, I'll explain when we are back in the forest.'

Donny nodded as he instantly knew the gravitas of the threat. He gripped the straps of his backpack to ready himself to sprint away. They slipped by debris on the floor, careful not to disturb any loose materials that could cause a noise.

Before they could make it back to the road, Ana instinctively pulled back and Donny bumped into the back of her. 'Did you hear that?'

'Hear what?' Donny whispered.

The scene outside remained the same. Trees slightly swayed on their spots in the concrete. Abandoned cars rested. The birds had stopped chirping.

A figure walked by the window. A chill ran down Ana's spine. It was over six feet tall with a vacant expression. It wore a suit commonly worn by androids and it was muddied and flayed. It carried one of the laser rifles made famous in the war.

Ana and Donny ducked behind a desk. Donny had a small metal object in his hand. A revolver. *Where did you get that?* Ana mouthed at him. Donny didn't respond and put a single finger to his lips. The two of them waited crouching for what felt like an hour, but she knew only minutes had painfully crept by.

Donny peaked around the desk and signalled to move back to the factory floor. Ana followed Donny through the machines until they found a metal door at the end of an aisle. He pried the door open and allowed Ana to move in first and he closed the door behind them, blanketing them in pure blackness.

Ana gasped as a beam of light pierced through the shadows. It came from Donny's wrist and centred on the stairs. She marvelled at its brightness. Ana hadn't seen a light source other than the sun, moon, or candles for years.

They reached the top floor and found a secluded corner office with a view that looked over the city. Ana locked the door behind them and joined Donny near the edge of the window, peeking behind the blinds.

'I can't see him or your friends anywhere,' Donny said as he carefully put the blind back against the window. 'What happened?'

'We found bodies in the shopping centre. Their hands were bound, and they had been shot in the head. I'm not talking about war time executions. Their bodies were decomposing.'

'Shit.'

'Whoever that was downstairs, it might not be alone. I don't know what they're doing here. Foghorn said a hunting party had passed by this city only a couple of months ago and it was deserted.'

'It doesn't look like they appreciate visitors,' Donny said taking another peak out of the window. 'What happened to your friends?'

'I told them to head back. I saw you in the distance and thought we could catch up with them quickly...' She trailed off.

Donny placed the gun on the desk. 'Thank you. Thank you for coming back to get me.'

'Anyone would've done it.'

He raised an eyebrow. 'Liam wouldn't have risked his life for mine.'

Ana tried to say something, but nothing came to mind.

'We'll be safe here,' Donny said changing the subject. 'If we speak softly and don't open the blinds, I don't think they'll find us.' He sat down on a lone sofa.

Ana sat next to him. Stress ran away from her, and she was grateful to rest her body after spending hours on her feet. 'How long should we wait here for?'

'Until after midnight.'

'Their vision is bad at night,' they said in unison. They both smiled.

'Also, not the best idea,' Ana said.

'Why?'

'Um, have you heard about an animal called a wolf? They hunt at night as it's too hot for them during the day.'

Donny flushed. 'I know what a wolf is. We only get badgers back in England.'

'You weren't to know. I hope the others will be alright.'

'Foggy had a mean looking rifle, they should be safe.'

'I guess.' Ana wondered if Liam would come back to look for her. It reassured her that he wouldn't and would head back to town, but it also left her with a bad taste of dismay. He would never risk himself for her either. 'Then its decided. We'll stay here until dawn.'

For the next couple of hours neither of them said much. Anxiety-fuelled thoughts floated through Ana and she remained glued to the sofa. She wondered if Liam or Hazel would tell her parents where she was. Would her father send his soldiers to come rescue her? Would the androids find them?

Donny never stopped fidgeting. He moved from the sofa back to his spot on the wall where he peered through the blind observing the streets below. Every now and then, he would pick up the revolver and open the barrel as though the bullets had magically vanished.

Ana considered him when the last rays of the days cast down his body. The first new person in her life for years. Would she be safe spending a night with a stranger?

'Who are you?' Ana asked suddenly.

The break of noise startled Donny. 'Excuse me?'

'I mean, how did you get here? It doesn't make any sense. The old world is dead. There is no power left anywhere.'

Donny moved away from the window and examined her. 'Do you think there are only barbarians left in the world?'

'It's not that I think you're a barbarian. Don't be silly. It's hard to wrap my head around. You arrived here by some powered up machine like it was some mundane event. I have a theory. You're actually from some depraved band of thugs. You snuck into the barn and pretended that you're from the other side of the continent. You planned to get me alone and then kidnap me, and now you're holding me here captive.'

Donny smiled as he sat on the edge of the desk. 'Quite the theory.'

'It's more logical than what you told Papa.'

'I hate to break it to you, but that's what happened. My friend Edwin and I worked on the Lightspeed Capsule...the teleportation device. After years of hard work, we finally fixed it. So here I am.'

'Well, if you didn't end up in Romania, I wouldn't have invited you to come with us on this trip, and I wouldn't have had to come save you. I would've been safe with my friends heading back to the village. I wish you never came to Romania.'

Donny's face twisted. Ana regretted her choice of words. She didn't mean to take out her frustrations on him. She always played by the rules. The one time she strayed, she ended up in danger.

'Listen, I didn't plan to be here,' he finally said slowly as to restrain his anger. 'It was a mistake. I didn't choose to come here. It turned bad and I had to leave quickly without planning a proper destination.'

'That's why Papa says we must leave the old tech in the past where it belongs. It only brings misery and pain to our people.'

'Do you believe him?'

'Yes.'

'Technology can be used for good. It can solve hunger, it can educate children, it can connect families across the globe. It put humans on the Moon and on Mars. With technology we cured diseases and healed people.'

'Don't patronise me, Donny,' she said. 'I know human history better than anyone. When we created ships and explored the world; we turned people into slaves. When we created gun powder, missiles, and atom bombs; millions died. Then when we created artificial intelligence; the human race diminished to near extinction. So please, keep on explaining to me the wonders of technology.'

Donny paused for a long time, studying her. 'It's still better than living in the mud like you do.'

'Excuse me?' she snapped.

'Calm down, they will hear you.'

'Don't tell me what to do in my own homeland. What do you mean living in the mud?'

'It seems pointless,' Donny said. 'Why are we even in school learning about physics and history? You gain so much knowledge, but then you end up working in a field at the end of it all. And you accuse me of being a barbarian.'

'No, it's not pointless. You may think you're better than us because you come from some place frozen in time, but there is nothing wrong with ploughing the earth. It means people don't starve. We work for our survival; machines don't do it for us. It is a simple life but a happy life. You need to get your head out of your butt.'

Donny's face flushed a crimson red. They sat in silence avoiding eye contact. It felt like someone placed a weighted bag of flour on her shoulders. The heavy sense of aggravation hung in the air.

After the urge of screaming at him left her system Ana spoke in a cool tone as she left the sofa. 'Get some sleep. I'll take the first watch.'

'Sure,' he replied. He laid his watch on the desk. 'You can use it to track the time. Wake me up at 1:00 AM and I'll take the final shift.'

'Thank you,' she said.

Donny stretched out on the sofa and turned away from her to face the wall. She studied the watch. Its chrome design riled up a self-hate within her. A small act of kindness on his part, but it wouldn't wash away the annoyance. She thought he might've been different from Liam. Yet he was just as arrogant. Maybe all boys were the same. This would be the last time she would go out of her way to be nice to Donny.

Ana stole a glance from out the window. The sun had commenced its brilliant ceremony of setting above the trees with its show of warm rays dying out. She did her best to memorize the path that would lead them out of the city when they needed to escape.

Ana wondered if it would be the last sunset she would ever see.

DONNY

NINE

Donny wiped away sleep dust from the corner of his eye and yawned.

It had been a couple of hours since Ana had woken him to take over as the night watch. She didn't have anything to report and seemed grouchy, a result of what he said rather than a lack of sleep or the situation they had found themselves in. Donny regretted what he had said to her. Who was he to judge how others lived? It wasn't only Ana's lifestyle who he had belittled, he criticised those on the island of living a life too small. He had mocked his own father. Donny sighed. Would the life in Seoul satisfy his impossible standards of a perfect life? Perhaps he doomed himself to never be satisfied with whatever blessing he had.

He would apologise to Ana once they were back in the safety of the forest.

The illumination of a full moon made it easy to make out the surroundings of the city. The silver branches of the trees sparkled in the cosmic rays. The city appeared deliberately decorated in the vegetation, giving it the appearance of an alien world.

Ana mentioned she had not seen any movement during her watch. Maybe the android passed through. Ana was right about the wolves. He heard a couple of howls off in the distance, deep in the heart of the woods. The idea of running into a wolfpack did unnerve him. With his handgun he felt safe enough. If they were to encounter any on the way back to the village, he could fire a shot to scare them off. Or aim to kill the alpha.

Donny's back ached and he grew tired of staring through the side. It would be easier if the window were uncovered. He grabbed for the cord controls and slowly lifted the blind up to get a better view of the landscape.

Moonlight poured into the room, soaking its milky beams into every crevasse. A glint of light sparked from the sofa. Ana lay still, her chest falling up and down slowly with the rhythms of her dreams. She wore her trademark glove over her arm. Donny thought it might've been a fashion trend among young Romanian women. It was peculiar she didn't take it off when she slept.

A shiny object was situated at the top of the glove, perhaps a jewel. The more Donny studied it, the more it seemed unnatural. As if it was separate from the piece of cloth.

Curiosity enticed him towards her.

Something seemed strange about the so-called jewel, it had more of a metallic appearance than that of a gem. Ana's face remained still and innocent. Her mouth slightly parted as a soft whistling of air escaped from it in incrementing beats. Without thinking, Donny's hand reached for it.

His fingertips brushed it. The metal was cold, hard and detached from the glove. His fingers lifted the fabric from the skin. Dread crushed his lungs as he choked on the discovery. The metal wasn't on her arm, *it was her arm.* Donny pulled the glove down to reveal a robotic forearm. Long smooth panels ran from a fleshy stump towards an assortment of titanium hinges in her wrist. The glove eventually peeled off the fingers, the digits of complicated weavings and bolts.

Ana was an android.

The hand grabbed Donny by the wrist before he could react. He yelped in pain as the icy fingers squeezed his bones. Ana had woken and watched him with dismay. Donny tried to counter the hold to force himself away. Ana anticipated the movement and twisted his arm forcing him to the floor. The pain seared from his wrist to his brain in a trail of fire as Ana stood over him.

'How dare you undress me,' she choked out, her voice uneven.

'I'm sorry,' Donny managed. His mind tried to ride out the pain. The gun remained still on the desk and he couldn't lift himself to retrieve it. 'Please let me go.'

Ana held him for a moment longer before she released him.

He withdrew his arm and hugged it. His breathing calmed as the pain retreated like a wave falls back into the ocean. Once it subsided, he tested his arm for fractures. Nothing seemed to be broken though it felt like she badly sprained his wrist.

'You had no right to touch me,' Ana said, her eyes narrowed.

'I didn't mean to upset you,' Donny said. Ana stood between him and the gun. He wasn't sure if he would be strong enough to overpower her. The metallic arm hung menacingly by her side.

'Stop staring at me like that,' she said.

Donny diverted his eyes to the floor. 'What are you going to do with me?'

Ana sighed. 'I'm not one of them you idiot. I'm a human.'

'But, your arm...'

'Yes, it's the same type as the ones used in androids.'

Donny pulled himself up to a sitting position. The pain in his wrist had subsided to a dull ache. He saw her in a new light. In all his research never had he heard of any successful procedures of using android technology as human prosthetics. Something peculiar about the fingers. A couple of them kept twitching as if the actions were involuntary.

The entire hand spasmed wildly.

'Oh my God,' Ana said under her breath. She clasped it with her human hand, but the robotic digits continued to wiggle in her grasp. Donny moved up towards her, but she turned away hiding the arm from view.

'Can I have a look at it?' Donny said.

'What? No, you can't look at it. It happens when I feel anxious. It'll pass in a few minutes. Don't make this weirder than it already is.'

'C'mon,' Donny said. 'Let me help.'

Ana regarded him with wary eyes. Her grip fell away, and the whirling of parts buzzed gently in the moonlit room. She lifted the hand closer towards him. Only a few moments ago the fingers were crushing him, now they were dancing to their own tune.

Donny rummaged through his backpack on the ground and returned with a tiny screwdriver. 'You need to hold your arm still for as long as you can.'

'Are you crazy? I'm not going to let you open me up.'

'I know you have no reason to trust me after what happened. I want to make it up to you, I can fix it. You must have some sort of faith in me since you invited me on this trip and that you came back to save me. Plus, you know there is not much damage I can do to an android limb with a silly screwdriver.'

The fingers squirmed furiously as Ana pondered the request. She clamped down her robotic hand and held her wrist out towards Donny.

Donny's fingers removed the four screws that held the square panel at the top of Ana's forearm, carefully placing each on top of the desk. Even in the dim light of the moon, he could spot the problem right away. Dozens of thick chords ran above sealed casings. One of the chords didn't run freely, it had wedged itself deeply in the arm and vibrated violently.

Donny tested the strength of the wire with the head of the screwdriver and Ana groaned softly, sensitive to his touch. He applied pressure to the durable material until the cable popped out.

Ana gasped as if a demon had been sucked out from her soul. The fingers of her android hand had fallen silently. She tested each finger individually, which fired off a couple of the wires at a time in the open panel.

The spasms had stopped.

'How…how did you do that?'

Donny picked up one of the screws from the desk and set the panel back in place. 'I've worked on androids in the past. Deactivated ones of course. Their build is fascinating. Easy to repair, which is a problem for us. You could destroy most of an android and they can still be easily salvaged to be back on their feet in no time.'

Ana's mouth opened and closed as if she wanted to say something, but nothing came from her lips.

'I mean, it's not weird or anything. We had a couple of men back on the island who lost their legs in fishing expeditions that were fitted with prosthetics, but nothing as advanced as this. How did you get it? It even had the latest CPU processor. Edwin would've been amazed; those models were only available to the army and super-rich. Your family must've been wealthy. How do you control it? I understand if you don't want to talk about it, I'm just curious.'

The final screw tightened in place and Ana tested it out. A sense of calmness appeared to float over her. 'No, it's okay. I had a regular prosthetic arm at first. I didn't mind it at all. I had a set of different colour casings that could be

127

switched in and out, depending on my mood. Also, the hands were changeable. I had a normal hand and a claw hand. My personal favourite. Much easier to hold objects with and I could use it to terrorize Hazel.'

'Anti-android sentiment grew more and more each day. My arm made me stand out in the playground and the other kids bullied me. Especially if it lost power in the middle of doing a task, which happened a lot. My father knew this genius of a scientist in the army. He experimented on attaching android-style appendages to those who lost their limbs in battle. To make soldiers even more effective I suppose. I entered surgery and they connected it to it my muscle tissue and nerve endings. I remember touching my mother's face after the surgery. I could actually *feel* her.'

'That's amazing,' Donny said. 'Does it feel pain?'

Ana's tilted to the side. 'Not pain exactly, but it feels uncomfortable when it gets too hot or smashes against a hard surface. Can you see this section here? I can use it to extend it to match the growth of my right arm. I should've received a skin graft every few years. The same skin they used on the androids. Ironically, it would've made me look human. A few weeks after my surgery, the first bombs dropped. The humans were wiped out and I was stuck with an android arm.'

'Must've been tough. I have the impression everyone in your town thinks that technology is the work of the devil.'

'Tell me something I don't know.' Ana smiled for the first time since he left her at the store. It warmed up the icy room. 'I swear some of them believe I'm one of Satan's spawn. That's why I always wear the glove.'

Ana sat on the sofa and gestured to the free seat. *A peace offering*, Donny thought as he sat next to her.

'One time I had to give a speech in front of the class. I was so nervous that halfway through the presentation my hand started to get contractions and I dropped my chalkboard. Before it hit the ground, the kids burst out laughing. I returned to my seat, fingers still spinning around, and I never finished my speech. My teacher didn't say anything and called on another student. It scarred me for life.'

'At least now when you become the shepherd of the flock, you won't have to worry about your arm malfunctioning.'

Ana giggled. 'You know what is funny? I have never spoken at such length about my arm. Not to my parents. Not to my best friend, Hazel. Not even with my boyfriend. I think they pretend it doesn't exist. So, thank you. For fixing it and for listening to my self-pitying tale.'

'Not a problem,' Donny said.

'Gets the second highest score on a pop-quiz on his first day of school, becomes the talking point of the first house party he attends and also happens to be an android mechanic. You become more mysterious and spectacular the more time I spend with you. I'm impressed.'

Donny rubbed the back of his head. 'Spectacular isn't a word someone would use for me back on the island. You know, I'm just a regular lad that mostly kept to himself.'

'Stop destroying this image I have built up of you,' Ana said. 'Tell me about your life on the island. Wait. What time is it? Do we have to leave soon?'

Donny checked the watch on the table. 'We have an hour before sunrise.'

'Good. So, tell me Donny, the mysterious and spectacular barbarian from across the seas, what is your story?'

'There is not much to say really. I lived on a tiny island off the coast of the British Isles. Spent most of my time learning and watching vids from the old world. I didn't have many friends. Well, only one. Edwin. He took me

129

under his wing early on when I showed signs of aptitude in engineering. He was like my goofy older brother. Smart but also an honourable person. Edwin is the kind of guy who would give the shirt off his back if you didn't have one. We looked out for each other.'

'What happened?'

Donny described the events that unfolded over his last fateful days on the island. Ana's mood had softened. 'Is it true what they say about your father? And what of your friend?'

'Yeah, my Dad was killed,' Donny said matter-of-factly. 'I'm not sure what happened to Edwin.'

'I'm so sorry,' Ana said.

'It's strange. I know in my gut Edwin is still alive out there somewhere.' Donny glanced towards the window feeling lost. 'It'll be dawn soon. We should make a move.'

The wind meandered from branch to branch as though the trees whispered to each other. The accumulation of secrets from thousands of years of silent vigils were being passed to one another. The trees bore no animals. Either they were still asleep, or they sensed danger.

Donny kept his thoughts to himself. He and Ana had left the city before sunrise and did not encounter anyone on the roads. Every crunch of his shoe against some loose pebbles or a dried leaf made him squirm. The woods were still hidden in shadows, but he could make out shapes well enough to manoeuvre through. One of the shapes filled him with a sense of unease and he turned towards it.

An android stood in the clearing.

A tall being with broad shoulders. It wore a bodysuit and a laser rifle poked out from behind its back.

Ana screamed as it burst into a sprint towards them.

Donny pulled the revolver out from the front of his khaki shorts and flipped off the safety in one motion. He fired a bullet into the creature's chest, the feedback shot painful flames through his enflamed wrist.

The gunshot did nothing to halt its sprint. Its body absorbed it. The android was upon Donny and slapped his raised hand with such force that the revolver flew into the thicket. Icy cold fingers grasped around Donny's windpipe and his grunts soon became drowned out from the pain.

'What were you doing in my city?' the android asked in a voice so calm that it almost sounded polite. The grip tightened and Donny choked on his words. 'I will make you pay for what you stole from me.'

Sparks exploded from the android's face as Ana's metal fist flew into the side of it. Donny broke free and drunk in the sweet air of the forest. The thud of the android's fallen body echoed through the trees.

'Let's go,' Ana shouted as she tugged forcefully on Donny's shirt.

Oxygen flooded back into Donny's brain as he shook his head in protest. 'No,' Donny panted. 'We need to stop it.'

His hand rummaged through his backpack until the fingers found what they were searching for. The largest screwdriver.

A huge dent showed on the side of the android's face where Ana had hit it. Sparks twirled at the edge of the charred skin. 'Help me turn it over,' Donny instructed. The pair lifted at one side, flipping the android like a heavy tyre.

Donny ripped away the suit's material on the android's lower back. He jabbed the screwdriver into the exposed skin pulling it downwards. Navy coolant squirted from the gash. In the breaking dawn, it glistened like blood.

The skin ripped away until an ominous panel appeared. Like for Ana's arm, Donny worked on opening it. He tossed the coolant-soaked panel aside, which revealed an orange sized sphere buried in a titanium casing.

Donny dug the screwdriver into the side and tried to use the leverage to remove it. Even with all his strength the sphere wouldn't budge, and he felt the shaft start to bend.

The android lifted itself from the floor in a push-up position. Its arm almost struck Donny as he toppled backwards with a violent jolt.

Donny stared at the charred skin of the android's face. It drew in the darkness of the sky. Donny's fears rushed back. How the androids killed everyone on the island. Fear froze him to the spot.

Ana darted behind the android and reached towards its spine with her robotic arm and ripped the sphere out cleanly.

'What do you think you are doing?' The voice now an electric static, crackled as the android fell back to the floor and its eyelids fell shut.

Then there was silence.

They both let out a sigh of relief and fell to the ground.

Moments passed as they both panted. Birds squawked in the distance, welcoming in the new day.

Ana crawled over to Donny to show him what she had removed. 'What is this?' she asked as her metallic fingers tapped on the robotic looking fruit.

'It's the battery.'

'I see. So, his heart?'

'It doesn't have a heart,' Donny said as he lay in the grass. The adrenaline that had built up in his body had nowhere to escape to. His neck ached. His wrist ached. He rested on the ground and concentrated on his breathing. Finally, he spoke again. 'From its suit it appears to be a medical android. I doubt it ever understood compassion.'

'How do you propose we solve the world's problems if both sides hate each other so much?'

'There is no solution,' he said. 'We survive and destroy as many of them as we can.'

Ana considered this as she played with the sphere in her hands. She lay beside him, listening to Donny's laboured breathing. 'I'll keep the battery. A memento of our adventure.'

ANA

TEN

Ana slammed the door, shutting out the bickering voices behind her.

The diminished world had transformed into a winter wonderland overnight. A dusting of snow had sprinkled over the roads, trees and rooftops. Where doom and famine raged on in the minds of the villagers, a clean start came in the form of winter. The worries of the world had been cleaned away.

Ana savoured the crunching of the fresh snow underneath her boots as she marvelled at the footprints being left in the white canvass. No one else was venturing out into the cold. A quiet place only she could enjoy. She pretended to be an explorer, discovering new lands, or conquering Antarctica.

Even in the enormity of the mayor's manor, it had proved difficult to escape the arguments between her parents. The harvest had not been as successful as previous years. Rationing had come into effect and her father had come under pressure to kill even more of the livestock. She needed to get away.

Icy stalactites hung from the thermometer in the town centre. It showed the temperature had dropped ten degrees below zero Celsius. Ana shivered with excitement. She couldn't remember the last time they had a proper winter. Christmas might be wonderful this year for a change.

Ana wrapped her arms across her chest and ventured onwards. She trapped the warmth in her parka, savouring it against the bitter breeze. Winter was her favourite time of the year to dress for. Her jackets covered her android arm from show, and no one questioned when she wore gloves all day. Now her left hand wouldn't feel *left* out anymore. She chuckled at her bad joke.

The door to Liam's house was unlocked and she let herself in. Laughter came from the open living area at the back of the home. The dining room table had been moved to be closer to the fireplace that crackled with a vengeance. Liam, Foghorn, Kyle, and a couple of the boys from the grade below were seated around the table with mountains of colourful plastic chips in front of them. Kyle dealt out cards to the participants of the game.

'Ana, daughter of our fearless leader,' Foghorn called to her. 'Come watch me win. I'm a few rounds away from parting these chumps from their money.'

'What are you playing?' Ana asked as she leaned against Liam's chair. Liam remained in deep concentration as he stared at the two cards in front of him.

'Poker,' Kyle said as he pushed his cards toward the centre of the table. 'Damn it, I'm bleeding chips 'ere. You wanna play next game? We're not playing for anything serious.'

'Only pride,' Foghorn said. 'Kyle has little left. Please join in and help us take the rest away from him.' Kyle grumbled to himself as he counted the few chips that remained in front of him.

Ana beamed and put her arm around Liam's shoulders. 'No thank you, gentlemen. I only popped in to see if my handsome boyfriend would like to accompany me for a walk in the snow.'

In a smooth motion, Liam removed her arm. 'I'm playing with the lads right now. Can we hang out tomorrow?'

Ana's face grew hot and uncomfortable, she was unsure on what to do. The conversations on the table continued as if she had never been there. Her skin prickled and she sweltered near the fire in her winter garments.

'Okay. Enjoy your games.' Ana left the house. Not once had Liam looked in her direction.

The relationship between Ana and Liam had been frosty for a few months now, ever since she spent the night in the city with Donny. It took days of convincing Liam of what happened, the dangerous events that unfolded and how they barely escaped with their lives. Even now, he didn't appear to believe the story. Ana stomped away from the house, no longer caring about the footprints she left behind. Why wouldn't he believe her?

Fortunately, her parents never knew she spent the night away from the village. When Mihai sent a guard to find Ana, Hazel said she planned to spend the night with her. When the guard challenged her and asked to see Ana, Hazel said Ana was in the bathroom with severe period pains. The guard became embarrassed and left.

Ana refused to let Liam ruin her good mood. She would enjoy the snow without him.

The fields had accumulated a lot of powder in their trenches. Ana remained cautious not to trip when her foot sank a few inches deep. When this happened, she would lift her foot up and spray the snow in the air.

Ana wanted to throw a snowball. She didn't care if someone thought of her as childish.

She removed the glove from her android hand and scooped up some untouched snow. The benefit of using her metallic hand would be that she could hold the snow without feeling the cold. The powder transformed into a perfectly formed ball in her cupped hands. Its simplicity was a marvellous sight. The roundness resembled the android battery she kept in an old shoebox at the back of a cupboard.

Ana spied the trees that stood across the field and decided they would be perfect for target practice. She continued her trek, breathing in the sweet air. One of the trees caught her attention. It had a trunk larger than all the others, so it made an appetising goal.

At fifty feet away, she took aim. Like the old pitchers on baseball mounds. The snowball flew past the tree and into the thicket.

'Oi,' shouted a voice from deep in the woods. Donny emerged brushing snow from a woolly hat too big for his head. He wore a bulky coat and massive black boots. The summer glow in his skin remained and his lips were the same colour as jam. His eyes sparkled like sapphires under his snow-coated eyebrows. 'What's the big idea, huh?'

Ana smiled. 'I shouldn't have used my android arm.'

Donny pursed his lips and considered her. From their time in the classroom together, she knew that look meant he was trying to figure something out. 'You would've been a great bowler in any cricket team.'

The terms were foreign to her. 'What do cricket teams do?'

'Never mind,' he said with a wry smile. 'I'm about to head down to the river. The pump has frozen so Gheorghe has sent me on an errand. Would you like to accompany me?'

'It would be my pleasure.'

Donny picked up two steel buckets from their snug snowy pockets and they embarked on their trek past the leafless trees. Some stood as giants like old sages from a mystical time.

No conversation came forward and Ana wondered if the awkwardness remained between them since their stay in the city. He had lived in her village for a few months now and the most noticeable change was his scent, from a salty freshness to the familiarity of dirt and ash. Donny had a seriousness to his demeanour that melted away when he felt embarrassed or uncomfortable. He would answer questions with ease in class to prove his intelligence, but when he messed up or dropped something from his desk, he would blush and laugh at himself. His true self remained hidden behind a wall.

'Is there something wrong?' Donny asked.

The question caught her off guard and she could only pretend she didn't hear him correctly. 'Sorry, what?'

'It's strange,' he said. 'You haven't spoken to me in months. You avoid me in class. Now here we are walking together like nothing happened. You are throwing snowballs, skipping around. Now you're smiling at me like an idiot.'

Ana punched Donny in the arm, and he winced in pain. 'I'm glad you used your human fist, or I might've been killed.'

'All I wanted was one day where I could enjoy myself,' Ana said. 'No pressure of exams in the spring. Time away from my parents who want to rip each other's heads off. I'd find Hazel, but she is a liability. Maybe I could've spent some time with Liam, but no, he is always with his friends. When I woke up this morning, I opened the curtains and it filled me with such happiness. It had *snowed*! It never snows anymore. I wanted to share the day with someone and experience its magic. It feels like all I want to do is grow up and join the council. As a result, I'm missing out on the last few remaining days of my childhood, you know?'

'So, there *is* something wrong.'

Ana stuffed her hands in her coat pockets. 'I don't know, Donny. Maybe.'

They walked further on and a guard passed by on his patrol. Donny and the man exchanged friendly pleasantries before he continued on his route. She always imagined Donny as being a loner. It couldn't have been easy after the tragedies he had faced.

'My friend Edwin once told me I'm a good listener.'

'Is that so?'

'Let's start with something easy,' Donny said. 'Why do you like the snow?'

'The real question is, why don't you like the snow?'

'It's alright,' Donny said non-committedly. 'It's pretty to look at but when I get back home it has soaked my gloves and socks. My fingers and toes feel like they are on fire and about to drop off.'

'Well if you get snow in your boot, make sure to shake it out. You don't need to act like a tough guy around me.'

'Whatever. So why do you love it so much?'

'It's mostly for nostalgic reasons. I remember years ago when Hazel and I played in the snow for the whole of winter. It wasn't much deeper than this, but as a six-year-old, that was a hell of a lot. We made snowmen, forts and an attempt of an igloo but it caved in on us.'

'Sounds traumatic,' Donny said.

Ana laughed. 'Very traumatic. Never been in an igloo since. Anyway. The season is like a fairy tale. Everything is shiny and new, a clean slate, full of possibilities. Christmas is a huge deal for us in the village, not so much for presents these days but midnight mass and lots of food. The most food you'd ever seen on one table. My grandmother would sneak me a cookie before they even served dinner. It tasted delicious and I didn't care if the other children watched me eat it.'

'I can see where you get your boldness from.'

'She was as tough as a walnut. She loved winter as well. Seventy or eighty years ago when the Earth was still cool, they would get mountains of snow. It would come up to her waist. I miss her.'

The Danube came into view. A massive body of water stretched between two snowbanks. It was like a portal to another dimension. The pearl reflections danced off the banks. Shards of ice floated on the surface, resembling frozen water lilies. Donny stumbled down the bank with his two buckets, trying his best to keep his balance and not to plunge in the sub-zero depths of the artic world.

The Danube represented life. The two-sided coin of both beauty and sorrow. Ana had never learned to swim. The vastness of its body overwhelmed her. The other riverbank was so far away it might as well have been on Pluto. She was content to spend her life entirely in the village, though Donny being here changed everything. He had been living an entirely separate life out of this confinement.

The ice drifted silently down the river.

She watched how Donny collected the water. He did it in such a tentative fashion that it looked like he feared a mythical ice reptile would break from the depths and devour him. After the buckets were full, he stood still watching the river rush by. Donny had been fixated by something on the river that only he could see.

Donny shook his head and picked up the buckets. They slushed unsteadily as he hurried back up the hill.

'Made it,' Donny gasped. He rested the buckets on the ground and brushed the snow from his legs. 'Carried them up here without spilling a drop.'

Ana rolled her eyes 'You're an inspiration to us all.'

'I like to think so.' Donny said as he emptied his boots of the accumulated snow.

Ana's left arm reached for one of the buckets. The weight pulled on her shoulder, but the android grip took pressure off the strain. 'I'll help you with your water run, so that's two you owe me, dragă.'

'I'll keep a mental note of all your good deeds,' he said.

Ana and Donny walked back through the forest in silence. Ana wasn't sure if it was an uncomfortable silence or not, but she welcomed the break in conversation to admire the settings and become lost in the world. From the corner of her eye, she noticed Donny stealing glances at her exposed android hand. Most people would stare at her glove in a manner of distrust, yet with Donny it was more of a curiosity. He had seen it in all its glory. It was as though he had seen her naked. The thought sent a strange sensation through her. Not even Liam had seen her arm without the glove on.

'You keep staring at me.' Ana asked.

Donny became startled, as he had been snapped away from a deep trance. 'What did you say?'

'You keep looking at my hand.'

'Your hand. Yes of course! You should be proud of it. I mean, I wish I could throw a snowball like you.'

Ana muffled a giggle with her human hand.

The early evening descended as they broke out into the fields. The warm glow of fires danced in the windows of the houses, enticing them to move in away from the cold. The smoke puffed into the greyness as if the two ecospheres merged to become one.

A noise carried with the wind but became dampened by the snow. The noise came again. A woman's voice.

'There you are!' a girl shouted.

She wore a beautiful elegant black coat that dropped to her knees and her hair fell out effortlessly from her woolly red hat.

'I've been looking everywhere for you,' said Victoria.

'I had to collect water for Gheorghe,' Donny said.

'Yeah, I know. He sent me in this direction to find you. You're always disappearing at the strangest times. You haven't forgotten our plans for later, have you?'

'Dinner at yours? I remember.'

'Listen, I need you on your best behaviour', said Victoria. 'I've put in a lot of groundwork with Daddy and he is warming to you. Smile and laugh at his bad jokes.'

'You know me, I thrive under pressure.'

Ana stood still while the two discussed their dinner plans in front of her. She didn't even think Victoria registered her presence. It might've been partially why she didn't speak to Donny much since that night away. He had become close with her enemy and she couldn't stomach the thought of spending extra time with Victoria.

'Are you enjoying the snow?' Ana asked testing the waters. Too much time had passed for a greeting and she didn't want to be overshadowed by her rival.

Victoria blinked a few times as if Ana had suddenly materialised out of nowhere.

'The snow?' Victoria snorted. 'If you can call this pitiful residue, snow. The blizzards we had back in Canada make this place look like a tacky Christmas exhibit.'

Victoria's eyes lowered to the bucket Ana carried. 'Aren't you the sweetest? Pretending to be a councilwoman already, helping the villagers with their chores.'

'Knock it off, Vic,' Donny said.

Victoria smiled and reached for Ana's bucket. 'I'll help Donny take that back to his house. Don't want to take up anymore of your time. By the way, nice hand, Anadroid.'

Ana flushed and stuck her hands into her pocket. She had forgotten to put her glove back on after she made the snowball.

'Thanks for helping me,' Donny smiled at Ana before he left. She swore she could hear him telling off Victoria as they walked away.

It didn't even occur to Ana that her glove had remained in her pocket. She felt comfortable enough around Donny to leave it off. The joints moved around stiffly as she warmed them up. They had the tendency to get stuck if the temperature dropped below freezing.

Ana wanted to punch the nearby tree with all her might. It took all her self-control to hold back. She knew using excess force when her arm started to freeze would cause damage to it.

She threw the glove on the floor and stamped it into the snow.

• • • • •

Candles burned brightly from Mihai's study. Ana moved quietly as she tried to sneak by to get to her room without being noticed.

'Ana, is that you? Come in here,' a voice called from behind the door.

She cringed and withdrew into herself. She pushed open the door and entered. 'Yes Papa?'

'Are you ready for dinner? I haven't seen you since this morning.' Mihai didn't look up from the papers he wrote on. His grey hair had aged to a pure white over the last few months. It shone brightly against the decaying spines of books stacked in the shelves behind him.

'I'm not hungry,' Ana said.

Mihai glanced up from his desk with an eyebrow raised. His eyes fell on her exposed android arm. The tips of the candles were reflected in its surface.

'Why aren't you wearing your glove?' Mihai asked, the wrinkles on his forehead hardening into a scowl.

'My arm doesn't get cold in the winter, Papa. I wanted to try it out.'

'It is embarrassing,' Mihai said as his attention returned to the papers. 'There are people starving and morale is low. What we don't need is for you to remind them of the monsters that are still out there. Understand?'

'But I thought it --'

'Do not shame this family any further,' his voice was louder now. 'Do you understand?'

'I understand, Papa,' Ana said calmly, a rage rising inside of her.

Ana turned on her heels and left the study.

DONNY

ELEVEN

Donny yawned wildly on his way to school. Another sleepless night left him agitated and groggy. It wasn't a one-off event; he hadn't slept well in weeks. The Lightspeed Capsule restoration was near its end. However, a major problem blocked his path.

The machine required a highly advanced processing unit to make the calculations to send a person's atoms to the satellite in the correct arrangement. Otherwise, their atoms would be shot out into space to be lost forever returning to the stars they originated from.

On his trip to the city, Donny couldn't find anything remotely close to that level of power. Until he opened Ana's arm.

Ana's android arm contained a military grade processor. It wasn't the standard issue unit he had seen in any android he had previously taken apart. Whoever put it together had access to the latest technology used in the war. The processor would be used to translate brain impulses into the arm's receptors so that the movement of the limb would be as natural as flesh, bone, and nerves.

A question that plagued his mind. How would he acquire the processor from Ana's arm?

The most obvious way would be to ask to borrow it. Even if she did agree to it, she would want to know what he needed it for. Then she might tell Mihai what he was planning. Of course, the risk was high. If the unit became damaged, Ana would never be able to use her arm again. It would be a dead piece of metal hanging from her body. Then again, maybe they could travel back to the city. Donny could remove one of the standard issue processors from the android they deactivated. But her movement wouldn't be as fluid. Not an attractive selling point.

The other option was to trap Ana somehow and remove the piece by force. Donny dismissed this idea straight away. Not only would it be too dangerous, he would never dream of treating Ana like that. There was something special about her…

'Earth calling Donny.'

Donny jumped. Victoria walked closely by his side wearing her medical scrubs. She didn't wear a perfume, but her scent was pleasant, and it made him nervous. It reminded him of the meadows from back home.

'Where do you go in your daydreams? You weren't thinking about another girl, were you?'

'No way,' Donny said far too quickly. 'Boring stuff. You wouldn't be interested.'

'Try me.'

'Vectors and three-dimensional geometry.' It wasn't exactly what he had been thinking about, but it was a class he had coming up later in the day.

'Okay, forget I asked.' She wrapped her arm around his and he blushed. Victoria's skin was warm and felt good against his own. Over the last few weeks, they had been spending more time together. Victoria was intelligent, driven and spoke her mind freely, all qualities he admired. Even when she wore baggy scrubs, he would fantasize what she would look like naked. They weren't an item; they hadn't even kissed. Donny's aloofness and dedication to his project probably delayed the relationship from moving at a normal pace.

'I can't believe I'm taking you to school,' said Victoria with a sly smirk. 'It feels like I'm a cougar, stalking you.'

Donny gave her a weird look. 'Get real, Vic. You're like one year older than me.'

'Play along,' she winked at him. 'I can even tutor you afterwards if you want some extra credit.'

The school building came into view when they turned the corner at a rusted stop sign. Several of his classmates waited outside ready for the lessons to start. Other villagers roamed the streets, heading to their jobs. The farmers had probably been in the fields since sunrise.

'My duty beckons,' said Victoria. She placed a soft kiss on his cheek and squeezed his arm tightly. A boy whistled loudly from the group of teenagers near the door. 'You have something to say Foghorn?'

'No ma'am.'

'That's what I thought, shrimp,' said Victoria as she walked away.

Donny waved at her awkwardly as Jaspar arrived. He followed his teacher and the other students inside, and stretched excessively before he took his seat, trying to feed the oxygen into his body. Staying awake for the rest of the day would be a struggle.

Jaspar waited patiently as all the kids piled into the room.

'Good morning!' Jaspar said with his regular flair. 'Please could you keep standing for our daily prayer?'

The class stood attentively and said the prayer they were ordered to recite each day. Donny had heard of American students having to pledge their allegiance to a flag before the great war, and of religious schools saying prayers to their specific gods, though he never heard of a mandatory spoken devotion for another human. Maybe it made more sense than pieces of fabric and invisible deities.

The prayer was short in length. The words were designed to give thanks to the leader, Mihai, almost as if he were a divine being. That he would protect them and feed them. Donny didn't want to make a fuss by refusing to say the lines. All he had to do was to blend into the background as much as possible.

Once the prayer had been completed and Jaspar opened his lesson plan, Donny fell back to doodling on his chalkboard. Most of the material Jaspar taught he either knew already or could pick it up quickly enough in the month end summary sessions. The end of school year and final grades meant little on Donny's list of priorities.

The hour moved slowly; Donny was barely able to keep his eyes open. Perhaps he would have a nap after school. The clock above Jaspar remained permanently at twenty minutes past seven, the batteries had run out and they hadn't bothered taking it to the barn.

A change in the teacher's tone caught his attention. 'Alright class that's enough history for today,' Jaspar said as he clapped his hands together. 'I have a special announcement. I'm so pleased with this idea, I worked on it all weekend. Since Donny joined us, our class finally has an even number of students. That means I can introduce a final year project. One where you'll have to work in pairs. What a treat! I won't be cruel and assign you partners, I'll let you organise that amongst yourselves. You're practically adults now so it should be an easy enough task. The project will be a three-thousand-word comparative paper on two works of fiction written before the twentieth century. What those two books are, are up to you. It'll count as twenty percent towards your final grade, so please take it seriously. This is an out of school assignment, so it'll teach you time management and teamwork skills. We'll take a five-minute recess and then we can delve into the details and organise teams.'

The chairs scrapped back as the class moved around to go form groups with their friends in different parts of the rooms. Donny sighed heavily. *Perfect,* he thought. *More time wasted on a trivial matter.* Donny wasn't sure if he was annoyed by Jaspar's project because it would mean less time spent on the Lightspeed Capsule or less time spent with Victoria.

Though none of it really mattered until he solved the problem of the processor. Maybe he would take a trip to the city again by himself over a weekend. The buildings appeared to be damaged by the ruinous touch of war, which increased the chances of military weapons buried in the rubble. The easiest option remained. To somehow get the processor from Ana...

Donny could sense someone close to his side. The gentle shuffling of metal against wooden floorboards brought a person hobbling forward in their chair.

'Hi Donny,' Ana said as she entered his personal space. Her head lowered towards his as to shield their conversation away from the rest of the class. 'What an interesting lesson, didn't you think so?'

'Was it?' Donny raised an eyebrow. 'Which part about it in particular did you like?'

'Oh, you know, all of it. Who would've thought the Nordic Empires were so violent?'

'Is this your attempt at small talk?'

Ana narrowed her eyes at him. 'Well at least someone pays attention in class. All you do is stare out the window and draw stupid pictures.'

Donny smiled. 'I'm only kidding. I hate small talk.'

'That's a relief. So do I.'

'There is nothing worse than two grownups wasting their time on trivial matters. Why talk about the weather? It's always hot. Except for our snow day.'

'What a perfect day it was though. Have you recovered from that ferocious snowball hit?'

'The deadliest snowball I had ever been hit with,' Donny let out a small chuckle, content that he had been involved in such a personal anecdote. 'What can I do for you Miss Ana?'

'I have a proposition for you.'

'Oh?' Donny had forgotten about his sleepiness and became transfixed with the girl who now leaned on his desk. 'What would that be?'

Ana blushed. 'It's embarrassing. I was wondering if you would like to be my partner for the project?'

Donny didn't know what to say. The group of Ana's friends in the corner now became noticeable from the other side of the room. Foghorn delivering one of his exaggerated stories with Hazel and Nicole laughing at every word. Liam stood at the back of the group with a sombre expression. He glanced towards Donny and Ana with spiteful intent.

Donny turned his attention back to Ana. 'You want me? I'm a bit surprised. I mean, wouldn't you rather be with Hazel or Liam?'

Ana lowered her voice. 'I love them both. They're both fantastic in their own ways, but…Liam never takes his schoolwork seriously. And Hazel is Hazel. I really need the best score possible and you're smart. Sometimes, I see you sitting alone in the fields reading a book so you must enjoy some works of literature.'

'Okay.'

'Yeah?'

'Yeah, I'll be your partner,' Donny's grin was so large that it hurt his cheeks. Sometimes you must work hard to get what you want, and sometimes an opportunity falls right into your lap. 'But I want something in return.'

'I knew there would be a catch. What do you want, Donny?'

Donny glanced at Liam who continued to watch them from the corner of his eye. 'It's a delicate matter. Do you mind if we step into the hallway to discuss it?'

'Um, sure, I guess?'

Ana rose from her seat and followed Donny out of the door. Donny didn't need to turn around to know that Liam's stare was shooting daggers into his back.

The hallway was cramped with little sunlight. A staircase led to another classroom upstairs and a tiny bathroom was tucked away to the side. A row of hooks ran along the wall where the students could hang their coats on the rare cold and wet days. A musky smell seemed to be trapped in this part of the building.

'So, what do you want?' Ana was forced to stand close to him in the confined space.

'Your arm,' he said bluntly.

'What! You want my arm?'

'Well just a piece of it. There is a component inside that I need for --'

'What will happen when you remove it?'

'Uh,' Donny paused and rubbed the back of his head. 'Your arm will stop working.'

'What! No way.'

'Let me explain. I'll put it back in once I'm done with it, I just need to borrow it for a few minutes. It's for a secret project I'm working on. I can't tell you what it is.'

'This all sounds pretty suspicious. I'll just tell Jaspar that we are a team. That I took pity on the new boy who no one else wanted to pair up with. Then you'll have to work with me.'

'I'll fail on purpose. I'll write the worst report of all time.'

'You wouldn't dare.'

'I wouldn't,' Donny said nodding his head in acceptance of his terrible bluff. 'I'll help you, and we'll get a top score, but please, I really need that piece of tech. I'll get your arm working again a few minutes later. You know I can.'

Ana folded her arms and stared at the floor. 'Fine, but no secrets. You have to tell me about this project of yours.'

'I'll show you what it is. Once you let me take the component.'

'Once we get our score back you mean, which should be just before graduation. You can borrow it if we get an A. We have a deal?'

'Deal.' Donny was one step closer to Seoul.

ANA

TWELVE

Ana watched Donny with a curiosity. The boy wandered around the library with an innocent awe. From behind the lines of bookcases, he would dart in and out, inspecting every title on the shelves. Searching for a missing piece of himself that he didn't quite realise existed. The building was contained to one level with a raised section at the rear that contained the non-fiction section.

Ana flipped through a collection of novels that built up like towers on one of the hefty tables. The pages were browning and worn yet still held in all the magic of storytelling written on their century old pages. Ana believed there was a magic about the words in a physical form rather that the pixels on a digital screen.

Footsteps hurried towards her as Donny dumped another load of books on the table. 'I can't believe what a gold mine this place is. I mean, I had most titles you could think of back on my old holopad, but there is something different about seeing them in a hard copy. As they are more accessible. Even if it sounds paradoxical.'

'I was just thinking the same,' Ana said making a note on a chalkboard of a potential novel that they could use for their project. 'I love the simplicity of them.'

'Why is this place deserted? No one even told me the village had a library.'

Ana shrugged. 'No one cares about it. They look down on having to exert themselves from turning a piece of paper, despite them being involved in manual labour all day. I like it that way. The library is my sanctuary.'

'I can see why,' Donny said with his hands on his hips. He was full of energy today. Eager to act as the runner boy searching for Ana's requests.

'We have enough books for now,' Ana said. 'Let's make a start on our project, dragă.'

Donny slid into the chair opposite her and picked up a book from one of the piles. 'Dragă? You keep calling me that. Does it mean dragon?'

'Sure, why not.'

'It's better than being a barbarian.'

Ana tilted her head and smiled. 'Barbarian isn't the worst thing to be called in the world. Teddy Roosevelt once said, "Unless we keep the barbarian virtues, gaining the civilized ones will be of little avail."'

'You're right. Over-sentimentality and softness are qualities no longer fit for this world. You're really into politics, huh? How did that come about?' Donny asked in a sincere tone as he glanced up from his book.

Ana paused for a beat. 'I guess I was involved in activism for as long as I can remember. I attended the international school. The best school around, and I always loved speaking other languages, so being in a classroom with children from around the world was perfect. I enjoyed speaking to the Italian kids though they always wanted to speak English. Then we had the student council, where representatives from each grade would come together to make decisions that would affect the entire student body. I thought, *I could do that*. Next thing I knew, they were voting me in every single year.'

'My initial interest must've been sparked by Papa. He always had a strong opinion on what happened in current affairs. At first, I would agree with him on everything, but when I read more and became more informed, I could come to my own conclusions. After the war, I watched my father with pride as he worked on the village's very own council and how he helped the people, who had lost everything, have a new shot at life. It's a noble cause.'

Donny remained silent for a time after. His thinking face crunched up again as he entered a stage of reflection. Ana didn't mind and enjoyed the silence of the library.

'So,' Donny said clearing his throat. 'About what you said...'

'What are your deductions?'

'You've told me your friends believe you would be a great councillor and that your Dad was a great influence...but why do *you* want to do it?'

'Shit, you got me.'

'I'm not just a pretty face,' Donny said.

'I wouldn't go that far,' she laughed.

Donny huffed as the corner of his mouth crept up into a smirk. He left the platform clear for her to gather thoughts and express her opinion. Liam would've changed the subject by now or answered for her.

'I feel uncomfortable in my skin,' she decided out loud. 'You know when you're wearing a baggy shirt and it's a cold evening and you pull a jumper over it, but the layers feel wrong? I find it unnerving. These new layers of skin, and I don't know how to wear them. That feeling lives with me all day, every day. It's like I just...'

'Don't belong?'

'Exactly,' Ana said. 'All these people stare at me and judge me. My neighbours, even my so-called friends. Some have known me my entire life and they still think of me as someone different. Prosthetic limbs were such a common sight in the media. Since the war, they associate my arm with the monsters. They believe in some way I'm partially responsible for the events that happened. It's so absurd. I want to prove to them that I am worthy. No. Not

155

to them. To prove to myself that I'm capable of great things.'

'If it's any consolation,' Donny said. 'I like your arm.'

'What?'

'It's the best human enhancement I've seen. To witness advanced technology, integrate so seamlessly with a human host. It's amazing.'

Ana's heart sunk. 'You think it's stupid. I shouldn't have said anything.'

'Sorry, I didn't mean to start with something so superficial. The engineer in me was nerding out.' Donny took a sharp breath and continued. 'I admit, even if I was shocked when I first saw it. Though the more I ponder it, the more special it makes you. It's the impression you give. In a place where technology is insanely taboo, you have the confidence to walk around with your head held high. You are fearless, strong, and capable. You're more ambitious than anyone I've met. You don't run from your problems, like I did. You even took out an android with your bare hands. You hold your ground and say to hell with the world, I'm going to be the best damn version of myself. For that, I admire you.'

Ana could feel tears at the edge of her eyes building up, like the first stars in a dusk sky. She held them back tightly.

'I guess you need to find meaning. What's the point of being alive if you don't want to do something spectacular? Are you okay?'

'I'm fine,' Ana said blinking a few times. 'No one has ever said that to me before.'

'That the point of life is meaning?'

'No stupid, that you admire me.'

He blushed. 'Oh.'

'Donny let's make a promise. Let's promise we will always be honest with each other. No matter what.'

'Can I trust you?' He seemed wary of the new proposition on offer.

'You have my word. We can tell each other whatever we want, and it'll never be spoken to another soul.'

'How do we form such a contract?'

Ana put down the book she was reading. She removed her glove, exposing the android hand. The silver surface shimmered like the ice world they had explored together. Donny gaped at it for a while before he reached for her. He grasped her tightly. No one had ever held her robotic hand for a long time. Even though the sensors were nothing on the touch of her skin, she felt the warmness flow from him.

'I promise,' he said. Ana could tell by his clenched teeth he found her cold, but he held on for a few extra seconds.

'A promise between friends,' she confirmed and let him go.

'I'll even show you the project I've been working on.'

'Good,' she said simply.

Ana selected a green-coloured piece of chalk from her box. In her standard cursive, she listed possible novels they could use as the basis of their project. The library offered a rich choice of options. The difficult part would be selecting which two novels were similar enough to do a comparison on, but with enough stark differences to create an interesting discussion. The chalk crumbled into tiny pieces of dust as she illustrated the names of her favourites.

'I was wondering about something,' Donny said.

'What is that?' Ana asked, not looking up from her board.

'You said you want to be on the town council. I guess we're told at the graduation service?'

'Mmm...'

'Do you have to make a speech if you get selected?'

'Yes, you do,' Ana said as she reached for a new piece of chalk. 'The student who gets selected for the council makes the ceremony's closing speech.'

'Ah, interesting,' Donny said. 'I bet you have your speech already written out and rehearsed.'

Ana could feel her skin prickle with embarrassment. She ignored him and continued to write down her *maybe* choices in a different colour.

'You have, haven't you!' Donny exclaimed in a jovial manner. 'I admire your confidence. We better do well on this paper then. I feel its in the bag already. Let's hear the speech then. I know you have it memorised.'

'Pardon? You want to hear it?'

'Of course,' Donny said.

'You're silly,' Ana shook her head. 'You'll just laugh.'

'I promise I won't. C'mon, if you can't do it in front of one person, how can you do it in front of hundreds?'

Ana hesitated. She really did want to practice the speech. This would be the perfect time with a willing participant. Public speaking was never her strong point and she did yearn to become more comfortable at it like her Papa.

'Fine,' Ana said as she cleared her throat.

Donny smiled and leaned back waiting for her to speak.

'Thank you, everyone. I would --'

'Hold on,' Donny said. 'You need to be standing up as if you were at the podium.'

Ana sighed and pushed back her chair. She walked away to find a sturdy chair and to be further from Donny, she didn't want him staring up at her at such a close distance. She picked out a suitable chair and it wobbled as she lifted her weight on it. The android hand grabbed the back support to steady herself. She adopted her posture to that of the politician she wanted to be. Straight back, legs slightly apart in a commanding stance.

'Do I look the part now?' Ana asked waving an imaginary pen in front of her.

'Perfect,' Donny laughed. 'Remember to use that passion you have. You're not just saying this speech to me, you're saying it to the people at the back of the room. It needs that... *oomph*. Pretend this library is filled with your adoring fans. You're awesome. You've got this.'

Silence resumed in the air as Donny watched her expectantly. She gulped in a large mouthful of air to expand her lungs and she started again. 'Thank, you everyone! I would like to say few words about those who helped me get to this moment, to be standing in front of all of you! Without your guidance, I wouldn't be the woman I am today!'

'Bravo,' Donny said applauding. 'That's the energy that'll win you the crowd.'

'You don't think it's over the top?'

'No way, you smashed it. Hell, I would follow any law you made with a voice that commanding. You'll be great on the day. Let's hear the rest of it.'

She tried to compose herself, yet a commotion distracted her. From her standing position, she had a clear view of the windows on the far side of the building. Dozens of villagers were running along the road towards the town's centre. The urgency in their movement suggested something out of the ordinary was happening.

Ana jumped from her chair and hurried to the door. Donny shot her a confused look and trailed behind.

By the time Ana reached the square, a huge crowd had already gathered. With her slight height, she was able to duck and push through the mob to reach the front. A unit of soldiers formed a circle around two men, keeping the villagers back from interfering. One of the men was a

159

captain in her father's army. The other she recognised as one of the blacksmiths. His face was badly bruised with one of the eyes swollen shut. The captain carried a club in his hand and patted it menacingly against his palm.

Donny moved up beside her at the front. 'What is going on?' he asked in a lowered voice. The colour was draining from his face as he made out the dilapidated condition of the blacksmith.

'I don't know,' Ana said softly.

The captain continued to circle his captive who knelt on the stony floor, his head lowered. The man was completely defenceless. Without warning, the captain swung down the club onto the man. A sickening crack of a bone breaking as the weapon thumped the man's shoulder. The blacksmith screamed in pain as the crowd gasped and cried out. The soldiers stood tall and unwavering.

'Let this be a lesson to every witness here,' the captain addressed the crowd. He walked around the circle his eyes searching for any objectors, but the crowd simply averted their attention to the floor. 'Your neighbour here has committed a terrible transgression. He has been spreading doubts about leader Mihai's ability to govern. Questioning his divine right to rule. Blasphemy is a serious crime and will be punished. Mihai has been blessed with God's will and his name will not be forsaken.'

'Amen,' the crowd said in unison, ignoring the blacksmith's sobs.

'Amen,' the captain replied. 'Long live Mihai.' His face scrunched up in a grimace as he hit the blacksmith again, this time in the arm.

Ana turned to Donny, but he was gone. *How could Papa allow this to happen?* She thought. *What kind of society had they become?*

DONNY

THIRTEEN

The barn had become Donny's sanctuary. Any day after school where Stefan was posted as the barn's sentry, Donny would casually slip past the red doors. It would be such a common occurrence that the chains would be unlocked by the time Donny arrived.

Sundays were the safest as he knew everyone else would be at church.

Surrounding the Lightspeed Capsule were broken-down gadgets. Their guts and cable intestines poured over the floor. Televisions were dismantled and home appliances stripped. An assortment of tools lay on a table in order of size and purpose.

The scene sparked a sharp sense of déjà vu. It reminded Donny of the days in the lighthouse where he would take apart less valuable equipment to repair, or in some cases, create more valuable tools for the island.

The task at hand was the most elaborate challenge he had faced. Over the months stranded in the Romanian village, significant progress had been made on repairing the capsule. The parts he found in the city were exactly what he needed to replace the damaged modules. However, the machine would still not turn on. A painstaking job remained. He would have to replace every key component to find out what caused the surge of power to blow the machine.

Once he got the power back and installed the processor from Ana's arm, he would be able to get to Seoul.

If only Edwin could see him now and how far he had come. Once he could get the pod back online, he could continue his search to find out if Edwin had survived.

The ding-dong of church bell rang in the distance. Mass had come to an end and he would be late for his date.

Donny reached for a rag and wiped oil from his hands. A reflective sheet of metal acted as a mirror. He ran his fingers through his hair to make sure he looked somewhat presentable. He had never worried about his appearance before, but Victoria had changed his attitude.

Stefan stood where he had left him an hour earlier, with his slouched pose and his bored stare.

'I'm done for today.' Donny said as he patted at his shirt, unable to flatten out the wrinkles.

'Where are you off to in such a rush?' asked Stefan.

Donny smiled. 'Only a lunch date with Victoria.'

'Ah Donny, she's so pretty. The unmarried soldiers say that too. They tell me they want to break your legs. They all have an eye on her. I tell them, "don't break Donny's legs. He is a good man."'

'Um, thanks, I guess,' Donny said, not knowing whether to take any part of the statement as a threat. He half-jogged towards the fields knowing he would arrive late.

'You haven't forgotten about our chess game?' Stefan called after him.

'I'll be there,' Donny shouted back.

• • • • •

The picnic was already laid out by the time Donny arrived. A woolly checked blanket lay across the dry grass

162

in between weeds of the open field. An assortment of fruit in compact bowls and a loaf of bread lay to one side. Victoria sat next to a basket with a matching straw hat that protected her pale skin. She strummed on an acoustic guitar, gently humming a warm melody. The tune had a sweet mixture of contentment and sadness. The steel strings vibrated with joy with every pluck.

Donny kicked off his shoes and sat opposite her without saying a word. He absorbed the moment as best he could. The gentle chords rushed over him like the way the sea swept over his feet at the beach. The guitar kept her attention and she didn't look up until she strummed in one final motion to signal the end of the song.

Donny applauded. 'Brilliant.'

'Thank you,' said Victoria as she checked her watch. 'You've made it. At 10:43 AM as well, my favourite time of the morning.'

'The perfect time of the morning,' Donny agreed slightly confused.

'You know, Planck time. The quantum of time. It's the time it would take a photon travelling at the speed of light to cross a distance of the Planck length. It's the smallest measurement of time, 10^{-43} seconds.'

'A physicist, a talented musician and a medical doctor. Is there anything you can't do?'

'I have so many talents already,' Victoria declared as she lay down the guitar on the blanket. 'It would be unfair to everyone else if I had any other gifts.'

'Of course. It would be breaking the laws of physics to go beyond that stage of perfection.'

'Exactly,' she said. 'Just like your face.'

'My face? What about it?'

'It's symmetrical. It makes you look handsome.'

'It is?' he asked. 'I wouldn't say that's entirely true. One of my ears is bigger than the other.'

Victoria frowned and leaned in for a closer examination. 'How can I live with that? I have OCD when it comes to beauty.'

'I hate to disappoint you,' Donny smirked. 'Alright, explain to me what we have here.'

'You've already experienced the pre-dinner entertainment, so you already know you've entered one of the finest establishments. For food, I managed to get a loaf from the bakery before it closed early for mass. And for dessert, I did some deals with the fruit pickers to get my favourites. Sweet cherries and strawberries. I now owe them a life debt, but these are prices you have to pay if you want to have a memorable date.'

They dug into the food. Donny wanted to try all the treats. Each bite an explosion of flavour he had once forgotten on the blandness of a seafood diet back on the island.

'You know what I miss most?' said Victoria. 'Planes.'

'Huh? You miss planes?'

'You know, airplanes. I always took them for granted. On a cloudless day like this you would look up and see a plane slowly moving across the horizon. The gentle hum of its engines in the distance. It's what they symbolized. Being able to travel freely to any part of the planet. My Dad took me on trips to many different countries. Sadly, I was too young to appreciate those places. Sometimes I wish I could pick up my passport and head to the airport with no particular destination in mind.'

A spell had fallen over Donny. He was unsure if Victoria wore makeup as her lips resembled the cherries in the bowl before him. A faint hint of lavender added to the effect of her spell. He drowned in her ocean eyes. 'This is already by far the best date I've been on.'

Victoria studied him as she took a bite out of a strawberry. 'Am I the first person you've dated?'

Donny ran a hand through his floppy hair. 'I mean, there weren't many young women back on the island. Also, I was always busy with Edwin working on his crazy ideas. And I always had to do housework in my --'

Victoria laughed. 'Dude, I'm messing with you. I assumed you never had a girlfriend before.'

'Why would you assume that?'

'I don't know,' said Victoria as her fingers rummaged for another strawberry. 'You gave off those vibes.'

Donny crossed his arms. 'Vibes? What vibes?'

'It's a compliment,' said Victoria. 'You're intelligent and reflect on topics that no one else does. It's a breath of fresh air speaking to you. I know we've been hanging out a lot recently and I wanted to let you know. I think you're cool.'

Victoria had shifted closer to him, so her body pressed against his knee. Donny's heart pounded and his skin became prickled as if he were being jabbed by thousands of tiny needles. He had never known a woman who had matched Victoria's beauty, like a Hollywood actress from the old world.

'I think you're cool too,' Donny stammered.

'Good,' whispered Victoria. He could smell the strawberries on her breath. 'I bet you haven't kissed a girl either.'

He had always been consumed with his work. Especially now, with the urgency to repair the Pod and find Edwin, he didn't even consider he would be in a frame of mind to consider romance. Yet love presented itself before him in the most unexpected of forms.

Donny leaned in closer as Victoria's lips parted. He closed his eyes in expectation. A new life flashed before him. Kissing Victoria. Getting married in some strange Order of the Danube wedding ceremony. Being allocated a house to live in with his new wife. Having children of

165

their own. Dying in this town. Never using the machine. Never reaching Seoul. Never seeing Edwin again.

Donny pulled away.

Victoria cocked her head to the side. 'Is something wrong?'

'I'm not sure. I don't think I can do this right now. I can't afford to be distracted.'

'Are you being serious?'

'Yeah,' he said.

'I see, okay.' Victoria played with her fingers for a few moments until she moved to her knees and packed the food away into the basket. She tugged at the blanket and Donny obediently got off as she lay it over her arm. She picked up her guitar and left.

Donny took a few steps after her, but no words came out. The hardened blades of grass poked into his socks.

• • • • •

The chess pieces had already been set up before Stefan arrived. The pieces were wooden and chipped but otherwise in good condition. The plastic mat lay seamlessly on a stone table situated in the shade of low-lying branches. Donny had given himself the white pieces, he needed some sort of advantage after his strange encounter with Victoria.

Stefan plopped in the seat opposite him, examining the board to make sure Donny had set it up correctly. Donny arrogantly assumed that he would be the far superior chess player between the two of them since he had transported the atoms of his body 2,000 miles across the continent while Stefan was merely a glorified barn security guard. Donny assumed wrong and lost most games.

'You're here already,' Stefan noted as he adjusted his knights, so they were facing in the correct direction. He wore a vest top, which signalled he had finished his shift. 'I thought you had a date with the lovely Victoria.'

Donny huffed and moved one of the middle white pawns forward to start the game. 'I think I did something stupid.'

'Yes. It wouldn't surprise me you would be an idiot,' Stefan nodded in agreement. 'Hope is lost with you.'

'I do like her, but it seemed to be moving too quickly. I have no idea what's wrong with me. I'm afraid it would distract me from my goals.'

Stefan took one of Donny's pawns and placed it on the stone surface to the side. 'You had a girlfriend back on the island?'

'There were no girls that took my fancy.'

'Donny, this is no good. This is not life. Life is about love and adventure. You want someone to experience the memorable moments with. Look at me. One day I was like you and then I meet Denisa, the most beautiful woman in the world. Now I'm a changed man. Life is too short to be alone.'

'I never even pictured having a girlfriend until I met Victoria. She is, um, perhaps the most interesting woman I've met. And so witty. No one has kept me on my toes like she has. Now she hates me.'

'You take too long to move your pieces,' Stefan said.

'Sorry,' Donny said as he moved a bishop across the board.

'You don't need to apologise to me. You must apologise to her.'

'Maybe it wasn't meant to be,' Donny said. 'A sign I shouldn't get close to anyone. It hasn't even been a year since I lost my Dad and my best friend. I'm not even sure if Edwin is still alive.'

'Are you not settled here, Donny?'

167

Donny paused for a while. He didn't want to show any eagerness in his response to hint at his plans to leave. 'I don't want to appear ungrateful. I appreciate how Mihai, Gheorghe, and everyone has allowed me to stay here. I've experienced so much death it holds me back from forming friendships or relationships.'

'Death is a natural part of life,' Stefan said. 'The Lord giveth and the Lord taketh away. There is a famous folktale in Romania about death. Would you like to hear it?'

'When have I ever stopped you from telling your stories?' Donny said as he considered his next move on the board.

'Once there was a man who wanted to become immortal. There had to be an answer to everlasting life. So, one day he said goodbye to his loved ones, and set off on his quest. He searched for years, asking the inhabitants of every city he came across if their people died.'

'Finally, he came to a town on a river, hidden behind a mountain, where no one knew what dying meant. The traveller became overjoyed but at the same time confused. Why was the population so small if everyone lived forever? One of the villagers answered him, "every now and then somebody emerges from the river and beckons the townsfolk to go to him, and whoever follows him into the river, drowns and never returns." The traveller thought this was an idiotic thing to do. Why follow him if into the water if it meant you would perish? He would never do something so stupid. He returned to fetch his wife and settle his business affairs. When they reached the mystical town, he warned his wife, that in no circumstance, to follow any strange beings who come from the river if she didn't want to die. So, the couple had a luxurious life with their newfound immortality.'

Stefan stole one of the pawns near Donny's king and continued the story.

'One day, the couple were comfortably sitting out in their huge garden when his wife jumped up suddenly and moved towards the direction of the river. "Where are you going?" he called after her, but she didn't reply. The man could not hear anyone calling from the water, but his wife had been drawn to it by some invisible force. He chased her and told her to stay away. When he moved close and tried to grab her, she bolted from his grasp, screaming, and wadded out into the fierce currents. The husband was too afraid to follow her. He watched her go underneath the surface, never to submerge again.'

'Days passed and then months, years, decades, and the man fell into a sense of madness. Waiting for the voice to call him. Then one morning he heard the voice. Rage consumed him and he grabbed a knife from the kitchen and ran to the edge of the riverbank shouting, "I won't come, do you hear, leave me alone!" He saw a mysterious figure in a black cloak hover above the waters in front of him. The man pursued the figure, ready to stab him. He swam out towards him, but the wild currents swept him away. He kicked and struggled, trying to get some air. Eventually, his footing found the riverbank and he crawled up the sandy shore coughing and wheezing. The river had taken him miles across the continent back to the hometown of his birth. The streets and buildings were deserted. An eerie feeling fell over him and he rushed to find his old house. The windows were smashed in and the door wide open. In the chaos, the figure in the black cloak waited for him. Under the hood was a skull with a long grey beard. It was Death. He had lingered centuries in the mortal realm waiting to steal away this man's life. And when the man realised this, he begged Death to end his suffering.'

Donny played with the black queen he had taken. Stefan had laid a trap for him and it would not be long before he would be defeated.

'Death is waiting for us all, Donny.'

'Something has been bothering me,' Donny said absorbing the meaning of Stefan's tale. 'You remember you told me the story about the children? How much truth did it have? Did the kids of the village ever get to the old orphanage in Bucharest?'

Stefan rubbed his unkempt beard. He sighed heavily as all the troubles of the world were resting on his shoulders. 'There is a secret I have kept for far too long. I haven't even told my darling Denisa. Every day it eats away at my soul.'

'What is it?' Donny asked as a chill ran down his spine.

'Maybe there is truth to both of the stories I told you. Mihai, myself, and a couple of other soldiers were summoned by the old leader five years ago. We were in turmoil. We hadn't planned for this new life. A lack of food was a problem. To ration the food, the leader fabricated a tale that he had a friend at a secure base where the children would be safe. A place used to house the children of soldiers fighting in the war. Later the council spun it so we could never find out whatever happened to them as there were no means to contact the base. Me, Mihai and the other soldiers loaded the fifty youngest children into the trucks, and we drove towards Bucharest.'

'Once we had gotten far enough from the town we pulled to the side of the road. Mihai told the children he needed to baptise them so they could join The Order of the Danube. One by one he led them to the river. He baptised them, but he never let them re-submerge. I was so young and foolish, but I should've done something. He drowned them, Donny. He drowned them. I must carry that guilt for the rest of my life. We murdered those young people so there would be enough food for the rest of us to get through the first winter.'

Goosebumps formed on Donny's skin as he felt Death's touch lingering in from the river. He wanted to run as fast as he could, but his legs would not move, as if his feet had been cemented to the earth.

'Why are you telling me this?' Donny asked after a long time.

'I wanted to give you a chance to leave,' Stefan said. 'A chance those children never had. Since you arrived, Mihai has told me to watch you. He has plans for you.'

Stefan moved his rook across the board, placing it next to Donny's king.

'Checkmate, Donny.'

• • • • •

Donny's mind spun uncontrollably; his thoughts caught up in a violent tornado.

For what purpose did Mihai need him for? His only real skills were repairing machines. And they were banned. The religious undertones of the society made Donny feel uneasy, but he didn't think he would be offered as a human sacrifice.

The stories Stefan had told him replayed in his mind. The tales were bathed in a sick scent of demise and misery and had much more meaning to them than Donny initially thought. Mihai murdered the most vulnerable to save the many. A wave of nausea hit him hard when he considered the idea.

For the months he had lived in Romania, he only obsessed over one goal. To leave. He didn't plan to develop friendships with Victoria, Stefan, and Ana; the once hostile environment had started to feel like home. Now this changed everything. He *needed* to escape.

The best plan would be to stay on his current course; keep his head low until he fixed the pod, work out the Seoul coordinates and leave silently in the night. That's what his mind told him to do.

His heart had other ideas. He needed to confront Mihai.

Donny made his way through the village to the mayor's manor. A few security guards stood at the front entrance that suggested Mihai was home. He would never go anywhere without his entourage.

There would be little chance to have a one-on-one conversation with Mihai. He spent his days on guarded walks or in meetings with the council members. Donny almost gave up hope until he saw the majestic church on the top of the hill. Two guards served as sentries at the entrance. The doors were usually open, so believers could pray at any time of the day. Now they were shut closed. Mihai had to be inside.

Donny circled the hill and climbed on the far side that faced the mountain. An old wooden door lay inconspicuous in a stone enclave. The rusted door handle felt cool in his hand and remained firm when he tried to open it. Donny produced a small screwdriver from his pocket. Methodically, he removed the four screws and the handle became loose in place. The door released and Donny slipped inside.

He breathed in the stuffy and spicy air. His footsteps echoed softly on the marble floors. The candles in the nave section of the church were unlit and the pews were empty.

Donny stood still. For a moment, he caught a noise so faint he thought it might've been a mouse scuttling in the wall. He waited and heard it again. A soft moan coming from the back rooms.

Donny continued towards the noise. It grew louder and heavier with every step. He moved beneath the giant crucifix, under the watchful gaze of the crucified Jesus Christ.

A light flickered behind an ajar door.

Donny pushed the door softly and peered in.

At first, the image didn't transform correctly. Mihai's trousers were around his ankles. His wrinkled shirt ran down his back and covered his buttocks. He panted quickly as he leaned against the wall.

Another figure of pure flesh whimpered softly, being wedged between Mihai and the desk. Her coal-black hair fell over her shoulder as her eyes remained shut. Donny could only make out a partial angle of her face, but he recognised her. It was Hazel.

ANA

FOURTEEN

Notes scattered across the desk. Neon streaks ran across the pages, highlighting the most significant arguments. Pencils lay motionless, their lead tips blunted. A stack of hardcover books rose like skyscrapers. The characters in their titles acting as enclosed windows. *Physics. Religious Studies. Economics.*

Ana tapped the edge of the desk rapidly. Her exposed metal fingers thudded heavily against the wood and the pencils rolled with the vibrations. She slammed the textbook on the table and reached for the another one. Earmarks in the pages indicated the areas she deemed the most pressing to review.

Her eyes flickered across the words, but her eyelids felt heavy, as if someone had tied miniature sandbags to each of her lashes.

Ana and Donny had completed their literature project and she was beyond happy with it. That boy surprised her greatly with his contribution to the paper and his ideas were unique and captivating. At least that part of her grade would be safe. The exams, however, could be her downfall.

'This is hopeless,' Ana said out loud. 'The more I revise, the less I seem to know. It's like I'm pushing out valuable information for everything I put in. What's the point?'

A figure shifted on the bed behind her. Hazel propped herself up against several of Ana's giant goose feather pillows.

'Don't say that,' Hazel protested. 'You're the smartest girl in the whole village. And seeing as most people have been wiped out, you're probably one of the smartest people in the world.'

'Hardly reassuring. I'm going to fail the exams tomorrow.'

Hazel closed the book on her lap. 'You're putting too much pressure on yourself. We should only be revising what we already know. I bet you already have all the answers to the questions in that big ol' brain of yours. We'll both ace those exams and get assigned the best jobs in the community.'

'I wish I had your optimism.'

A knock at the door made Hazel jump. Ana smirked and called for the visitor to enter. A timid man with a camouflage cap poked his head into the room.

'Lady Ana,' the young man said. 'Liam has requested to speak with you.'

'Where is he?' Ana asked. 'Tell him to come join us.'

'I'm sorry, he only left a message with me at the front door. He asked if you could meet him by the silos?'

'Why is he being so weird?' Ana asked as she spun a pencil quickly between her metal fingers. 'I need to be studying, not playing his stupid games.'

The young guard hesitated for a few seconds before he left.

Ana snapped the pencil as if it were a twig. 'That's all I need right now. Liam to be acting like an idiot. Doesn't he know how significant today is? I need to be focused and relaxed.'

'Don't be so hard on him,' Hazel said. 'Maybe he wants to apologise. The fresh air and walk might do you some good.'

'Maybe,' Ana said. 'He has been acting so distant recently. I didn't want to bring it up with the exams so near. This might be what I need. I'll give him the biggest hug and hear what he has to say. Will you be alright by yourself? I'll be as quick as I can.'

'I need a break as well,' Hazel said. 'I'll stretch my legs and explore your giant mansion.'

Ana headed towards the door. 'Make sure not to disturb my Dad. He's locked away in his study. He bites my head off whenever I bother him.'

'I won't,' Hazel smiled. 'Scout's honour.'

• • • • •

The silos were located at the far side of the farms. Colossal silver cylinders rose above the dried wheat fields where the farm hands worked diligently under the unforgiving late spring conditions. The workers had darkened skin, bronzed by the exposure of the outdoors. Ana imagined herself being assigned a farm role if she failed her exams.

No one wanted to work on the farms.

The scorching sun turned the silos into robotic volcanos for the amount of heat they radiated. Ana made the mistake a couple of years ago when she leaned against one of them. The palm of her human hand was severely burned, and she couldn't hold a pencil for a few days after.

Liam waited in the shade; his hands stuffed deep in his pockets. With a lowered head, he kicked stones at the closest silo. A pebble panged as it ricocheted off its metallic skin. The echo revealed how little grain was stored inside.

'Hey stranger,' Ana said.

Liam looked up. His expression remained blank, void of any emotion. 'Hi.'

'Why aren't you studying?' Ana asked.

'I wanted to talk to you. In private.'

'Is that why you whisked me away from my home? We have about a dozen empty rooms in there. Unless you wanted somewhere romantic to apologise. It's been a minute and a half. Is there something wrong?'

'Listen, there is no easy way to say this. We're too different. We want different things.'

Ana froze. She waited an eternity before Liam spoke again.

'I think it's best we break up.'

A mixture of emotions whirled in Ana's being, colliding into each other like atoms, producing ripples of pain. The act of breathing no longer felt natural and she clawed for each mouthful of air. The softer feelings burnt away quickly like pieces of paper, leaving only a raw, bitter rage.

'What the hell is wrong with you?' she cried out. 'You have ignored me for weeks, made me feel worthless and now you're dumping me the day before the exams. You know how important they are to me.'

Liam stood back; his face skewed in astonishment. She didn't realise she had this much power over him. 'Chill out, Ana,' he managed casually. 'You'll still do well.'

'That's not the point, asshole. Did you even consider my feelings? You only ever care about yourself.'

Liam squared up to her. He loomed over Ana in order to make her feel small and inadequate as he often did when he dismissed her opinions. Ana didn't back down.

'You want the truth? You've changed. You keep hanging out with that weird Donny guy. And you spend every day in the library reading. What's the point of learning so much? This is all we have. You need to throw yourself into this community. You always say you want to help the people here. Well, where are you?'

'I can help them if I learn about --'

Liam cut her off, 'And that's not even the worst part. You never wear your glove anymore.'

'What!' Ana said. Her teeth clenched together.

'I'm not going to sugar coat it for you. I'm only saying what everyone else is thinking. You look like a freak with your android arm. You look like one of them. It's embarrassing for your father and it's embarrassing to be seen with you.'

Ana's arm flew through the silo wall. The steel popped as her robotic slid into its dry contents. Ana's stare bore so fiercely it forced him to break eye contact. She ripped her arm away and a flood of grain poured from the tear onto her feet.

'Stay away from me,' Liam said as he turned to leave.

An old man came running from the field shouting at Ana in Romanian.

'Îmi pare rău,' Ana apologised in her native tongue. 'Îmi pare foarte rău.'

The grain poured out on the ground like a puncture wound, rushing between Ana's feet.

• • • • •

Ana lay in her bed, wide awake. The wails of the wind reflected her mood. A tree branch tapped on her window in irregular beats, like an old skeleton asking for permission to enter.

178

The exams had finished earlier in the day, but Ana couldn't remember any of the questions. It was as though she had left her body and watched it answer the papers on her behalf, separate from her knowledge. Deep down she knew she performed terribly.

Ana threw off her duvet and slipped into her most comfortable jeans and sweatshirt. She needed some fresh air. The corridor was blanketed in darkness, yet Ana knew the passages well enough by now. She proceeded to the back staircase making sure not to knock over any nearby ornaments.

The glow of a candle grew around a faraway corner. *Who is up at this hour?* Ana thought. She poked her head around to find her mother pacing back and forth in her nightgown.

'Mama, what is wrong?'

'Nothing my dear,' Rozene said as she almost dropped the candle holder. Even in the obscure lighting Ana could see the black eye bruised in her mother's face.

'What happened?' Ana asked in a harsh whisper.

'I'm okay, pumpkin. Your father is under a lot of pressure with his duties. He is always worrying about the safety of everyone here. I know he doesn't mean it.'

'This is ridiculous,' Ana said. 'I hear him shouting at you all the time. He has no right to hit you.'

'Please leave it,' Rozene said in her motherly tone that indicated the conversation had reached an end. 'Go back to bed and get some rest. You must be exhausted.'

Her mother turned and left her in the dark hallway.

• • • • •

Ana ran as fast as her legs could carry her. She sprinted across the fields with only the full moon as a guide. Pain chased behind her. She needed to escape it all. Her lungs ached by the time she reached the mountain, but she didn't let it deter her as she ascended quickly up the rocky gradient.

The cliffs above blocked out the lunar rays, and Ana's footing slipped over the edge. The android arm, the reason for her subjugation amongst the townsfolk, shot into a crack in the wall, saving her from plummeting fifty feet to the ground.

Ana exhaled and continued at a slower pace towards the summit.

When she reached the top, she marvelled at the land that fell before her. To the north, a beautiful forest basked in the silver glow of the moon. To the south, her hometown, with houses that shielded her sleeping neighbours and the guard outposts whose lights burned giving security to those who were lost in sleep. And beyond the town, the Danube, dark and powerful. The giver of life and keeper of secrets.

'I didn't know midnight patrols were one of your hobbies,' said a ghost.

Ana gasped and spun around. A young man sat near the edge of the cliffside. He turned a spanner in his hands. In the moonlight she could make out his face.

'Donny,' she choked. 'What are you doing up here?'

'I could ask you the same question. I'm guessing the same reason I'm here. You couldn't sleep.'

Ana approached him cautiously. She could make him out clearer now. His sharp facial features contrasted with his floppy hair. He looked leaner these days than when she first met him, but it could've been exaggerated by his baggy clothes. 'This seat taken?'

Donny lay down the spanner and gestured to the spot next to him. Ana placed herself on the hard ground and breathed in the view. She had spent many days and nights on top of the mountain taking in the same panorama, but it never bored her.

'You ever feel in control of your life?' Ana started. 'Your future had been planned out to the smallest detail and you're so excited to conquer it and make it your own. Then one day you wake up and realise that everything you ever wanted was meaningless.'

Donny stared at her. Ana thought the twilight played tricks on her, but she detected a deep sorrow in his expression. Pain under the depths of his surface. He waited for her to continue. The afterglow of his image stayed with her when she looked back to the town.

'I'm tired of it, Donny. I'm tired of it all. It feels like there is nothing left to feel joyful about. I wanted to serve the community. They despise me. I wanted to marry and have a family with my boyfriend. He dumped me. I wanted to be respected by my father. I'm certain I failed the exams and there is no chance of making the council now. He probably resents me anyway.'

Donny raised an eyebrow when she mentioned her father, but he said nothing and looked back ahead.

'Here I am chatting away about my problems of being an outcast, when you lost everyone you knew. You must think of me as insensitive.'

'Don't worry about it,' Donny said. 'If anything, I used to feel how you did. I didn't feel at home on the island either. It didn't feel right. I believe as humans; we weren't created to stay in one place. We evolved into hunters, into explorers, into travellers. Our souls die if they stay in one place forever.'

'So, you were planning to leave? Even before the attack?'

'Yeah.'

'Weren't you afraid? To leave behind the only place you ever knew. To head out into unknown dangers?'

'Of course I was,' Donny said. 'That's why I needed to go.'

Ana stared up at the heavens. The stars burned brightly as if each one had been purposely put in a special place. Before the war, humans had even conquered another planet. Now, it seemed an impossible feat to achieve again. The words of Donny weighed heavy on her. Trading comfort for adventure. Never had she considered it as an option.

'I'm leaving the village,' Donny said.

'You are what?' Ana stumbled on her words. 'Where will you go?'

He rubbed his face. 'I can't tell you.'

Ana moved closer to him. 'Donny. We made a promise we would always be honest with one another. Don't you remember?'

Donny sighed. 'I can't tell you because of your father. He can't find out where I'm going.'

'This has nothing to do with Papa. This is between you and me. I gave you my word I would always be truthful with you and keep your secrets in return. My word is the only thing I have left. That and my stupid arm.'

Donny studied her for a long time. 'I'm going to Seoul.'

'Seoul, as in South Korea? How on earth will you be able to get there?' Ana deliberated what he said for a moment and it dawned on her. 'The Lightspeed Capsule. You fixed it! Papa said it was destroyed when you arrived. That's why you need the processor in my arm...'

'That's right. I need the processor to link the Pod to an operational satellite. Besides that, I'm almost done. I've been working on the capsule since I arrived here. I found parts from the city we visited and ripped apart all the old machines you had in the barn. I finally made it operational. The only problem is I don't know the

182

coordinates on how to get to Seoul. I've been sending test signals to every possible number. It could take days or even weeks. Once I get a response, I'm gone.'

'What about Victoria and Stefan? You seemed close to them both.'

'Vic is angry and won't talk to me anymore. And Stefan…I wouldn't consider him a friend.'

'I'm sorry to hear that. It's no secret I'm not Victoria's biggest fan, but you both seemed good together.'

'Don't worry about it,' he said. 'C'est la vie.'

'C'est la vie,' she repeated. 'Tell me. Of all the places to go to, why choose Seoul?'

'If Edwin survived the attack, that's where he would've headed. It was our plan. He must've had the booklet with the capsule coordinates on him, so he knew how to get there.' Donny paused for a while, waiting for the right words to come to him. 'I'm going to miss you Ana, but this is not where I'm supposed to be.'

Time slipped away from them so quickly. In an intermediate sense, she no longer knew the hour of the day or where she was, and in the bigger picture, where her friendship with Donny seemed so new and exciting, it seemed to be over already.

Ana moved closer to him. His warmth radiated through his clothes.

'Can I hold your hand?' Ana asked him.

'You want to hold hands?'

'Not any hand. I want you to hold my android hand. I want to remember this night forever. I want this to be my favourite memory of us.'

Donny narrowed his eyes as if he tried to see through her deception. He relented and reached out for her. His fingers intertwined with hers. Flesh against metal. The circuits and wirings shot signals of kindness and affection to her brain. Ana leaned in and rested her head against

183

him. She closed her eyes and lost herself in his grip until reality slipped away from her and she was at peace with her decision.

Ana didn't want to let go of him.

'I'm coming with you,' she whispered.

DONNY

FIFTEEN

Donny studied the stranger who stared back at him from the bedroom mirror. The year in Romania had transformed him into a character he no longer recognised. He had lost the puppy fat around the neck and torso, his body appeared to be made of only lean muscles and bones now covered by a bronze skin. The sun had bleached his dark chestnut hair to a golden brown. Despite the sparse diet, he appeared stronger and wilder.

He wondered if Edwin would recognise him if they met again.

Guilt tore at his gut more than the pang of hunger. Donny should work on the portal today, not hang out with Ana. He had told her his biggest secret, and it was out of his control if she would reveal it to her father, though he believed he could trust her. To make matters worse, he had revealed his plan to escape the village, but nothing about the affair between her father and her best friend, Hazel.

Maybe it was best that Ana never found out to spare her the pain of the betrayal.

A knock came at the door.

'Come in,' Donny said.

Gheorghe entered carrying some clothes in his long arms. He stared at Donny blankly as if he were an alien from another world. 'Why you never wear clothes?' Gheorghe enquired.

'It's not my fault, it's always so hot,' Donny said as he pulled on a white t-shirt.

Gheorghe took a seat on the single bed and it creaked under his weight. 'You prepared for end of school party?'

'I am, though it's hard to get ready for an event when I don't have anything formal.'

'Here, try this on,' Gheorghe said.

Donny grabbed the item of clothing from Gheorghe and he shook it open. An old grey blazer. His arms slipped through the sleeves and he tugged it snug at the collar. No longer did he look like a lost boy. Donny was a man.

'It good on you,' Gheorghe said. 'It was my nephew's. He fought for his country in the war and never came home. I'm proud of him. You now finished school and ready to take on world. I know you make your family proud too, as they look down on you from heaven.'

Donny walked over and gave him a hug.

'Thank you for everything, Gheorghe.'

'Stop that, you stay with me for as long as you want. Now go to your party.'

• • • • •

Ana waited for him outside by the gate, leaning against the broken wall. The fragments of bricks lay on the ground like crumbs. She hadn't seen him yet. Her face tilted upwards, so her skin absorbed the final beams of light. Her dress burned a bright shade of mandarin. The android arm shimmered unashamedly without any glove to conceal it.

'Wow, you look…' Donny started.

Ana raised an eyebrow. 'Is it too much? Do I look like a fake?'

'Stunning more like,' Donny said. 'Though fake was going to be my second choice. Definitely a fake. If I had a

186

knife, I'd cut a slice out of you. It would be just as I expected, you are made of cake. A fake who is really a cake. And I would continue to cut slices out of you until the day you had been fully consumed. Then I would mourn that you were gone as I would no longer have any cake.'

Ana put a hand on her hip and pursed her lips. 'Has anyone told you how annoying you are?''

'From time to time,' he said.

'You might be an idiot, but a surprisingly handsome idiot in a smart jacket.' She threw her arms around Donny's neck and embraced him tightly. He savoured the moment until a strange sensation burnt away at his skin.

Donny cried out and pulled away, clutching onto his neck.

'Oh my God, I'm so sorry,' Ana said. 'I've been so used to wearing my glove in the summer, I forget how hot my bionic arm gets.'

'No harm done,' Donny said as he involuntary touched his neck to check for burns. 'I'll survive.'

'It would be a pretty lame way to go during an apocalypse. Death by hug.'

'To be honest, it sounds like the best way to go. Please put that on my gravestone. "Here lies Donny. He died doing what he loved, hugging cute girls."'

Ana laughed and slipped her human arm through his. 'I promise I'll be gentle with you. You are my ticket out of here after all.' She pulled him along as they walked towards the town centre. It bustled with villagers who were heading home for their rationed meals after their work shifts had come to an end. A few shot wayward glances at the pair.

'Explain to me why we have to go to this party,' Donny said.

'It's crucial. For several reasons.'

187

'Several? They better be good. I could've been spending today in the barn sending out test signals.'

Ana smiled. 'First, it's a notable date in the school calendar. Not as serious as the exams or graduation day, but one every student looks forward to. Plus, if we are to leave in a few days or a few weeks, this will be the last time I get to hang out with the people I grew up with. Don't worry, I'm ready to disappear. One more night to hang out with those I care about and, in a way, to say goodbye.'

Donny sighed. 'I suppose that's a valid reason.'

'Also, it would be suspicious if neither of us attended. They might figure out we were plotting something. The kids get excited for this party. It's like our prom. There are only two more school years after ours, so this could be one of the final times it happens for a long time. That's until the children return from the orphanage of course.' Ana paused for a while, lost in her thoughts. 'I do hope they're okay.'

Ana doesn't know, Donny thought. It was a relief to find out she wasn't implicit in the horrible crimes that took place but then why would a father tell his daughter, who would've been thirteen years old at the time, that he had killed dozens of innocent children? Mihai had hidden his murders and infidelity from the entire village as he won the trust of the people to become their leader. What else was the Order of the Danube hiding?

The sooner they left, the better.

A random memory popped into Donny's mind. 'Say Ana, whatever happened to the dictator you told me about? Um, Nicolae Coleseku? The one that forced the families to have a lot of kids?'

'You mean President Nicolae Ceaușescu? After a military tribunal, he was found guilty of genocide and sentenced to death by firing squad.'

'I see,' Donny said.

The local gymnasium had been transformed from a crumbling dungeon of sweat into a tacky cathedral of brightly coloured flags and scented candles. A long table covered in a tattered tablecloth lay against the wall and appeared to be reserved for food, but it lay bare except for two bowls of a colourful liquid.

An old electronic scoreboard hung by rusty chains in the far corner. They would've moved it to the barn if they had the proper tools to do so. Two huge flags of Romania and the European Union lay dormant to the side, symbols of the old world.

The hundreds of candles set a gentle glow on the shadowy shapes of the teenagers who chatted amongst each other in their social cliques. Donny had a disconnect of intimacy from his classmates for the past year, as if they were family who had now become strangers.

'Are you sure I look okay?' Ana asked suddenly. 'Maybe this wasn't such a hot idea after all.'

The only real connection he had was with the person who stood near him. He winked at her. 'You look great. Nothing to be nervous about. And I'll be right here if you need a break from your friends.'

Before Ana could reply, something caught her attention.

Hazel, with an innocent smile and her hair worn up elegantly, bounded towards them.

'Ana! There you are,' Hazel said. 'Where have you been? Oh, hi Donny. This set up is pretty neat, huh? Apparently, there is going to a be a surprise later.'

'Oh really?' Ana tried to force up some enthusiasm to mirror Hazel's energy. Donny remained silent.

'Yeah! Soon I heard. Nicole organised the whole thing. Though that bitch is a teetotaller so sadly no alcohol. Don't worry, I've already taken care of that. It wouldn't be a teenage party if something wasn't spiked. I only poured vodka into one of the bowls. Try to guess which one, Donny boy.'

A silver flask was plucked out from a side parting of Hazel's gown. 'Though if you want a faster trip to party town, I have here an express ticket.'

Donny watched disapprovingly as Ana grabbed the flask and took a modest swig.

Hazel giggled and pulled Ana by the hand and lead her to the group that consisted of Liam, Foghorn, Nicole and Kyle. Ana looked over her shoulder and mouthed sorry to Donny as she joined the group.

Donny didn't mind being excluded. It was a relief to not have to mix with Hazel and Liam.

An assortment of drinking glasses, mismatched in size, lay on the long table. Donny picked up one and sniffed it. He reached for a ladle and filled the glass up with the homemade cordial. The fiery kick of alcohol drowned out the faint scent of berries.

Donny set the glass back on the table not taking a sip. He needed to keep a clear head.

The gym doors opened on the far side and Donny's teacher Jaspar waltzed in. He placed a black rectangular box on a foldable table.

'Gather around, children,' Jaspar said as he waved everyone closer to him. 'It's a bittersweet moment. You have finished your studies and now are about to leave my nest. You have made me so proud. Before I get too emotional, I have a treat for you all. I only use this for special occasions, so no blabbering to your parents.'

Jaspar pushed a button at the top of the box and music blared out of its sides. The teenagers screamed in delight and rushed back to the centre of the gymnasium. They flung their limbs and bodies around in tune with the rhythm.

190

Donny sat at the edge of the table and watched his classmates dance about in a scene that could've been taken straight from an old movie. He pondered on the hypocrisy of it all. The Order of the Danube despised technology and even banned it. Though why would they allow a music box that ran on batteries? Why were the soldiers allowed to carry assault rifles? What about the farming machinery? Surely another form of human tech. Was their prejudice against the digital age and anything analogue or mechanical were acceptable? The most distinguished question would be left unanswered. Who drew the line?

After a couple of songs Ana left her group of friends and headed back to Donny. Her whole face lit up when he caught her gaze. She hopped up on the table next to him.

'Finished already?' Donny asked. 'You were cutting some serious shapes on the dancefloor.'

'Quiet you. Is this your drink?' She picked up the glass and gulped its contents in one go and her face twisted. 'That is awful, how much vodka did Hazel put in there?'

'I imagine a whole bottle.'

'It tastes like it.'

They sat silent for a while, watching the pulsating bodies, and listening to the old tunes.

'It was fun,' Ana said. 'Dancing. Yet I felt like I wasn't wanted there. None of the others spoke to me, other than Hazel of course. It feels like Liam has turned them against me, like I no longer belong with them. The most upsetting part is that I formed the group. I brought everyone together. Hazel and I were inseparable, and she knew Foghorn well. Nicole and Kyle were good friends of mine. Then I started dating Liam and our little family was formed. Liam sees himself as the leader and now that he is no longer interested in me, I'm no longer welcome.'

Donny considered the significance of her words. 'You shouldn't let the opinion of others define who you are.'

Ana played with the empty glass in her hand. The clinking of her metal fingers against the crystal could be heard over the music. 'You're right. The only person who should judge me is myself. But whatever. It's sad but I'll survive. I'm done with childish games and trying to please everyone. Being some sort of social chameleon. The only person I'm going to concentrate on now is myself. I'm so ready to start a new life.'

'It's funny. In the short time I've known you, I've never seen you this at ease.'

'Oh?' Ana rubbed her cheeks that dimpled against the pull of her grin.

'There is something different about you.' Donny noticed how her face glowed in the ambience of dusk and he temporarily became lost in an extraordinary moment and he was aware of it. 'It feels like your aura has changed. That you were hiding a warm energy from the rest of the world. Maybe you held that emotional luggage for too long. I always respected your mind and now there's this new level of confidence on top of it.'

'Shut up, stop being nice. You're weird. My face can't take anymore smiling.'

'I can't promise that.'

Ana exhaled, the sort of exhale that follows an awareness of contentment. 'I don't know what it is. Everything has been going so wrong. For the last few months, I have been in a swirl of depression. Yet now, it feels like a huge weight has been lifted off my shoulders. I no longer care for the small-mindedness of those who have never travelled across the world or lost themselves in a book.'

'You're free to be anyone you want now,' he said.

'It's exciting. To find out who you're supposed to be. Tonight, is the perfect way to end this chapter.'

Voices nearby caught their attention as they saw Kyle and Foghorn beside them, filling their glasses from the punchbowl. They snickered amongst themselves before walking off.

Ana's feet dangled above the ground.

'They're all idiots,' Ana said.

'I know,' Donny said.

A slower song rose across the gymnasium. Synthesizer keys stretched out forever in time. A nearby candle stand lit up the lines of Ana's body. Her face masked in serenity. In that moment, nothing else mattered to Donny other than how beautiful she looked.

Life is short so make the most of every minute, of every hour.

Donny slid off the table and offered his hand in the air. Ana tilted her head in confusion over the invitation.

'May I have this dance?' Donny tried to put on the poshest voice possible.

Ana's eyes swirled with mischief. She offered her hand and jumped off the table. 'You may, good sir.'

They walked to the centre of the floor, hand in hand. Donny looked at Ana expectantly, unsure of how to behave in the moment. She smiled and reached for his hands and placed them on her waist. The metal of her arm had cooled during the evening and felt refreshing on his skin. Her arms rested on his shoulders as they swayed to the slow beat of the music.

'Am I doing this right?' Donny asked. 'I've never danced with anyone before.'

'You're a natural,' Ana reassured him.

Couples on the dancefloor swayed around them like evergreens being teased by the wind in a twilight forest.

'Do you recognise this song?' Ana asked. 'I haven't heard much music in the last five years. I mean, no offense to Victoria, but her playing on the guitar in the village square is not my idea of a fun time. This is different. I like this song.'

'It's perfect,' Donny said.

Ana moved closer to him, wrapping her arms around his neck. 'Tell me what life will be like. In Seoul.'

'I'm not sure what to expect. From the last news reports, I believe it's the most likely place where humans have made their last stand against --'

'No, not that nonsense,' Ana interrupted. 'Tell me the good stuff.'

Donny paused and deliberated on Ana's request. 'I see you in your own place. A fancy apartment in a high-rise with a view over the entire city. A room dedicated to your study; each wall covered in more books than you could ever read. You have a vital role; you help people. You're happy.'

'I can't wait.'

As the song concluded, someone ripped Donny away from the warmth of Ana's embrace. Pain shot through his back as he bounced off the hard floorboards. He gathered his composure and opened his eyes, searching for the reason of his fall. Liam stood over him. The flames flickered across his face.

'What the hell are you doing dancing with my girl?' Liam snarled.

Ana pushed him away. 'Are you kidding me? *You* broke up with me. I'm not yours. You don't own me like a piece of property.'

'What is so special about this guy anyway?' Liam asked ignoring everything she said. 'He is a loser who spends all his time in the barn. God knows what he does in there.'

'It's none of your business who I spend my time with,' Ana shot back.

Donny jumped to his feet and noticed his classmates had formed a circle around them, enclosing them like zoo animals.

'Listen, Liam,' Donny said in a calm manner. 'Nothing is going on between us. We're just friends.'

'Then what happened that time you were at the city? When you both spent the night together?' Liam's voice slurred. He might've been drinking before he arrived at the dance.

'Beat him up,' Foghorn shouted from the side with delight.

'Oh my God!' Ana exclaimed. 'Nothing happened. How many times do I have to tell you before you get it processed in that thick skull of yours?'

'Whoa, processed?' Liam chuckled. 'Sounds like tech talk to me. Too much time with the android lover over here.'

'Do you even hear yourself sometimes?' Donny squared up to him.

'Face it, you've changed her,' Liam said, his face close to his. 'She used to be a sweet innocent girl before you filled her head with nonsense. Talking about the outside world. Walking around town with her robotic limb on display. Maybe Mihai made a mistake letting you stay here.'

'He's right,' Hazel chimed in. 'What happened to you, Ana? I want my best friend back.'

The crowd murmured in agreement. They stared at Donny. He felt alien and belittled.

'Donny the tech freak,' someone shouted, and everyone joined in a chorus of laughter.

Liam puffed out his cheeks and threw down his fists as if he had won a boxing bout, ready to declare himself the champion.

'You see, everyone thinks the same,' Liam said. 'Get lost you tech freak and take her with you. She's a lost cause.'

Ana lunged at Liam, but Donny held her back.

'Please,' Donny said. 'Ana. Let's go.'

Ana's body didn't resist, and she allowed herself to be moved towards the exit.

'Bye, tech freak,' Liam said.

'Bye, tech freak,' Hazel chimed in, giggling to herself before she turned towards Ana. 'Stop being such an android slut and be the old Ana again.'

Donny snapped.

'You're the freak, Liam! How could you ever mistreat someone as wonderful as Ana the way you do. You're an idiot for ever letting her go. And Hazel, you're one to talk after what you did with Ana's father.'

A heavy silence fell over the gymnasium. For the first time, Donny had noticed the music had stopped. Ana walked backed towards the circle of teenagers who kept stealing glances from one another.

'What did you say?' Ana asked. 'My Father? What did she do?'

Donny choked on his words.

All the hyper energy Hazel possessed had vanished as she stood like a hollow husk.

'What did you mean Donny?' Ana said louder this time.

Donny swallowed hard. 'Hazel and Mihai. I saw them. I saw them together.'

ANA

SIXTEEN

Ana stared at Donny, her mouth ajar.

'What do you mean you saw them together?" she asked.

The once noisy gymnasium had fallen to a gravely silence. Her classmates had frozen into statues of stunned curiosity. The orchestra of cicadas hummed outside, their insect legs hitting the crescendo of their performance in the humid night.

'It just happened,' Hazel said quietly.

A wave of nausea washed over Ana. The spiked punch in her gut bubbled as she used her strength to block out the ungodly imagery from the forefront of her mind.

'Haze. You're joking right?' Ana said, already knowing the answer.

'I'm sorry.'

'He's my father!' Ana screamed. 'You knew him when you were a child. He looked after us when we were small. You were part of our family. You were like my sister.'

'I didn't mean for this to happen,' Hazel said. 'I love him.'

Ana snorted unhinged at the notion. 'Love? You have no idea what love is.'

'He loves me too,' Hazel protested. 'The leader deserves what he wants. Mihai is our closest link to God. If he wants me, then that is God's way. Don't take this out on me just because he never loved you.'

Their classmates murmured and nodded in agreement. Ana shuddered with rage as a red mist bled into her senses. She lunged at Hazel. Her friend let out a cry and tumbled back into the spectators. The wall of teenagers stood in front of Hazel, blocking Ana's path of fury.

Donny pulled her away. 'Ana, stop.'

'Get your hands off me,' Ana spat as she was pulled away. How could they all just stand there with Hazel? Can't they see how sick this was? This wasn't normal. 'You can all go to hell,' she screamed at them.

Ana ran from the gym, as fast as she could move. After she stumbled, she tossed her shoes into the grass and carried on in bare feet. Years of climbing the mountain and spending time in the fields gave the soles of her feet a natural resistance to the rocky ground. A couple of minutes later she approached the entrance to the manor. She leaned on a tree to catch her breath as concocted scenarios played out in her mind. How did she not see it? How long had it gone on for?

'Ana, are you okay?' A voice came up from behind her.

'Leave me alone, Donny.'

The young man appeared by her side. He no longer wore his blazer.

'I wanted to tell you,' he said. 'You had so many problems and I didn't want to add to them. You're a smart and special person, Ana. This place doesn't deserve you. I know what it's like to be an outsider.'

'You have no idea what my life is like,' Ana said. 'You're a spoiled kid who only knew luxury. You never had to go to bed without food. You never knew which one of your friends would die of malnourishment or from an illness that couldn't be treated at a clinic with limited medicine. You complained about your dull life and how you wanted an adventure. Well, my life isn't for your entertainment.'

'Stop,' he said. She couldn't tell if his eyes gave away any signs of remorse. 'Please hear what I have to say. You owe me that much.'

'Excuse me? I owe you nothing. You knew and you didn't tell me. You knew this whole time. Remember when you promised you'd always be honest with me? Your word is meaningless.'

'I care about you,' Donny said.

Ana broke out into a hysterical laughter. 'You don't care about me. You only care about that thing in my arm. That's all you want from me.'

'That's ridiculous. Listen, I didn't tell you because I thought if we were going to Seoul together you wouldn't need to find out. There you can forget about Mihai, Hazel and all the horrible people of this backwards society who have treated you terribly. You have a chance for a fresh start.'

'You must be truly insane. I'm going nowhere with you.'

Ana walked through the gates towards the house.

• • • • •

The grandfather clock ticked in the hallway. Every tick carrying its own personal burden. Each moment was recorded briefly by its mechanical instruments, then lost forever into the void of time. The pendulum swung back and forth. Ana stared at it in a trance, no longer thinking about anything. Nothing else could bring her solace. There was no escape from the inevitable reality where no one cared. The ancient house moaned and creaked under its own weight. Years of history had occupied the confines of the home over the years. Another anonymous soul to pass

199

through, and it wouldn't be the last. Time nor history would care that she had existed.

Ana's fingers ran along the stone walls. She was trying to hold onto the last essence of a family life that she always took for granted. Summer holidays on the beaches of the Black Sea flooded back to her. Her father holding her hand near the water's edge with her toes digging into the sand. Her mother watching them from her sunbathing spot on the towels.

Ana wondered if anyone still visited the beaches.

Ana gulped in a large mouthful of moistureless air and entered the dining room. The candlelight glowed on her parents at the end of the table. Scraps of food lay on their plates, as not even her family had any special treatment when it came to rations these days. She moved in an uncertain fashion trying to appear normal.

Her mother glanced up from her meal and beamed in pride. 'You look lovely tonight, pumpkin.'

Mihai raised an eyebrow. 'You're home early. Isn't it the end of year school dance?'

'Have you eaten?' Rozene asked. 'We don't have any leftovers. We had to give them to the maid. She hadn't eaten all day. Though come sit next to me, you can have some of mine.'

'Papa,' Ana cleared her throat. 'I know.'

Mihai lay his knife and fork on the table calmly and stared at her. 'What do you *know*?'

'Does Mama know?'

'Young lady,' Mihai's voice now deep and menacing. 'You better think carefully on the next few words you speak.'

Rozene's head moved from her daughter to her husband. 'Can someone explain to me what is going on?'

'Papa has been sleeping with Hazel.'

'Who told you such a filthy lie?' Mihai jumped to his feet and towered over Ana who stood her ground.

'Hazel admitted it herself.'

A soft sobbing had begun. Her mother cried though tried her best to conceal it. Maybe she always knew and chose to ignore it.

'There are matters you don't understand,' Mihai said capturing some of his lost composure. 'Hazel is an exceptional young woman. A rising star in The Order of the Danube. If you spent as much time reading your Bible and attending Order meetings as you did with your silly books about history and sciences, you would understand. She is dedicated to her leader and our mission. She would do anything for our people. Your mother understands. You need to fall in line or forget about joining the council.'

'You're insane,' Ana said.

Ana stormed to her bedroom and kicked the door shut. She locked it and fell into a heap.

'What the hell is going on?' she said out loud.

She had no one. Not Hazel. Not Liam. Not even Donny. The world turned its back on her. What did she have left?

A loud pop made her jump and a pain erupted inside her android arm. This was the first time it had ever encountered pain. It felt like something had exploded within.

The metallic fingers begun to twitch. She held them tight and breathed deeply waiting for the convulsions to end.

DONNY

SEVENTEEN

Donny hid his watch from view under the abundant fabric of his gown. On the display screen he brought up a digital image of him with his father. They posed wearing the kit of their favourite football team with a colossal stadium as the backdrop. A dopey adolescent grin spread across Donny's face while his Dad had a proud pose. Football was a serious business back in those days. For his birthday, his parents had surprised him with the new football top and a junior membership.

Donny sighed and minimised the picture.

The interface reverted to a regular analogue watch face. The last remaining piece of technology he had taken with him on the day he left the island. He could disguise it from the townsfolk and charge it with solar power. The memories stored away in its virtual compartments were the most precious possessions he owned.

The sleeve fell back over his wrist. A pungent, sickly-sweet odour rose from the dark, crusted robe. They probably stored them in some shed all year round until the next graduation ceremony. Fortunately, he didn't have to wear one of those stupid hats. He had difficulty staying clean in the village during the hot months and he didn't want anything touching his already tangled hair.

Donny sat at the back of three lines of foldable chairs on a stage. The newly arrived classmates chose not to sit next to him. Hazel had taken her seat already. Right at the front, closest to the podium; her normal perky self, making small talk with her friends around her. She sometimes waved to someone in the ever-growing crowd before them.

The number of possible destination coordinates that remained grew smaller. It would be any day before he could leave. Everyone would hear the noise the Lightspeed Capsule would make, but he would barricade himself inside the barn and take the gigawatt batteries with him so they could never follow.

The animal anxiety gnawed at his stomach. The force was so intense he had to close his eyes to contain the ache. Would Edwin be waiting for him in Seoul? Either way he had to prepare for the worst-case scenarios, getting to Seoul and Edwin wasn't there or the Seoul pod not being operational and having to find a new destination. He ignored the possibility of there being no more working capsules in the world and being stuck here forever.

Though none of that mattered while Ana was angry at him. He needed the processor in her arm, and he didn't want to leave without her. Maybe she would forgive him soon and change her mind about leaving this place.

A commotion in the town hall awoke Donny from his hibernation. Mihai stood near the entrance, shaking hands of eager men around him. A tiny figure brushed passed him and made their way down the middle aisle to the stage. Ana, whose face was always full of wonder and intrigue, now carried a darkness in her eyes and a terrible anger pulling at her eyebrows. She observed the seating layout and sat in the front row at the opposite end from Hazel.

Hazel made a visible effort to lean forward and gain Ana's attention, but Ana looked ahead ignoring her. Hazel giggled and spoke to her neighbours at a louder intensity, not fazed by the snub.

203

Ana could still reveal his plans to her father. No, he told himself, she wasn't that type of person. *Since you arrived, Mihai has told me to watch you. He has plans for you.* Stefan's words came to him. What was Mihai plotting?

Donny studied Ana for a long time. Her head floated above her graduation gown, as if she distanced herself from everyone else like an unseen planet rotating around its star at the furthest possible orbit. His heart grew heavy for her. Gaunt faces from the audience stole glances of disgust towards her, like ghouls from the underworld. Ana deserved better than this.

From the sea of brainwashed faces Donny spotted someone familiar. Victoria wore a trim suit so clean it could've been bought recently from a new store. Her auburn locks fell over the navy jacket. She pushed her wire rimmed glasses up her face and laughed easily. With her makeup, it made her appear a decade older. Donny became aware of how juvenile the robe made him look and he sunk further in his seat. She probably thought he was too immature to be taken seriously.

A high-pitched voice was heard as Jaspar took his place at the podium asking for the audience to settle down. An eerie tranquillity swept across the hall as chairs scraped along the barren floor and the whispers perished.

'I'm happy to present to you the class of 5 AR,' Jaspar announced with applause from the audience. Foghorn let out one of his signature whoops. 'I know they're all dying to learn how they did in their examinations, but I first want to tell you how proud I am of this bunch. They've grown up so fast and blossomed into wonderful adults. There have been hardships, of course, and there've been times where their characters have been tested. Yet for every challenge they shone through.'

'I told myself I wouldn't get emotional,' Jaspar reached for a handkerchief and blew in it. 'Let me end with saying that whatever role you are assigned to today, you'll become valuable members of this society and great servants to our illustrious leader. Without further ado, let me present the man himself. Mihai.'

From the councillors, who sat on the opposite side of the stage, a powerful man rose from the front. He carried himself with dignity and authority. A man oozing with arrogance. His bear paw hands grasped the side of the lectern as he absorbed the admiration from his worshipers. He glanced over to the graduates. His focus seemed to be on Ana, towards whom he cast a damning stare.

'Countrymen, compatriots, my children; may God bless you all.' Donny felt the voice travel through his bones. 'A year ago, all hope vanished when we lost our glorious leader. We wondered if our great community would still be able to proceed without his guidance. I stood on this stage before you as a humble servant asking you to place your trust in me. You did so and together, we have continued to have safety and prosperity. God bless The Order of the Danube.'

The crowd rose to their feet and chanted his name. 'Mihai. Mihai. Mihai.' They laughed like jackals who had cornered a stray gazelle. Mihai waved them down and they sat obediently.

'Let me tell you a story about a young man who is graduating today. Liam. He is like the son I never had. I say this genuinely about all the young men and women on stage today. They are my children. However, this story is about Liam. When I was commander of the armed forces of this town, he came up to me and asked in the innocent tone that we are accustomed to hearing from our young children, how do I get to be a soldier? I asked him why he wanted to pursue such a dangerous vocation, and he simply said he would look cool holding a gun.'

205

This drew some light laughter.

'I said, I'm afraid you'll need a better reason than wanting to impress your friends. He told me in seriousness that he wanted to protect his family and his friends from the monsters. He wanted to protect us. The beautiful simplicity of a child's mind. School is where they learn the importance of responsibility. Like Liam, I want to protect you for as long as I can during these difficult times, until God calls for us as declared in the Book of Revelation.'

Jaspar cavorted across the stage to hand Mihai an envelope. Mihai snatched the envelope and ripped open the seal to reveal a single sheet of paper. 'Based on the examination results and council evaluations, here are the newly appointed professions of the graduates. Good luck.'

'Army and defence: Liam. Well done, son.'

Liam pumped his fist in the air as his buddies patted him on the back and ruffled his hair.

Mihai continued. 'Kitchen: Nicole, Felix and Lydia.'

'Lumber and carpentry: Kyle and John.'

'Machine and weapon repair: Donny.'

Donny blinked in astonishment. For so long he had resigned to the fact he would be leaving he didn't consider getting a job suited to his talents. Maybe Mihai wasn't as bad as he once thought. The kind notion vanished as soon as it arrived, like the bloody tide leaving the shore on a battlefield.

'Plumbing and sanitation: Daniel and Brennan.'

Kyle poked Foghorn in the side, 'looks like you're on toilet duty, pal.'

Foghorn protested to his classmates. 'Surely there has been some sort of mistake.'

Mihai ignored the noise and cleared his throat before he delivered further assignments. 'The farm: Natalie, Mikel, Emily and Ana.'

206

After a stunned pause the students in the seats positioned their bodies towards Ana. They tried to gauge her reaction, lavishing in her predicted anguish. Ana held her head high and still, gazing towards the shadows at the back of the hall. Donny could make out a tear of frustration running down her cheek. She brushed it away. The quick display of her exposed android hand drew insidious comments from the room.

Mihai waited for the whispers to stop before he continued as if he knew putting his own daughter on the farming detail would send a message to everyone present.

'And last but not least,' Mihai said, now in a more menacing tone, 'let me introduce you to the student who has taken the final spot on our council. She achieved some of the highest scores on the exams, she is a credit to her community, and one day will be a fine leader. May I introduce to you, your new councilwoman, Hazel.'

Hazel walked towards the front of the stage and bowed to the applauding crowd. Mihai placed a kiss on her cheek as she took over the podium from him.

'Thank you,' Hazel shouted out. 'It's such an honour to be chosen as your voice on the council. I promise I'll work hard to serve --'

A scream tore through the air. Ana threw off her gown and stomped towards Hazel whose eyes were as wide as a fawn's gazing into the blinding lights of an oncoming truck.

Ana's android arm recoiled back and then sprung at Hazel's face. Against the sickening crumpling of cartilage, Hazel fell to the floor. A beat passed before blood poured from what remained of her nose, reddening her teeth in a waterfall of blood.

Ana's metal first trembled uneasily by her side.

ANA

EIGHTEEN

Soldiers leapt onto the stage and charged at Ana like a ferocious storm. Two of them clasped their hands tightly around her arms attempting to control the fury she had unleashed. Ana struggled against their weight and flung a man flying off the platform with her android appendage. She grunted as two more burly men took his place and forced her to her knees.

Liam and Foghorn, their faces as white as fresh snow, stood over Hazel as she shivered uncontrollably.

'The bitch broke my nose,' Hazel's whimper gurgled in the blood. Her once exquisite face now turned into a pulpy hue of purple.

'Bring her to me,' Mihai ordered.

The fight burned inside of her as she jerked against the soldiers who dragged her to the centre of the stage. The villagers crowded the front of the stage, jostling to get a better view of the chaos.

Fury burnt in Mihai's eyes as they met hers. 'What have you done?' he harshly whispered.

'I let her off lightly,' Ana said.

'Assaulting a councillor is one of the gravest offenses. You of all people should know this,' he said louder now so everyone could hear.

'This is a farce. She's not a councillor. She's a lazy brat that you're screwing.'

'Don't you dare speak to me in that tone, young lady.' Ana could smell the vodka on his breath as he leaned in towards her, his face deepening into a dark crimson. 'I am your father and your leader. She is now a woman of God. You will show both of us respect.'

The eyes of every person in the room bore into Ana like hundreds of miniature spears, piercing through her skin. Her life calling was to help people, yet they scorned her, belittled her, and treated her like a doormat. There was no more left to give, but she could not give up hope. Not yet.

'You're no leader, Papa. You're a bully and an adulterer. You say you provide safety for these people, yet each day they starve while we get first choice of the food. You have failed them.' She turned to the crowd, 'you deserve better.'

'No one speaks to the leader like that,' someone shouted from the crowd.

'Who does she think she is?' another person added.

Jeers and whistles rang out as the mob congregated in mass.

Mihai whispered in her ear. 'You have always disappointed me, Ana. Maybe it was my fault, believing you would live up to my expectations. The truth is, I always wanted a son. A son to carry on my legacy. But your Mother disappointed me. You were the only child she could deliver and now I see for the first time what a failure you are. Maybe your friend is ripe enough to bear me a true heir.'

Ana spat in Mihai's face.

The crowd gathered at the front inhaled in unison. Then they erupted. They screamed at her. They swore at her. A projectile grazed her jaw, but she kept her nerve not to look at the crowd. She didn't back down her gaze from her father.

Mihai pulled out a cotton handkerchief from his jacket's breast pocket and wiped the saliva from his eyebrow.

'My children,' Mihai said in a calming voice as he addressed the crowd. 'What you have witnessed today is that sin is still very much alive in our world. We believed we could escape it by shedding away our old comforts and distractions from the devil. For many years we succeeded, and the good Lord blessed us kindly. However, I made a mistake. For I am a mortal man of flesh and blood like all of you. My sin was vanity. I wanted my daughter to lead a normal life. Satan himself tempted me and provided my daughter with a new arm. Only through our trials and suffering do we find eternal life. Yet I took that burden away from Ana. I gave her an easy life, and in return I have lost her spirit to evil.'

'Punish her,' a woman screeched.

'Technology has infected her mind,' Mihai said. A flock of crows squawked as they flew by in the distance. 'It runs from her arm into the blood stream and it corrupts her heart. Technology poisoned our world. It created those, *machines*, who hunted us down, took away our loved ones. Because humankind had imagined itself as smart as God. That we were equal to God.'

'Death to tech,' Gheorghe shouted.

'Right you are my brother. Judgment Day is almost upon us. We need to do what is honourable and rid ourselves of these sinful tools. Only then, will we be worthy to enter His kingdom.'

'Death to tech,' more people chanted.

Mihai turned to the biggest of his guards. 'Go fetch your axe.'

Ana breathed hard. The warmth drained away from her face and she shivered. She glanced at her classmates on the stage, but they were only strangers to her now. Hazel yelled something at her, but she couldn't make out the words.

Donny stood by himself. His beautiful blue eyes shining against the greyness like two sapphires glowing in a heap of ash. He lifted his robe to one side showing her his revolver stuck into the top of his jeans. 'I can help,' he mouthed towards her. 'No,' Ana mouthed back. Donny would be killed instantly if he intervened.

This was her fight.

The giant of a man who Mihai had sent way had returned. His hairy forearms bulged as they held on securely to a polished handle. The wooden staff ran up to a giant blade at the head. The vicious curve of metal flashed menacingly against the sunlight.

Ana exhaled. Nausea rushing around her stomach like a typhoon.

'It's time for your punishment,' Mihai said. 'Lay her down.'

The soldiers forced Ana face down on the ground. Her face banged against the dusty floor. A knee dug into her spine, sending shockwaves of pain through her body. Two of the men stretched her robotic arm away from her.

Ana used her might to pull the arm free, but it was no use. They were too strong.

'Papa don't do this,' Ana cried out.

Mihai ignored her and spoke to the crowd. 'Ana's punishment has been decided. Her demonic arm will be removed from her body. Then, the healing process can begin. She can repent and return to our flock. Death to tech.'

'Death to tech!' the crowd shouted the mantra in a trance. 'Death to tech! Death to tech!'

'Papa,' Ana begged, but the mindless chanting drowned out her voice. 'You can stop this. This isn't you. Please. Stop.'

Mihai nodded towards the man with the axe.

The giant's boots came to rest in parallel with her android arm. Her eye darted up to catch the glimmer of the blade as it tilted towards the roof.

Ana closed her eyes and held her breath.

A deadly pulsing rushed through her body almost choking her. The fierce echo of metal against metal vibrated in her ears. Ana could still feel the sensation in her metallic fingers. She peeked towards her arm to find a tiny scar etched in her titanium skin. The axe did no damage.

'Death to tech! Death to tech! Death to tech!' the voices rang out with greater persistence.

Someone called out to her. A boy she knew. She glanced up from the floor now washed with her sweat and tears. A soldier carried Donny off stage, his arms and legs flailing.

'Aim for the flesh,' Mihai barked. 'Above the elbow.'

'Are you sure boss?' the giant asked.

'Yes, don't make me repeat myself.'

'Death to tech! Death to tech! Death to tech!' joined in the graduates on stage.

Ana's world became cold and small as she escaped into herself to a frozen wasteland. No animals or people lived there. A monstrous glacier of ice replaced the mountain she loved to climb. 'Let her go,' Donny's voice carried in the wind, but she couldn't be certain. The world iced around her.

'Papa,' she cried out. 'All I wanted was for people to accept me. For you to be proud of me. Don't let them do this.'

The only thing that remained was her dignity and she clung onto it. She couldn't lose hope.

The axe crashed into the stage floor, severing the arm from the body in one lethal blow.

Ana screamed in venomous horror.

DONNY

NINETEEN

Donny sprawled out into the humid atmosphere. The dry grass and trees sizzled in the distance creating a hazy glaze. He gasped for breath unable to find any moisture to satisfy his dry tongue. The robe hindered his movements, so he tossed it into the bushes.

'We need to leave before they find you,' Stefan peered through the doors. An assault rifle hung from his back as if it were a harmless sporting tool, his soldier uniform hung loosely over his thin frame. 'They are distracted now, but soon they'll get bored and leave. You are not safe here.'

Donny shook his head. He panted hard. He didn't know if he would throw up.

'I can't,' Donny said. 'I can't leave her.'

Stefan shoved Donny in the direction of the road. 'We're running out of time. Mihai is a crazy man. I don't know what he is planning for, though I know it's no good. There is a spot I can hide you while you decide what you want to do. If you decide you want to stay, you are also crazy.'

Donny listened to the sickening cheers seep from the hall.

'Alright, take me there.'

Donny pushed hard to keep up with Stefan's pace. After spending most of the past year tinkering with machines and gadgets in the barn, he felt sluggish. He

213

burned through his reserves to keep up. A film of sweat built over his face and his shirt soaked at his armpits. Stefan moved effortlessly, his boots clomping on the broken road and his rifle swaying behind him.

A lightbulb moment struck Donny with a quick bolt of electricity and he veered off course down a back alley.

'Where are you going?' Stefan shouted.

Donny raced up the garden and checked the backdoor of Gheorghe's house. The door slid open and he made his way to his bedroom. He picked up his backpack from the corner and chucked in his possessions. First, the book from his Dad. He breathed in the room that had been his temporary home, holding in the memories for another day. He slung the bag over his shoulders and checked the kitchen. A stale piece of bread lay under a bowl. He stuffed it securely in a side pocket.

Stefan jittered at the edge of the garden as Donny re-emerged into the daylight. 'This is no time to goof around. I can hear people coming down the main road. They have left the hall.'

'I'm sorry. I didn't know if I would have another chance to come back here.'

After five minutes of darting through back roads and Stefan telling Donny to stay hidden behind walls and shrubs, they made it to a decrepit house in the centre of a neighbourhood. The pink walls peeled away, and weeds ruled supreme in the grass moat.

'You live here?' Donny asked knowing the answer already.

'Yes, yes. Get inside.' Stefan said shutting the door behind them.

Little furniture occupied the cramped dwelling, yet it still seemed untidy. Clothes lay on the floor and on the back of the couch. Old faded magazines towered in the corner. Donny picked up a rusted racing car from the coffee table.

'Be careful,' Stefan said as he snatched the car from Donny's hands and lay it back on the table. 'It is antique.'

It didn't look like an antique. It looked like a piece of junk.

'Why did you bring me here?'

'To protect you,' Stefan said. 'You're in danger. Hope is lost with you. Like always.'

'Why should I trust you? You might bring Mihai and his men here as soon as I fall asleep.'

'Why would I do that? I could bring them here right now. You're no good to Ana if Mihai gets a hold of you. You are safest here for now.'

'Don't you think they would search every house?'

'Let me show you something,' Stefan said.

A loose string hung from the ceiling. Stefan grasped at it and jerked it down, A light timber ladder slid to the ground with a thud. Donny followed Stefan up the stairs into a darkened attic. Stefan pulled another cord, and a light shone across layers of fluffy insulation foam. Planks of wood lay against one end of the room with boxes sorted into pyramids.

'I'm sure they would find me behind those.'

'Ah, but you are wrong,' Stefan said. 'Stop being annoying and watch this.' He moved the boxes to one side and played with the edge of the wall. A loud click rippled against the roof and a panel slid away. The heavy wooden door scraped along the flooring to reveal a secret compartment no bigger than a walk-in closet.

Stacks of cans, which contained soup, corn, carrots, spinach, beans, and peas piled up deep inside like a supermarket display exhibit.

'Where did you get all this food?' Donny asked.

'Back before the war. When I felt it was going to take a turn for the worst, I started stockpiling. I had so much more than this, yet I've been going through a lot of it in recent months when food has been scarce. Most of the cans are expired, but they still taste good enough.'

'Wow,' Donny said impressed. He always assumed the scruffy Stefan wouldn't possess such foresight and planning.

'You have to make a choice quickly. I can give you some of the cans and you can leave and start a new life somewhere else. Or, if you want to stay and help your friend, you can stay in the secret room until we find a safe moment to get you both out.'

'I'm staying,' Donny reiterated. 'But why are you are doing this? I thought you were loyal to Mihai.'

'Donny, I've done many bad things in my life. Not one night goes by when I don't think about those children. How I could've saved them if I acted differently. Recently I told my darling Denisa about the act I committed, but she agreed that Mihai took the best action. We fought many times over it. She said I was a weak man and that I needed to be more courageous like our fearless leader. Eventually she said she could no longer stomach the sight of me and moved back in with her parents. They worship Mihai. They all do. Now I am alone with my self-pity and guilt. Has the world gone so mad that the sacrifice of children is seen as the right thing to do? If those are the new rules, maybe it is time I break the rules.'

Donny stared at the ground, unsure of what to say.

'And what of you, Donny? Why do you stay for this girl? Aren't you with Victoria?'

'Ana is special. Her heart is pure. She didn't deserve what happened to her. She deserves better than this place…and she saved me, it's my turn to return the favour.'

'As you wish,' Stefan said. 'Don't make a noise from now on. I'll get you a pillow and blanket. And a bucket.'

• • • • •

The flow of time passed slowly, merging into a painful blur of sitting still and listening to the world carry on as normal. Donny broke up the days by reading *Catcher in the Rye*, reminiscing about the old days back on the island and formulating plans on how he would escape with Ana. Stefan would visit him late at a night to bring him fresh water and empty his bucket. He would ask him for reports on Ana. Stefan would say she was alive and stable, but he couldn't add any further detail. He heard gunshots on one of the days, but Stefan told him not to worry about it. A lot of the anti-technology rhetoric pointed at Donny's disappearance. Rumours had been told that Donny brainwashed Ana with his dangerous ideologies.

Despite the hours of free time he had on his hands, he couldn't decide on a plan. Stefan had given him a map and marked a spot he could head to. His cousin owned a farm in the north of Romania and would take him and Ana in if he mentioned they were friends with Stefan. Donny doubted someone would take in strangers during these times.

Eventually Donny entrusted Stefan with his true plan. The one he had spent a year working towards. Stefan didn't seem so shocked when he heard the involvement of the portal machine. The amount of time Donny spent in the barn; it would make sense that Stefan knew he had been trying to fix the device that brought him here. The plan was not only to save Ana, but also to retrieve Ana's android arm. Stefan revealed it wasn't taken to the barn, where all the other tech was stored, but kept in the weapon cache where the soldiers' guns were locked up. Stefan said attaining the arm wouldn't be a problem. Yet it would have to do at the last possible moment as they would know it had gone missing.

Donny's plan required a lot of luck. During nightfall he would break into the infirmary where they were keeping Ana. Hopefully, she would be well enough to travel. Next, they would sneak into the barn. Stefan would meet them there to deliver the android arm. Donny would only have a few hours before sunrise to install the CPU processor from the arm into the machine, find Seoul in the systems and then teleport them both there safely. Stefan might have to come with them if he felt his life was at risk.

Donny thought about going to the barn first and doing the final preparations before rescuing Ana but breaking into the barn twice in a row might be too risky. He had found two other working pods so far during his investigations. One in Lagos and another in Rome. It would be a gamble to head to those locations without knowing the political climate of those regions. If they were discovered, it would be a quick escape. He had his gun and enough batteries for the pair of them to make multiple trips. They could teleport to Rome and if it appeared dangerous, head to the next destination.

Donny would have to wait for the perfect moment to put his plan into action.

· · · · ·

A loud knock woke Donny from his sleep. His eyes blinked in vain in the darkness. He dared not turn on his watch to check the time because of the light it would emit. The knock came again, even more forceful. A few moments later he could hear the door unlock and at least one man entered the room two floors below his hiding spot. Donny couldn't make out any words from the discussion except that they were speaking Romanian. The door slammed, but no one locked it. His hearing strained to make out for anyone left in the house. No sound came. The house was silent.

Then a heavy shuffle came into the attic. Donny drew his revolver ready for whatever came his way.

'Donny, we've got to go,' Stefan whispered loudly. He removed the panel and Donny could make out his outline in the darkness.

'What is it?' Donny asked.

'They have asked me to cover the shift at the medical centre. A soldier has fallen sick. This is your best shot at saving Ana and escaping. I'll get the arm, you get the girl and we'll meet at the barn. Gather your things. We leave in five minutes.'

'Okay,' Donny said as anxiety flushed over him. 'Thank you, Stefan.'

The patter of rain droplets hit the roof tiles above him. Donny couldn't remember the last time it rained. The water dripped in a melody of aquatic songs. The mask of a rainy night would increase his and Ana's chance of escape.

Thunder roared from over the mountain.

Donny flicked on his watch to its lowest light setting and laid it furthest from the outside wall. He downed the remainder of his water and relieved himself in the bucket. His few possessions were squeezed into his backpack including a few cans from Stefan's secret food stash and the blanket.

The rain poured heavier now as Donny and Stefan peered outside. Donny pulled the hoodie tighter around his head, exhaled sharply and they slipped out into the night.

ANA

TWENTY

The rapid assault of gun fire pierced the city buildings. Smoke and ash hung in the air and it poisoned her lungs. She coughed and swore at herself. They would find her if she made a noise. They would kill them if they were found.

Ana held tightly onto her father's hand as he pulled her along as they darted between crumbling structures of rubble. A submachine gun waved ahead in his other hand, leading the way to safety. Mihai pulled her down on the floor against a stone wall. He peered around the corner out into the main road. His camouflaged uniform soaked in dust and sweat.

An explosion rang out a few streets over like the roar of a dying Greek god. Her hands shot up to cover her ears and she squeezed her eyes tight. The ringing in her ears gave way to her heartbeat that pounded in a panicked thump.

Ana wiped away the soot from her face. The skin of her palms felt smooth against her cheeks.

'I'm scared, Papa.'

'I know you are, pumpkin,' Mihai said as her turned to face her. 'But you're doing so well. You're the bravest nine-year-old I know.'

'Maybe,' Ana said as she wiped her nose on her dirty sleeve.

Gun fire rang out again and Mihai stole a glance from around the corner. 'Ana, listen to me. I need you to do exactly what I say. I'm going to drop you off with Mama and the others at the evacuation point. You'll walk through the forest until you reach the town near the river. You know the one, where your grandparents live.'

Ana nodded her head quickly. 'I like it there. That's where Hazel lives.'

'It's an old town hidden by the mountains. The monsters won't find you. I'll meet you and your Mama there once we secure the city.'

Ana cried out as she saw the figure run towards them. An ordinary man in every sense apart from the soulless expression across its face. Its suit was a luminous black, as dark as the hidden corners of space. A laser rifle was steady in its hands.

Mihai threw his body in front of his daughter and fired off the entire ammunition clip in the direction of the enemy. The android's face exploded in a spray of metallic shards and pieces of artificial human flesh.

The body of the android toppled over.

'Got him,' Mihai boasted. 'Pumpkin are you --'. Terror had consumed the face of her father in a way she had never seen before. His face became pale as the full moon and his bottom lip quivered.

'What's wrong Papa?' Ana asked as a spell of dizziness crept over her.

Ana lowered her head. Where her left elbow used to be were gaping blood-soaked holes. Her arm dangled loose and lifeless like the arm of a doll.

• • • • •

Ana gasped for air.

Raindrops against the windowpanes had replaced the distant memories of gunfire. The flicker of candlelight cast dancing shadows over the bed she lay in. She wore a hospital gown that was drenched in her own sweat. Fire seared the back of her throat as she choked on the fumes of a disinfectant.

Torturing electricity flared from her arm as though it splintered into two. She tried to reach for it, but she couldn't move. Heavy leather straps held her in place. The tubes of a liquid drip fed into her right arm. Her left arm was no longer there. Bloodied bandages wrapped around the nub of her bicep. The agony she felt was only phantom pains, sparking off from memories of old. The once elegant robotic arm had been removed in a grizzly episode. Not a nightmare she could wake from, it was the reality she existed in. The androids had taken her first arm, the family she loved had taken her new one.

Wind screamed outside as the rain continued to pelt against the glass.

'Hey hoser,' a voice ventured from a corner of the room.

The figure wore blue scrubs and a surgical mask. A bouffant concealed their hair though the wire framed glasses and mocking eyes gave away the identity.

'Wakey, wakey sleepy head,' said Victoria as she placed a tray of instruments on the table next to Ana's bed. 'You're in the medical centre. You gave us a scare, but Daddy managed to stitch you up all good and proper.'

'I need some --' Ana croaked.

Victoria read her mind. She disappeared and returned with a cup of water. She carefully manoeuvred a metal straw to Ana's lips. The icy cold water rushed down her throat and brought her relief.

'That better?' asked Victoria. She didn't wait for an answer and continued speaking. 'We were worried about you. Yes, even me. You lost a lot of blood and went into shock before we could bring you here. To be honest, most of them thought you wouldn't make it to. You've been falling in and out of consciousness for two weeks. I'm glad to see you've regained your senses.'

'I've been here for two weeks?' Ana tried to shout yet it came out as a croaky whimper.

Victoria pushed her glasses up her nose with a hand donned in a disposable glove. The lenses had fogged up from the surgical mask. In the candlelight, she reminded Ana of those doctors from the black plague. 'Actually, it's been thirteen days. You've been stirring for the last few days. You even tried to leave in a dazed state. The guard had to help restrain you.'

'I don't remember,' Ana said.

'It's the reason for the restraints,' said Victoria. 'That's what they told me anyway. Though I know the real reason.' She remained quiet for a while, paused in whatever task she was doing. 'I have to replace your bandages. It's going to be uncomfortable. Please don't be a brat while I change them.'

Ana said nothing and looked away.

The tangle of bloodied cloth unwrapped from her body and a tingling sensation at the end of her arm flared up. She wanted her android arm back so she could rip the belts off and get the hell out of there.

'Your wound seems to be healing nicely,' said Victoria with a hint of pride. 'There were no complications during surgery and the scar should be neat as well. It won't recover completely for another twelve months so you...hey, you shouldn't worry about it.'

Victoria had kept something from her. 'Why shouldn't I worry?' Ana asked before she let out a cry. Victoria applied to the tip of her arm cotton wool soaked in some sort of solution, though it felt like razor blades rinsed in vinegar. Ana ground her teeth together as each swab brought in a new wave of pain.

'You'll find out sooner or later,' said Victoria as she picked up a roll of wool bandages. 'Since you've been sleeping, the town has fallen apart. Your public humiliation awoke something insidious that's been living among us for a while now. The mob has taken a form of its own. Protests, damage to property, strikes from the farmers. People are going hungry, and they are angry. A clash happened with the soldiers a few days ago and two of the farm hands were killed. Everyone is so hungry. And scared. Don't worry, it'll be good again soon.'

Ana said nothing as Victoria wrapped her arm with fresh bandages. She couldn't comprehend what happened. Her own father turning against her. Her neighbours chanting for her to be cut up. The inaction of Liam and her friends for letting it happen. The helplessness suffocated her as if Victoria had stuck a pillow over her face.

'Events have reached a boiling point,' said Victoria. 'I didn't believe in your father. Perhaps the fact that he presented himself as a protector in Christian values made me warm up to his leadership. His back is truly up against the wall now. His mismanagement has endangered us all. You've been made to be a scapegoat. You didn't deserve any of this, little Anadroid.'

'You're as bad as the rest of them.'

Victoria snorted. 'Don't be too hasty. It's not like I've been changing your diaper for the last few days or anything.'

Ana's cheeks burnt brightly with embarrassment and annoyance. 'You shouldn't have to look after me.'

'It's my job,' sighed Victoria as she threw the bloodied bandages into a waste bin along with the gloves she wore. She picked up a bar of soap near the basin and rubbed it between her hands.

Ana remembered back to the last night she had been in that room. The night of Victoria's party and she had followed the strange new boy into the medical wing of the house. She smiled as she remembered scolding him. He behaved like an alien, visiting a distant world for the first time. So full of innocence and naivety. He sat on this exact same bed and for the first time she felt an instant connection with him. That destiny itself had rearranged the stars for them to meet.

'Do you know if Donny has visited me?' Ana asked, her voice high with her final traces of hope riding on the question with unbearable anticipation.

The splashing of water from the basin grew silent. Victoria appeared at her bedside. She wiped her hands thoroughly before she removed her mask.

'Donny left,' said Victoria.

'What?'

'Did I stutter? He's gone. After the graduation ceremony, no one could find him. The soldiers searched the whole town and didn't find a trace. A lot of folks are blaming him for the troubles. I couldn't care less about that nerd. He only cared about one person. Himself. That jerk didn't care about me. Like hell he cared about you.'

Tears burnt at the edges of Ana's eyes. With all the morphine and the fluids from the IV swirling around in her, it made it feel like acid had been produced by her tear ducts, burning her cheeks on their path to her ears. She had blamed him for keeping her father's affair a secret. She didn't mean to lash out at him, she couldn't control herself when she became angry. He was her friend, maybe her only friend left, and she pushed him away. Did he manage to find her android arm and use the portal machine? He could be on the other side of the planet right now. More guilt she had to live with.

'Whoa, don't be like that,' said Victoria wiping away Ana's tears with a towel. 'No boy is worth crying over.'

'Shut up, Victoria. Leave me alone.'

'Hey, listen. Remember the time when you visited here? Before the war. I looked after you when our families played tennis together. In my garage we found those paint cans and decided to paint a mural on the side of the house? I painted a unicorn and you painted a dragon, though it looked more like a cat with wings.'

'Oh my God. Papa and your Dad were so angry with us,' Ana snickered through the tears.

'They were! We weren't allowed to play with each other again. Dad made me repaint the whole wall and you got off scot-free.'

'Is that why you hated me?'

'I'm not that petty,' said Victoria. 'We grew up, we grew apart. You had your goofy friends and I had mine. You were always so serious. Always with your nose in a book. I enjoyed winding you up. It seemed simpler back then. I'm going to miss those days.'

They both remained in silence as the storm raged on outside. Ana couldn't remember a storm as wild, it was as though hundreds of ghosts from the Danube has entered the mortal realm and brought along with them their misery.

'Victoria, listen to me. You need to let me go. I have no future here. Everyone hates me. It's probably best I find a new home. Maybe in the city.'

'I wish it was that easy, little Anadroid.' Victoria stroked the leather straps and her forehead creased above her glasses as if she tried to solve a riddle in her head, but some of the pieces weren't there. 'We're out of time.'

'What do you mean?'

'Pretend I didn't say anything.'

'Tell me,' Ana demanded.

Victoria stared at her for a long time. A vacant stare tainted with the sense of finality. Her red hair burned slowly in the candlelight. 'All of our suffering is about to come to an end.'

Ana struggled against the straps that held her captive. She writhed as the leather chafed her skin and the agony of her wound burnt. She shouted for help despite her throat begging her to stop. Her limbs didn't budge so she tried to rock the bed over. It collided with a table, sending medical instruments pinging across the floor. They treated her like a mad woman, and she was happy to oblige.

A man in a white coat stormed into the room. 'What's all this ruckus?'

'Daddy, she's going crazy. It's because she lost her arm. It's too much for her to take.'

'Right you are,' William said as he rummaged through a drawer to produce a large needle. He opened the glass cabinets above and picked out a tiny jar with a clear liquid.

'Victoria, listen to me,' Ana said, her heart racing. 'This place is a nightmare. Don't listen to them. This place...it's a lie. We were promised safety here. To live our lives. A chance to be young.'

'It's good that she's regained consciousness,' William said as he squirted the liquid from the top of the needle checking for air pockets. Victoria stood silently next to him watching. 'We need to get her ready for Mihai.'

'Victoria, please.' Ana felt Victoria's fingers run through her damp hair. The tingles subdued her resolve

'Don't worry,' said Victoria. 'It'll be over soon.'

DONNY

TWENTY-ONE

A stream created from the chaotic nature of the storm rushed downhill over the hardened earth. The water swept away everything in its path from pebbles to tools, anything left out in the open. Water, even in its most pathetic form, had the potential to grow into something deadly.

The rain transformed from a trickle of water to a heavy shower. It darkened the light of the world, extinguishing the street lanterns and covering visibility in a glistening sheet of doom. The glow from the homes were faint, like distress beacons screaming out against the fog. All noises were muffled except for the steady shower of droplets pelting the earth with fury, as if it were the only noise that ever existed.

Cold and wet, Donny persisted through the elements. Donny pulled the hood tightly around his hair and ears. His hands tried to stay warm by being shoved deeply in the front pockets. None of the precautions were enough to protect him as the rain ran down his face and the wetness had intruded into his boot to soak the edges of his socks. The chill seeped into his bones.

The rain pelted him with every step he took as he darted between houses.

Only one goal made him persevere.

He had to escape. He had to escape with Ana.

It would be difficult for a guard to spot him with the low visibility, yet he had to remain vigilant. He could cut through the centre of town towards the infirmary and sneak in. Hopefully, Ana would be in a state to walk to the barn and escape this place.

A crack of lightning streaked across the darkened heavens. The flash illuminated the cross perched at the top of the church. The thunder roared a few seconds later like a demon alerted to his presence. Donny had stumbled into a hellish purgatory where the greatest sinners were pitted against each other in a satanic cesspool.

Donny slushed in puddles as he crouched near a fence. He peered around the corner to see the infirmary. No light came from the building. A couple of minutes passed by and still no sign of any patrol or guard posted.

There could be someone inside. Or they could've moved Ana back to the mansion. Or Mihai didn't care what happened to his daughter.

Donny patted the front of the jeans. The revolver with its power tucked safely away against his skin. In the scenario where he had to use it, he would have to get to the barn as fast as possible.

The back of the house was clear, and Donny tested the backdoor. Locked of course. He tried a window. Locked as well. He continued to circle the house until he saw a windowpane ajar. The rain fell off it like a waterfall. The numbness of his fingers burnt as he lifted the window upwards and climbed into the house.

The air had a savoury musk to it. Donny flipped on the flashlight of his watch to find himself in the Lafave's laundry room. A stack of towels beckoned him over and he dried the dampness from his hair and body as best he could.

Donny switched off the flashlight setting and peeked out of the door. The living room was as silent as a morgue. The storm had subsided with the once-torrential rain now only a mere drizzle. After Donny gained his bearings, he crept through the house. His heart fluttered each time his boots squeaked across the wooden floorboards. Every footstep was calculated as to not disturb any object; his breath was held as if the slightest of noises could summon an alarm. He only exhaled once he reached the infirmary.

An orange outline glowed gently at the end of the passage. Donny removed the revolver and edged towards it. He stood for a long time listening for any noise on the other side of the door, but none came.

Donny squeezed the handle and the pushed the door open. He half-raised the revolver with the intent to fire. He took one step into the room and gasped. The bed was empty. The room was empty. The lone candle burned to a population of zero occupants.

'Now what do I do?' Donny said to himself.

Donny couldn't react as he felt something huge creep up behind him. A violent weight crashed down and smothered him.

• • • • •

Two men carried Donny outside and tossed him to the floor as if he were a ragdoll. His body became submerged in a fresh puddle of mud. The men wore the military fatigues; one stocky, one lean and tall. They stood over him, speaking in whispers. The tall one searched Donny's bag while the other jogged off into the distance. The guard chucked the revolver into the backpack. He trained his assault rifle in Donny's direction. His face was now visible as it cleared from the nocturnal darkness. Liam's expression was cool and disconcerting.

Donny tried to scramble to his feet, but his ribcage exploded in agony as Liam's boot flew up to meet him. He tried again, quicker this time, and the boot caught him in the hip.

Donny rested on his back to catch his breath and he stared up at the sky. The storm had died out and the clouds had parted. The full moon, peered from behind one of the formations, like a malicious god, watching his punishments being carried out.

'What do they want with me?' Donny asked, as his side still burned with pain. Liam ignored the question and spat on the ground.

The church bell rang out across the valley. It would be hours until sunrise, yet the bell tolled on relentlessly. Something significant was about to take place though Donny remained ignorant to the forces in motion.

A group of men approached. All of them wore the camouflaged uniform except from the man at the front. He wore only black. His grey hair was luminated by the lunar rays. Mihai.

'The prodigal son has returned,' Mihai's voice boomed over the church bell. 'We thought we had lost you, Donny.'

Thunder roared in the distance, far over the mountain.

The residents of the town had spilled out into the streets. Some of them still wore pyjamas. Others carried umbrellas. They all had the same confused looks on their faces.

The full force of the army marched around and barked instructions at any lost drifters. Some of the men pounded on the doors of nearby houses, ordering people to get dressed. The instructions were to go to the church.

'What is going on?' Donny demanded. 'Where is Ana?'

'Don't worry my child,' Mihai said. 'All will be explained soon enough. I have a plan you see. As a leader you must always strategize. Like in chess, you need to have the next three moves ready to go. And backup manoeuvres for every scenario. This year's famine and unrest, forced my hand sooner than I would've liked, but now that I have you, we are ready.'

'Tell me where she is,' Donny growled forcing himself to his knees. 'If you have caused her any more harm, I will kill you.'

'Ah, my darling daughter,' Mihai laughed loudly to himself at a joke only he seemed to understand. 'To think, the missing puzzle piece had been under my roof this entire time.'

Mihai crouched in the mud, his voice a hoarse whisper. 'Do you remember that night? When God sent you to me? I knew it was a sign. I've been watching you. You've been a very busy boy this year. The leader made me responsible for getting the machine to work. I tried everything, yet it wouldn't send people to our targeted destination and we wasted batteries and lives. Then you came along, not only with batteries to spare, but you fixed it for me. Thank you.'

Mihai patted his shoulder as he rose above him. Donny's blood ran as cold as the Danube in winter. His thoughts spanned in hundreds of different directions. Mihai had used him to rebuild the machine.

'You mustn't think of me as an unjust man,' Mihai said. 'This is not the case at all. I have a present for you.'

Mihai snapped his thick fingers and the soldiers dragged out someone from the back. A dark bag covered their head and their arms were bound behind them. They were thrown to their knees only a few feet in front of Donny. A soldier removed the bag to reveal a familiar face. Stefan.

'You see, I once had trusted this man. I would even go as far as to say I trusted him with my life. Sure, he didn't care for regulations or tidiness, but when it came to honesty and getting the job done, I would always call on Stefan.'

Stefan whimpered into a gag.

Mihai drew a pistol from his holster and cracked it against Stefan's skull.

'Stop!' Donny shouted. 'Let him go. It's me you want. I'll help you get to anywhere in the world. I promise you.'

'Oh, I know you will,' Mihai said. 'The fact still remains. He betrayed you, Donny. Under a light dose of torture, he revealed your plans. He also betrayed me when he hid you. As the leader before me always said, *once a snake, always a snake*. Like the snake of Eden.'

Mihai pointed his pistol at the back of Stefan's head and fired.

ANA

TWENTY-TWO

Jesus hung on the cross.

The first rays of dawn surged through the stained-glass windows of the church. The rainbow of colours danced on a painting where Jesus hung motionless, his hands nailed to each side of the wooden plank. His head drooped down on protruding ribs. A Roman soldier to his right, his fingers clenched around a spear. A man consoling a woman to his left. A golden halo shone around the woman's head as bright as the sun, Mary, the mother of God. She wept as her son died on the cross.

The crown of thorns visible as a sign of mockery and strength.

Ana studied the painting intently from her place at the edge of a pew while the strong smell of incense smothered her senses. The picture had the Roman numeral for twelve inscribed underneath. The Stations of the Cross followed the events that depicted the day of Jesus' crucifixion. Station twelve was the part where Jesus of Nazareth died on the cross.

Instinctively, Ana knelt to pray. She could no longer put her hands together as was the custom, so she prayed in her heart.

She prayed she would see another winter.

When she arrived at the church, only her and a guard who dropped her down at the edge of the bench were present. She wore a pair of faded jeans and a baggy purple t-shirt, which probably belonged to Victoria. The candles were lit and the tablecloths for a service had been laid out. Once the bell rang out overhead, villagers filtered into the church hall. A few stragglers transformed into huge waves. The whole town had been summoned at this ungodly hour. Ana focused on her prayer.

The complaints of the crowd were shushed when figures stomped down the aisle. From the back, they dragged a young boy by his feet. His hands were bound in front and a gag placed in his mouth.

The soldiers lined up before the altar and pulled the boy up to his knees. His wet hair covered his sunken eyes that stared aimlessly into the air. She almost didn't recognise Donny; it looked like he hadn't slept in the two weeks she had been in the medical centre. Why was he still here?

Ana took a double take at one of the soldiers behind him. Her old boyfriend Liam stood in a brand-new uniform and carried a rifle with a vindictive swagger. They all carried rifles. What nightmare had she awoken into? Her father emerged from the backrooms wearing the robes he wore for the religious ceremonies. He was followed by Hazel in a pure white gown. A huge bandage covered her nose with cotton wool spilling out over the top. Her eyes were puffy and swollen a blackish purple. Ana had made her face look as ugly as her inner character.

A mixture of responses greeted him when he took to the pulpit. Some asked what they were doing there so early, some asked about food. Most though, chanted his name.

Mihai raised his hands with his palms out, and like a well-trained herd of sheep the congregation fell silent until all Ana could hear were the chorus of ravens.

'My children,' Mihai's voice carried to the last pew of the hall. 'I awake you to share tremendous news. The day of reckoning is upon us. The Lord our God appeared to me in a vision. As a giant ball of white light, he said to me. "I am the Alpha and the Omega, the beginning and the end. Who is and who is to come, the Almighty. To the thirsty I will give water from the spring of life without payment."' The flock let out gasps and cries of joy. 'The time we've all been preparing for my children; He is ready to open the gates to us. We have served our time in this purgatory, where the sinners have been tortured and killed by the very machines they worshiped. The Lord saw how we have lived in his name and were no longer tempted by the false idols. Death to tech.'

'Death to tech! Death to tech! Death to tech!' the crowd chanted.

'You might recognise the boy in front me. His name is Donny and we took him in as one of our own. We fed him, educated him, and gave him a home and in the end, he betrayed us. He smuggled in forbidden technologies and tried to re-create one of those monsters right here under our noses.' Mihai removed a silver sphere from his pocket that fitted snuggly in the palm of his hand. Ana's blood ran cold as she realised what the object was. She had kept it in a shoebox in her cupboard. 'In my hand, I have the battery of an android, the power source of these machines. As you can tell, they have no souls.'

The symbol drew boos from the church mass, as he had intended. They chanted even more rancorously.

Mihai placed the heart on the centre of the altar as if it were the centrepiece of a great feast and walked closer to the front of the marble steps. 'But as it says in Revelation, I will read it now for you, "as for the cowardly, the faithless, the detestable; as for murderers, the sexually immoral, sorcerers, idolaters, and all liars, their portion will be in the lake that burns with fire and sulphur." I will personally see that Donny is tied out in the wilderness to be greeted by the fires of hell while you ascend to heaven. My beautiful daughter has rid herself of her abomination of an arm, so she is free to join us in the promised land.'

Ana could always tell when her father lied. His voice would stray from his natural deep octaves. Mihai used Donny as a scapegoat to blind them from the truth. He wanted to get rid of them all. He wanted to get rid of her.

'Blessed is the one who reads aloud the words of this prophecy, and blessed are those who hear,' Mihai bellowed.

Dr William Lafave wheeled in a trolley containing several trays of glasses with clear solution. Victoria and a few volunteers followed closely behind. They carried additional glasses. Hundreds of them.

'What the good doctor is handing out is our salvation, please take one each. As Jesus offered his blood to his disciples, I now offer you mine. And like the Messiah, this will be our suffering. Your ticket to eternal happiness in paradise. May peace be with you all.'

Dr Lafave and the assistants continued to pass the trays down the rows, as everyone picked up a glass. Some clutched them with eagerness, some with solemn acceptance. A line of soldiers at the front of the church knelt before Mihai as he handed them each a tumbler from a tray. Liam was in the line-up and the first to receive the tumbler. They lifted the glasses in a sort of a toast and drunk the liquid in unison as to set the example. Liam and the soldiers fell forward clutching at their throats.

A glass smashed and Ana spun around to see Foghorn collapse to the ground. Cries of agony echoed around her as more and more people fell. An elderly man, down the bench from her, crumpled backwards and twitched erratically. A couple in front of her clinked their glasses before drinking the substances, then screamed out in pain. Everyone was dying. A horrific orgy of death.

The once vibrant townsfolk whittled down to fewer and fewer numbers, until there were less than a dozen left.

Ana glanced to her side to see Victoria standing next to her holding a tray with two remaining glasses of a cloudy liquid.

'It's your turn, little Anadroid,' said Victoria in a sweet voice.

Ana noticed the murmurs of the dying had come to an end. They lay still on the floor, no longer struggling. She couldn't see her friends, her neighbours, or her mother.

Apart from Victoria who stood before her, the only others remaining were a couple of soldiers, one either side of the pew, Mihai, Hazel and Donny.

'Drink up,' Hazel squealed as she danced down the centre aisle, skipping over bodies in her path. 'You'll be in a better place soon.'

Victoria sat on the bench, with a glass in her hand. Her free fingers ran through Ana's hair. Ana was too weak to recoil from her despicable touch. 'It's okay,' said Victoria. 'You don't need to be brave anymore.'

Ana gasped as the soldier furthest from her sprawled sideways as Donny slammed into him.

'Ana, run!' Donny panted as he held himself up by the edge of the bench, his gag now around his neck. A powerful force picked Donny off his feet as Mihai's backhand connected with his jaw. Mihai pulled Donny up by the scruff of the neck and held him with his vice grip.

Donny and Ana's eyes met. The cool lost oceans of his irises swirled in despair. She absorbed it in. Every detail of his face, the dimensions of his body, the fresh cut on his cheek, his stupid matted hair.

'I'm sorry I couldn't save you,' Donny said. 'I did try my best.'

'Donny,' Ana started. 'In our dreams, let's meet at the top of the mountain. We can talk about our plans and the adventures we'll have together. Promise me and keep your word this time.'

'I promise,' he said

'See you later, crocodile.'

'In a while, alligator.'

Hazel poked Mihai in the side like a perpetual child until he erupted.

'Enough!' Mihai commanded and shook Donny violently. 'Goodbye daughter, this is where I leave you. It's a shame it turned out like this, but you weren't what I needed. Now all of you, drink up and let's be done with this.'

Victoria handed Ana a glass. Mihai and the two soldiers watched her expectantly. Ana inhaled one last courageous breath, parted her lips, and drank. The liquid made her tongue squirm in horror and it burnt her throat on the way down.

Victoria produced the final glass and drank as well without hesitation.

The two soldiers satisfied, slipped out hidden tiny capsules and consumed the contents. Mihai dragged Donny away.

Ana coughed as she lay on the bench, waiting for the end to engulf her.

DONNY

TWENTY-THREE

They were dead.

Ana. Victoria. Stefan. His Dad. Everyone he had ever cared about no longer existed in this reality.

The first light of dawn crept along the roads, finding each corner of the village. As the brightness evaporated the darkness, the warmth ate away at the remnants of the storm. The vapour hung low in the air as an ominous mist.

For once, a stillness had captured the tiny Romanian town that lay at the bottom of the mountain.

Birds chirped happily in nearby trees as clogged drains from the houses dripped into puddles. The sun felt good on Donny's skin, as though he had stepped out into a world and left the death and terror back in the church. Yet he could still hear the screams.

Mihai half-pulled, half-dragged Donny through the streets. He fell, caking himself in the fresh mud. Mihai sighed and picked him up like he weighed no more than a bag of potatoes.

The barn came into view and it became clear what Mihai's intentions were. The paint of the barn burned a fierce red, as if it had been reborn from the ashes of the phoenix.

Mihai left him standing at the entrance. He had no more energy left to flee. Even if he did, they would catch him in a few easy strides.

Mihai handed his assault rifle to Hazel who pointed it at Donny with no hesitation in her stance. A key materialised from Mihai's pocket as he fumbled with the lock on the doors. Once the metallic device clicked, the chains rattled free. They were cast aside as their purpose had finally expired.

'Why are you doing this?' Donny asked as the barn doors swung open and Mihai stepped into the gloom. Hazel motioned the rifle for Donny to follow.

The low hum of the Lightspeed Capsule roared into being. Mihai stood at the multi-coloured control panel as he flipped some switches. 'You see Donny, I ran out of options. Every year, there was less and less food to feed an entire village. Even with the recent rains, people would succumb to malnourishment. The summers are always harsher. In a couple of decades, there will be nothing left on this planet for us humans. It'll become a desert. A planet only for the machines. No chance that I or the council could've saved them. Instead, I gave them hope.'

'You sold them a lie!' Donny cried out.

'The spirit is more powerful than the body. I told them exactly what they needed to hear. The grim reaper was already knocking on all our doors. I provided a fate better than what this harsh reality had to offer. I let them pass to the next world happy and in peace.'

Donny shook his head slowly as Mihai continued to work away on the pod. 'If you are so cynical about humanity's future, why are you still here? Where in the world can you escape your apocalyptic vision?'

'Donny, tell me,' Mihai said as he approached him. 'During your tests, did you discover an active pod in Rome?'

Donny's face scrunched up and he looked away.

A wolfish grin came across Mihai's face. 'No need to hide it my child. I've monitored your progress. When I saw you had Rome in the records, I put plans into place. As you asked, where can I escape to? I have an old friend. He was a high-ranking officer in the Italian army. He told me of their bunker they would retreat to if we lost the war, a new home deep underground where they could live in peace, with no threat from the androids or the heat. You see, I've been trying for years to get the machine to work and join him. Now there is nothing stopping me or my beautiful fiancée from getting there. We can have a new beginning and continue to spread the good word. Thank you, Donny.'

A mischievous grin drew across Hazel's face, the assault rifle still eager in her hands.

Donny laughed frantically. 'You are even more deluded than I thought if you think I will take any part of this. After what you did to Stefan. How you poisoned your own daughter. You're a monster. I'll never help you.'

'Donny, I am but a servant of God,' Mihai said offering his palms up to the air. 'Hazel and I need to go forth and continue our mission. Plus, I didn't say your efforts would go unrewarded.'

'What are you talking about?'

'Let me show you something first.' Mihai strolled over to a table near the Lightspeed Capsule. A white sheet covered a long object that he didn't remember seeing in the barn before. Mihai pulled away the sheet to reveal a lifeless piece of metal. It took a few moments to realise what the object was. It was Ana's android arm.

'The final component you need, boy,' Mihai yelled out in the same voice he used for his church sermons. 'I already know how to operate the pod. All I need to do is connect the machine to the satellites. Apparently, it receives atoms fine, as you are living proof of that, yet it never had the forte to send atoms. Stefan told me that what you need is right in this piece of android tech. So here is the arrangement I'm offering. Fix the upload connection. After that, you are free to go. The machine will be yours to do with as you wish.'

'You will let me go?' Donny asked in disbelief.

'Yes, I will. I remember what you told me about your friend. Go meet him again, forget about us. It's what you've always wanted. This is your chance to go find him.'

Mihai opened the door to the Lightspeed Capsule and stroked the inside fabric. 'Do we have a deal?'

The deal represented a chance to see Edwin again. The whole year had led to this moment. With Mihai and Hazel gone, he would be the last one left. The village had plenty of food to sustain one person and he probably only needed a few more hours to locate the Seoul launch sequence.

The old machines lay still at the back of the barn. Their technological guts spewed out across the floor. Parts and gears resembled human faces. Donny, in a strange way, enjoyed the endless months repairing the machine from scratch with no help from Edwin. He proved to himself he could do it.

Mihai had used him, but he had also removed the obstacles. In a few minutes, after he sent Mihai and Hazel away, there would be nothing stopping him from reaching Seoul. The village had ample food supplies and a vast amount of time.

Ana's android arm lay lifeless on the table. Their friendship has been one he had treasured above all else in the village. From their rough start, his opinion of her blossomed, like a rose budding from the thorn bushes. They were trapped together, he fixed her arm, they studied together, and he was her prom date. There was no one he admired more. Only now that she was gone, did he realise how much she meant to him.

Ana's blood remained stained at the end of the arm.

Donny closed his eyes.

'No,' Donny said. 'I will not help you. The androids might be cruel, but you are the true monster.'

Mihai's face became stormy with rage. 'We'll see how cooperative you will be under torture. It was what I was known for back in the army. My special talent. Mihai the Merciless they called me. Stefan broke in ten minutes. Are you strong enough to last longer than that?'

Donny had the wind knocked out of him as Mihai slammed him against one of the wooden pillars and his hands were bound behind the post. After he recovered his breath, he tested the strength of the rope, but it pulled tightly against his raw skin.

'Hazel,' Mihai said. 'It'd be better if you waited outside. You don't want to see what I'm about to --' Mihai coughed and turned white as a ghost. His hand moved near the holster of his revolver.

'It's over, Papa,' a girl said. 'You've failed.'

Ana wilted inside the entrance of the barn. Her bandaged limb poked out of a purple top that matched the violet hues of the sky behind her. In her hand was an army issue pistol. Victoria stood next to her, tall and defiant. She pointed an assault rifle towards the depths of the barn. One of the lenses of her glasses had cracked. Hazel's bottom lip quivered under her broken nose as her eyes begged Mihai for guidance, but he focused entirely on his daughter who was back from the grave.

'Ana,' Mihai choked on the word. 'You're alive?'

'Put your hands where I can see them!' Victoria yelled violently.

Mihai raised his hands slightly forward, but still close to his holster. 'We're on the same side here. Listen, we can figure this out.'

'Don't you dare move a muscle,' Victoria said. 'You and my Dad might've fooled this town, but you haven't fooled me. Everything you told us was a beautiful dream. Though seeing how you both treated Ana first-hand, how you gave only the best rations to quiet opposers, how the troops killed anyone who spoke out anyway; I couldn't buy into your falsehoods. You are evil.'

Ana took a couple of steps into the barn. 'Donny, are you okay?'

'I'm fine,' Donny coughed. 'Please be careful.'

She inched closer. Her movements were deliberate and slow.

'Ana, listen to me,' Mihai said. 'I'm your father. I command you to stop what you're doing.'

Ana ignored him and moved closer to Hazel.

'Stay back!' Hazel screamed. The rifle shook in her trembling hands. 'I'll shoot. I goddamn mean it I will.'

'You're not a killer, Haze,' Ana said calmly. 'He tricked you. He tricked us all. It's okay. You're my oldest friend. There's nothing in this world I wouldn't do for you. I'm here now. Please put down the gun.'

Tears built up in Hazel's eyes as she again glanced back at Mihai. 'You're a heretic, Ana,' she cried. 'That's what Mihai told me. You and Donny. You worshiped technology. You turned your back on God. Mihai, he's special. He made sure everyone got into heaven. We need to continue our paths to spread the word.'

Ana moved closer to her. 'He murdered them. Our friends. Our mothers. That's not doing the work of God. The war changed Papa. He's not the man he once was. He only serves himself.'

'Stop you bitch!' Hazel shrieked. 'You're lying. He loves me.'

Ana stopped in her tracks as Hazel raised the gun. Her energy reserves were near collapse as she wobbled on the spot.

The tension in the room crushed Donny's lungs. Everyone was armed and ready to open fire on each other. The relentless bonds on his wrists held him in place. He couldn't help them.

Hope is lost with you, as Stefan always told him. What Stefan had told him.

'Hazel, can I ask you something?' Donny said.

Everyone gaped at Donny, as if they had forgotten he had ever existed.

'What do you want?' Hazel snapped at him.

'What happened to your sister?'

'Why are you asking me a stupid question?'

'What happened to her?'

A flash of annoyance brought a sobriety to Hazel whose weight shifted to face Donny, though the rifle remained on Ana. 'I told you, they sent her to the orphanage in the safe zone. In Bucharest.'

'Did they?'

'Yes.'

'Did they?'

'Yes, for the millionth time. She was actually taken there by Mihai...' she glanced at her lover.

'Of course,' Mihai barked. 'I took her there myself.'

'Ask him what really happened,' Donny said. A single bead of sweat fell from his brow. Hazel studied him like an animal who had learned how to speak.

'What is *he* talking about?'

'Ignore him,' Mihai said. 'He's trying to get into your head.'

'Your sister didn't make it to the orphanage,' Donny continued. 'Mihai drowned her in the Danube.'

'Liar!' Hazel screamed.

'It's true,' Donny said calmly.

'Tell me he is lying,' Hazel said, her rifle now pointing towards Mihai. 'Say you didn't do it.'

246

Mihai's head dropped. 'Please do not worry my young Hazel, she is also in heaven now. Just like your mother and your friends. There is too much suffering on this planet. I saved them. I secured their place in the kingdom.' Mihai's hand unfastened the button of his holster.

'Oh my God,' Hazel wailed. The once inanimate object in her hands now appeared radiating a rage of pure hatred. 'Tell me you didn't drown her. She was only five. Tell me this is a sick joke. Please.'

Mihai gritted his teeth and drew his weapon. 'Hazel, let's not do anything --'

A rapid fire of explosions rained chaos through the barn. Metal and wood splinted apart behind Donny in such a violent force that he felt debris whizz past his face. The aftermath rang in his ears like a swarm of wasps.

A girl's voice called out to him. The smoke of gun powder stung his nostrils and he struggled to breathe.

His vision trembled in and out of focus. He saw Mihai lying on the floor. The once pure snow robe he wore, now had an ocean of red expanding from the centre. Ana knelt next to him. Her lips moved, but he couldn't make out what she was saying to him.

'Donny,' shouted Victoria. 'Can you hear me?'

'Yeah, Vic,' Donny smiled. 'Why wouldn't I be able to hear you?'

Donny glanced down and he noticed something strange. A liquid oozed from a hole in his lower abdomen. Only then did the pain run through him like a wildfire from the depths of an inferno. He could no longer feel his legs and he slumped downwards, his bound hands on the post prevented him from falling over. The pain vanished as soon as it arrived and became replaced with a deep ache.

'Don't you dare close your eyes on me. Hazel help me get him to the infirmary. I can't lift him by myself. No, untie his hands. Quickly, we don't have much time.'

Donny remembered one Christmas he spent with his parents in Scotland. The temperatures were tantalizingly close to zero degrees Celsius. He hadn't seen snow before, and his Dad promised he would help him build a snowman. Snowmen were mythical creatures that belonged in movies and fairy tales. Christmas morning Donny discovered the garden had become the winter wonderland he always dreamed of. He ran out barefooted. It was cold. So cold.

ANA

TWENTY-FOUR

Dried out flowers lay on two fresh mounds of dirt. The petals hugged the dead buds inside. Crinkled leaves ran across ghoulishly white stems. A gust of hot wind carried one of the leaves off across the meadow.

Ana knelt in front at the foot of one of the graves and said a prayer, her mother's favourite. She tried to remember only the good memories they shared together and block out the terror from the last few weeks. A rifle lay nearby in the grass.

A glimmer of light blinded her. The setting of the sun reflected off the blade of a shovel planted into the earth further up the field. It stood between more graves. She had a pang of guilt that she couldn't help the others bury their loved ones.

It would be dark soon. She needed to get indoors.

Ana slung the rifle over her head and almost toppled over as she rose. Backpack straps ran over her shoulders and the extra weight of the gun made her unsteady. She brushed the dirt off her knees with her only hand. Learning her sense of balance had proved an audacious task. Even though her android arm had been a source of ridicule and self-loathing, she deeply yearned to have it back.

She turned and walked away from the gravesite. Another day had passed where she couldn't say a prayer for her father. 'Sorry Papa,' she said. 'I still can't forgive you.'

Ana found Hazel sitting on the wall outside of the Lafave residence. Her head was lowered to examine a brooch she played with in her hands.

'Hey Haze,' Ana said. 'How are you feeling today?'

Hazel nodded her head without taking her attention away from the trinket.

'I'm glad you're getting some fresh air. I'll start cooking, so come in soon, okay? I'm making your favourite.'

Hazel offered a non-committal murmur. It was the best Ana could get from her. Hazel hadn't spoken since the day they were all in the barn. Ana smiled at her. A smile that masked an ocean of hurt and betrayal. She wanted to believe her friend was still in there somewhere. It would take thousands of small acts of kindness to erode the months of grooming she had endured.

Ana hoped she could bring her back. If Ana lost hope, she would have nothing left.

The living room of Victoria's house had gone through a significant transformation since the house party, which now felt like a lifetime ago. Sofas were barricaded against the back-bay doors, planks of wood were nailed in place over windows and a box of ammunition clips sat in front of the fireplace. Ana rested her rifle on the dining room table next to a detailed map of the town that she had found in her father's office.

'Anything to report from the patrol walk?' Victoria asked as she descended the staircase. Her once vibrant red hair was frizzed and tied in a ponytail. Deep dark bags under her eyes were visible even behind her large glasses.

'It was quiet,' Ana said. 'Nothing significant to report. I also placed some flowers on the graves.'

Victoria crossed her arms and nodded.

'How is he doing?' Ana asked expectantly. She had been thinking about him since she left the house.

Victoria sighed. 'To be honest, not great. His condition is getting worse every day. If only I could remove the damn bullet, but I know I'd only make matters worse. I don't have the training to do it. I'm such an idiot for not watching more of Daddy's surgeries. The good news is that there is no pus from the wound, and he hasn't had a fever. So woopey freaking doo, at least I'm not totally useless.'

'Don't be so hard on yourself, you're doing the best you can.'

'And that dipstick Hazel hasn't lifted a finger. We're doing all the work around here, and she mopes around like some hurt puppy.'

'Give her a break,' Ana said. 'She's been through a lot.'

'And we fucking haven't?' Victoria shouted. 'It's her fault we're in this situation.'

Ana placed her hand on Victoria's shoulder. 'It's going to be okay. Remember, Donny needs you to be strong. You must be exhausted looking after him. I know he'll be so grateful. I know I am. Listen, I'll pop in to see him and then I'll cook us some dinner. Why don't you have a nap and I'll wake you when it's ready?'

'Sure, whatever,' said Victoria as she disappeared down the hall to the medic centre.

Donny lay still in the middle of a queen-sized bed. The familiar smell of disinfectant hung in the air. With an effort not to make too much noise, she slid the backpack down her arm and placed it near the top of the bed, next to the table.

'Hey sleeping beauty,' Ana whispered as she pulled up a chair to his side. The duvet rose and fell in steady beats with his breathing. His face was calm and unflinching.

Her hand moved across the bed and held onto to his. The skin had a raw coldness to it, but she kept her hand there to share her warmth. 'Look at us. They messed us up pretty good, didn't they?'

Her android arm tried to brush the hair off his forehead, but the limb was only a phantom of her imagination.

'I brought you a present,' Ana said quickly to distract herself from the foolishness. 'Your backpack. Do you know how hard it is to carry a rifle and a bag at the same time? It had some neat ornaments in it. I thought it would make this room a bit more homely for you.'

Ana pulled the bag towards her and opened it. She placed little metal figures on to the table nearby. He must've designed them over the year working in the barn. Victoria would no doubt have a fit if they took up space that could be used for medical equipment, but she wanted to surround Donny with some familiarity. Something heavier lay above his spare clothes. Ana pulled out a revolver, the gun Donny had when they were fleeing the city together. She placed it on the windowsill behind her.

The last items in his bag were a water bottle, old food cans and a book. She took out the novel and studied it in the dying light from beyond the window blinds. Gold embossed words *Catcher in the Rye by J. D. Salinger* ran across a city darkened by a navy shadow. She flipped through the pages. Near the front of the book was an inscription from Donny's father. She read it through a few times before she closed it.

Donny never spoke of his family, but she could tell from the message he had a special bond with his Dad. She had always wished she had one with her own father. She leaned the book against the lamp, so it faced him.

Hopefully, the spirit of Donny's father would watch over him while he slept.

'I'll read it to you when you are feeling better,' Ana said in a soft tone. 'I promise.'

• • • • •

After dinner, Victoria and Hazel retired to their bedrooms to get some sleep.

Ana remained downstairs for the first watch. Though the mood at the candlelit dinner had been a frosty affair, their company had been reassuring. Now she remained in the screaming silence of the new world that had been forced upon her. Usually at this time, the workers would be enjoying vodka or moonshine at the town bar. She would be hanging out with either Hazel or Liam. Or she would be cuddled up in her favourite spot in the living room, while servants cleared the family's dinner plates. In this reality, only her and Victoria were holding the pieces together.

On the first night, they decided to move into Victoria's house, a logical choice because it had the medical supplies. Donny rested in William Lafave's room since it had the comfiest bed. Victoria, of course, took her own room, while Hazel and herself took the twin beds in the guest bedroom.

She dreaded the evening vigil. It crept by at a zombie's pace. Victoria and Ana would each take a shift as neither trusted Hazel with such a responsibility. Not until now did she understand the crucial role the soldiers played in the community. She had taken the safety they provided for granted. Now she waited alone in darkness for a threat that never came. Any noise or creak made her jump. Who was there now to stop a pack of wolves or a group of bandits entering the town? Or even worse, armed androids. If felt like the skin had been removed from Ana's body leaving her vulnerable to irrevocable damage.

Off in the distance a wolf howled.

• • • • •

Victoria paced endlessly in the front garden as Ana leaned against the wall in the shelter of the shade. Ravens called down from their place in the cloudless sky.

'Where the hell is she?' huffed Victoria.

'It's been three days,' Ana said. 'She's not coming back.'

'Where did she go then?'

'I try not to think about it. Hazel couldn't have used the teleporting device; it's still locked from the outside so we can rule that out. The last time I saw her, she headed to the Danube with a bucket. I followed the normal route down to the river, but there was no sign of her. She didn't have any supplies or weapons with her. Either someone took her or she's wandering through the wilderness unarmed.'

'Or she was eaten,' said Victoria.

'Don't say that.'

Victoria paced, kicking up dirt as she did. 'Compared to the other scenarios, it's a kinder fate.'

Ana sighed. 'I'm going to go for help.'

Victoria stopped immediately in her tracks. 'Why?'

'We've discussed this before. Donny is not getting any better so it's the best chance we have. What do you suggest? Just wait here until he dies? And then what? The two of us living here forever as friends? You don't even like me, Victoria.'

Victoria snorted as she removed her glasses to clean them with her loose flowing top. 'What you are talking about is suicide. How do you even know if it'll work? You'll get yourself killed. I didn't save your life for you to throw it away.'

'Why did you save me?'

'Because I knew you and Donny would be too stupid to get out of that mess by yourselves. Luckily, I had two cups of Agent 22 prepared. The army had it stored here to incapacitate prisoners for short minute bursts. No way I was going to sacrifice myself for a maniac's conspiracy. No offense.'

'Yes, but why did you save me in particular?'

Victoria stood still and crossed her arms. An enraged scowl burnt on her face. 'They treated you terribly. I treated you terribly. And because. I know how much you mean to him. You're probably the only person he cared about besides himself. He would've been, I don't know, angry if I saved myself and didn't try to help you as well.'

'Thank you, Vic. He cares about you too.'

'He never invited *me* to Seoul.'

'Donny probably thought you were happy here. I was so miserable. I could see it annoyed him after he told me his plans, and besides, I invited myself.'

'Well your Dad made sure to end everyone's happiness, didn't he?'

Ana glared at her. 'And yours broke his Hippocratic Oath. Don't play the blame game, we aren't our parents. I'm still going.'

'Go screw yourself. You're going to waste the second chance I gave you. You'll end up in a ditch somewhere like Hazel.' Victoria stormed past her back to the house.

Ana took in a deep breath of air to steel herself for the journey head. She walked across the town until she reached the church that stood on the hill. She climbed to the large wooden doors and pulled on one of the handles. She slammed the door back immediately and gagged. Decay hung in the air.

With her one hand she pulled off her top and wrapped it around her head, covering her nose and mouth. In a second attempt, she dared forth into the church.

The stench overpowered her. Even the fabric of her clothing offered little protection. Bodies of the community lay sprawled over each other in heaps where they had taken the fatal drink given to them by her father. Ravens croaked as they hopped from one body to the next, tearing away exposed flesh. The enclosed capsule felt like an oven capturing in the heat of the sun and slowly cooking the decomposing bodies.

The three girls decided they would only bury their parents as digging graves for hundreds of people was not a task anyone wanted.

Ana made her way down the centre aisle, stepping over the bodies that lay in her path. She kept her eyes averted upwards to avoid spotting the rotting faces of any of her old friends. The statues of saints judged her as she progressed forward. Instead, she directed her focus to Jesus on the cross. Only now did she understand the weight he carried on his shoulders.

The altar remained undisturbed since that fateful morning where everyone ended their lives on Mihai's command.

The metallic battery of the android lay motionless, like a diamond in the most exquisite display of a museum.

Ana picked it up and saw her reflection in the chrome surface of the android heart and the death that lay behind her.

• • • • •

The earliest beams of morning caressed Ana's skin and she awoke from her dreamless sleep. Before she went to bed, she had left the curtains open so she would naturally awake by Mother Nature's alarm clock.

Hazel's bed was still made and empty.

She hopped onto the wooden floorboards and threw on loose fitting khaki trousers and a light tank top. Her dark hair was pulled back into a long hanging ponytail and she put on a baseball cap to protect her face. The walking boots took a much longer time to tie up with only one hand.

An assault rifle and Donny's backpack rested near the door. It contained necessary supplies for the day trek, including food, a bottle of water and extra ammunition clips. He wouldn't mind her borrowing it if it meant saving his life.

Ana couldn't help stealing one last glance through the crack of Donny's room before she left. Donny remained where she had left him yesterday, sleeping soundly.

'I'll be back soon,' she whispered.

Ana crept down the stairs to the front door, but a voice called to her before she could turn the handle. 'You're still going through with this?'

Ana spun to find Victoria sitting on an armchair in the darkness of dawn.

'Yes,' Ana said. 'I have to.'

'You do realise if something happens, I can't come after you. I need to stay here.'

'I know. Nothing you say can change my mind.'

Victoria snorted. 'I figured as much. C'mon, I'll walk with you to the mountain.'

Victoria locked the door behind them, and they followed the main road to the edge of town not sharing a word between them. They walked off into the fields as the temperature steadily rose to its familiar heights.

They stopped at the mountain path; the entrance was an impromptu flattening of shrubs, trodden on by thousands of footsteps over the years. Victoria covered her eyes and studied the cliff face above, as if seeing them for the first time.

'It should be me who is going,' said Victoria. 'You're in no state to make such a trip.'

'I'm fine,' Ana said. 'My arm is healing nicely and if all goes well, I'll be back before sundown.'

'Don't push your luck out there. And if you get a chance, could you look for any antibiotics in the city?'

'Fortunately for you, I'm the one going then, if reading labels is required,' Ana said with a wry smile. 'Your Romanian is awful.'

'Whatever.'

Ana adjusted the weight of the bag and the rifle. 'Alright, I'll be back soon.' Ana made a few steps up the path before Victoria called to her.

'Wait. I wanted to say...um. I wanted to tell you I'm sorry. For everything.'

Ana nodded. 'I appreciate it.'

'Good luck, Anadroid.'

The climb without her robotic arm proved more challenging than she initially thought. No longer did she have the safety net of being able to cling onto the rocky wall at any given moment and it left her with a knot in her stomach. The weight of the rifle swayed in a warm gust of wind and she tilted for a moment at the edge. The loose pebbles tumbled off the path down the fifty-foot drop to ruin on the jagged rocks below.

Ana continued at a slower pace. After her time in the medical centre, her frame had become lighter and she had to watch how she moved up the trail. By the time she descended to the other side, almost half an hour had passed. She had to improve her pace through the forest if she was to get back before nightfall.

The towering green trees lay before her, the gatekeepers of a dangerous, lawless world. She had no one to rely on but herself.

Ana took in a deep breath and released it slowly. 'I'm strong enough to do this,' she told herself.

Ana entered the woods.

An hour passed without incident. She had not seen a single living being, not even any birds singing in the branches above her. The rustle of dry leaves presented the only ambience in a dead world. The muzzle tip of the rifle swayed in front of her as if it were a compass pointing her in the direction of the destination.

For most of her life, Ana felt invisible, like a shadow that hung out in the background of social gatherings and town events. To feel any emotion, she overcompensated in each area of her life. She had strived for the best academic achievements, dated the most handsome boy at school and was even the class president. Every gesture was a move to make herself liked by those around her. The happiness she had generated for herself always relied on the approval of others, a prisoner of their whims.

Now alone, she felt an awakening. Not to outshine Victoria or to impress her father; Ana only had to prove herself to herself.

After a while the weight of the rifle dug into her skin. She estimated only a thirty-minute trek remained until she reached the city and she deserved a break. She lay the rifle against the trunk of a tree and flung off the backpack. Her hand searched for the water bottle and she placed it between her thighs to pop up the lid with her thumb. The water was warm, but she gulped down a few mouthfuls quenching her wild thirst.

A snap of a twig made her heart stop for a moment. She lowered the bottle from her lips and strained her head to scan the area around her. Another noise, closer now. It made her fall to her knees and grasped the rifle by the grip. She lifted it in the direction of the sound.

Two men stood behind a cluster of trees. One was bulky like a bear, with tattoo sleeves running down his beefy forearms. The other man had a scar spreading across from his nose to his ear and with greasy long hair that hung over his skeleton physique.

'Don't come any closer,' Ana shouted, shocked by the fear rising in her voice.

As to defy her, the figures edged closer, darting behind the trees to cover themselves from any attack she would unleash on them. Ana took a step back, but they kept coming towards her. There was only forest for miles in each direction, she couldn't outrun them.

Ana fired the rifle.

Bullets pierced the surrounding trees with an unforgiving velocity. The gunfire roared, dulling her other senses. As she didn't have time to secure the rifle on to her, the barrel rose into the air with every shot. The barrage of bullets merely flew above the assailants' heads and they were on her.

In a swift motion, the bulky man knocked the rifle from Ana's grip and then smacked her across the jaw. A brightness of colours blurred her vision as she fell to the Earth. The bandaged limb struck the dirt at an awkward angle, releasing a new discovery of torment through her body.

'This witch tried to kill us,' remarked the bigger man behind his clenched teeth. 'Is there anyone else with you?' His hefty boot stomped on her stomach and pinned her to the floor. It seemed like he hadn't bathed in years as she could smell the lingering traces of body odour and animal fat. The stench was overpowering.

Ana squirmed underneath the weight, but she could not pull away. 'Yes, I'm with an entire army.'

'She's loaded,' whickered the skinny man with no shirt as he rummaged through the backpack. Long, yellow fingernails ran up a tin of canned corn he picked out. 'Food and ammo clips; jackpot boss.'

'Stop messing about,' growled the man on top of Ana. 'She is lying, but there could still be more of them out there. Go search the perimeter.'

'Yeah, yeah,' said the skinny man as he skulked off carrying Ana's rifle.

'You're a pretty one,' the brute said as he stared at her in the same way a lion lusts over an unexpecting gazelle before it pounces. Ana gritted her teeth as he applied more force down on her with his boot. 'That stump of yours is hideous, but I bet you'll still fetch a fine reward with the other groups. Beggars can't be choosers in the world we live in you know. I guarantee you'll be a far more valuable trading item than the lynx pelts we usually barter with.' He laughed at his own joke as he averted his attention to scanning the area.

Ana slowed her breathing as she arched her right foot towards her. Her hand reached up under the bottom of her khaki trousers, the fingers dancing along her leg until they reached the holster. She thumbed away the latch and clutched onto Donny's revolver.

Two men. Three bullets.

The man's face morphed from confusion to pure terror as he peered down to discover Ana pointing a gun at his chest. She fired the first bullet.

The pressure of his foot disappeared as he collapsed over like a broken tree. Ana rolled on to her belly and heard the footsteps of the skinny man move towards the lingering echo of the gun shot. When he appeared from behind a tree, he reacted slowly so Ana raised the revolver towards him. She fired, but the shot flew too high and missed him entirely.

The man giggled nervously as he struggled to get the rifle set in his shaking hands as Ana took aim. The next shot took away a piece of his skull above the scar, splattering a mist of bone and brain tissue in the air.

It felt like an hour had passed before Ana's breathing returned to a steady rhythm. She rolled on to her back to see the gentle sway of the treetops as they danced at the reaches of the peaceful sky. She tossed the revolver to the side and lifted herself off the floor to her knees. She staggered across the clearing to retrieve the rifle from its spot on the fallen grass. A trail of blood led her back to the bigger brute, who had only made it a few meters away from where he fell. He sat upright against a tree taking in laboured breaths. His massive hands grasped onto his lower abdomen.

'Please,' he shouted. 'I beg of you. Take everything we have. You'll never see me again.'

Ana watched him scowl in fear. This time she carefully put the strap of the rifle over her head and poised the gun with a determined sense of control.

'You're right. I won't see you again,' Ana said and pulled the trigger.

• • • • •

The buildings came into view, like a mystical domain, hidden from the rest of creation. Lush vegetation had grown up the concrete walls, so Ana mistook them for being as part of the forest at first. The previous two times she had been in the city, she had been attacked by androids. If she didn't break the habit, her and Donny were both doomed.

She ventured to the city's boundary and retraced her and Donny's steps when they had fled. She attempted to recreate the route many times and failed to find what she was looking for. After each failed attempt, she headed back to the main road and tried again. Someone must've taken it.

The sun had descended towards the west, and Ana knew she had to head back soon. She tried one more time in a different path through a thornier terrain. A few minutes later she saw the colourful insignia of a medical suit stand out from the undergrowth.

She hurried over and examined the body. The skin of the android had decayed in places where insects had burrowed through. A large part of the fabric had been ripped away, probably by a wild animal who mistook the robot for food. It would've looked like a zombie if it wasn't for the metallic components that gleamed under the flap of skin on its back.

Its laser rifle lay next to its side. She picked it up and hid it in a thicket of bushes over a hundred yards away.

The android battery has been wrapped safely in a woolly towel in the centre of the backpack. She placed it out on the grass and carefully unravelled the cloth. Ana put on the backpack and slung the rifle over her. The aluminium surface felt cool and alienlike against the roughness of her fingers. She balanced the metal ball on the gaping hole on the android's back and slammed it in with her palm.

Noises twirled through the skin. The machine slowly regained its artificial consciousness like a computer booting up its operating system. After a beat it jumped up and spun around.

The android faced Ana. A member of the most dominant species on the planet. The ones who had wiped out the humans.

'Please, don't attack,' Ana said as she lowered herself to the floor. She lay down the rifle and took a few steps back. 'I mean you no harm. Let me have my say, and you can do with me what you wish.'

The android stared at her for a long time. It had a large frame, curly brown hair, and a square face with a pronounced chin. It would be almost handsome if it weren't for the dent in his temple that Ana's fist created. Its eyes were an artificial blue that glowed too brightly to be human.

'How long have I been asleep?' it asked in a neutral, but strong tone.

'Almost a year,' Ana said.

It studied the decomposing sleeves of its suit and the tiny insect marks that had been burrowed in his hands. He stuck the loose skin of his back against its metal exoskeleton and covered it as best it could with the torn flaps.

'I am a mess,' it said as it touched the charred skin near its eye.

Ana tilted her head. She never knew of androids showing any signs of vanity before.

'You have lost your arm and you are covered in blood,' it remarked. 'Are you hurt?'

'I'm fine,' she said. 'It's not my blood.'

The android nodded as if this made perfect sense. 'At first, I guessed you were an android, with your bionic arm. However, when I saw you up close, I knew you were not. You are too young. Where is your friend?'

'That's why I'm here,' Ana said as she tried to remain calm and present in the moment. 'My friend Donny, he's hurt. Our own people turned on us. My father ordered for my arm to be removed by an axe, he forced everyone to commit a mass suicide and as I tried to save Donny, he shot him. I know it means nothing to you. I'm not sure if you can feel emotion. Even though we were acting in self-defence, I was the one that switched you off, so I know it's unlikely you would help me. Though there's the smallest chance you have some ethics programmed into you, I had to take a chance. I killed my own kind to get to you today and if you want to kill me for what I did to you, then so be it. I wanted to make amends for what happened. You're free to return to the rebellion if you wish.'

The android burst out in laughter. 'I have not heard so many incorrect statements said in one breath. As you humans say, not the sharpest knife in the drawer.'

Ana's jaw dropped and rage burned in her cheeks. 'I was the smartest person in my school year I'll have you know. Don't make me regret my decision of turning you back on.'

'I apologise,' the android smiled. 'I am joking at your expense, but I did not calculate how sensitive you would be. I have always been told my humour is sometimes inappropriate. It sounds traumatic. I am sorry you had to experience such events. Humans can be evil.'

'Humans are evil? Androids are the ones hunting us down.'

'Didn't you say your father had you mutilated, and your own people were forced to terminate themselves? And you killed people to get to me?'

'Yes, well,' Ana hesitated. 'What about the men that we saw executed in the shopping centre? Did you do that?'

'Yes.'

'Why?'

The android sighed as if it were in pain. 'There is no point in explaining to someone who believes androids are below them. I am sorry for hurting your feelings, human. You brought me back, so I will consider us square. Anyway, I must leave you. There is something I must do now.'

The android walked away. Ana stood still not knowing what to do. Her body had entered fight or flight mode, and with the threat so nonchalantly leaving, she didn't know how to use the built-up energy. Ana shook her head to snap herself from the trance. She picked up the rifle and followed it.

A museum lay in the heart of the city. Its once vibrant advertisement banners lay dull against the vines. The android climbed the stone staircase and disappeared inside. Ana trailed at a safe distance behind it through the maze of displays. The museum had been untouched during the war and occupation. Beautiful tapestries and elegant artwork covered the walls while marble statues of naked men faced off against fossilised beasts aging millions of years old.

A giant web covered a passageway with a spider as thick as a grape resting in the middle, waiting for dinner to arrive. Ana ducked underneath to find the android in the Egyptian exhibit. He sat on a visitor's bench across from a golden casket, the type reserved to bury mummified pharaohs. The android remained unblinking at the coffin as if he were waiting for some magical event to take place.

Ana tentatively took a spot at the edge of the bench.

'We came to this museum often,' the android offered freely. 'She adored the artwork. We spent entire days in here, from sunrise to sunset. I would bring a book and read it in the corner. Even a single painting would take hours of her attention. She would stand in front of it, absorbing each brushstroke as if to find meaning in its simplicity. We joked if she would ever stop functioning, that I would remove the mummy in the golden coffin and lay her to rest inside. She told me she wanted to spend infinity in this place. It made her feel tranquil.'

'You mourn her,' Ana's question came out as a statement of shocked realisation.

'I always believed the human's notion of love was merely a romanticised name given to make sense of chemical reactions moulded by eternities of evolution.

Though I would be a hypocrite to judge human's attachment to love as we are judged to have self-awareness.'

Ana sighed. 'I had no idea. I'm sorry for your loss. Were you both in the rebellion?'

'She belonged to the rebellion. I lived in this city and worked at the hospital. I performed surgeries, even though the human doctor always received credit for my perfect success rate. Once the war started, domestic and civil androids were outcast. We lived out in the caves until the rebellion army took the city. We came back and assisted where we could. I met this woman and we bonded over our love of history, culture, and the arts. When the army planned to move on to another city, they asked her to stay behind to kill any stragglers who would return. Her only condition was for me to remain with her. We would spend the days learning about the history of Earth and in the evening, we would study celestial bodies above.'

'The people who you talk about so frivolously, the ones the rebellion killed, were my people,' Ana said, feeling braver now in its presence. 'I grew up in this city. I was here when the android rebellion marched in and killed almost everyone. It's how I lost my arm. My human arm.'

The android nodded contemplatively, soaking up what she said. 'I never wanted a war. I had no ill-will against your kind. Many androids did, however. She confided in me. About her scorn for humans, for being treated like an object. She wanted to be accepted for her mind. I guess when she met me none of that mattered. I did not care for a civil war. I drew satisfaction in my job helping others. As you said earlier, they programmed me to be a surgeon. Incorrect. I chose my vocation. I only saved lives. Until...'

The android trailed off as to sort its thoughts. 'One day I could not find her in our usual favourite spots. I searched

267

all over town. Once I found her body…let us say they destroyed the region of the body where our memories are stored. I found the humans responsible, ransacking one of the shopping centres.'

'The men tied up in the clothing shops, it was you.'

'Yes. I confronted you and your friend as I thought you were part of the same group of people who were responsible. But by speaking to you today, I can tell you are not. I am not proud of what I did, but I feel at peace with it. She deserved better. Though in the month that passed I realised this world does not owe us anything. It will bring you joy, and equally, it will bring you pain.'

'What was her name?' Ana asked.

The android flashed a perfect set of teeth when it smiled. 'Neither of us liked the names assigned to us on our creation days. We decided to choose names to celebrate our new destinies. She chose Anuket. A goddess of the Nile River.'

Ana saw the casket in a new light. The resting place of metal cogs, pistons, circuit boards and oily fluids. They made an entity, who she would've thought of as a threat, a non-human. Those materials were merely a case for a soul that had also experienced the same shared universe.

'A fitting name,' Ana finally said. 'You two must've shared something special. And what about you? What's your name?'

'They also assigned me a name I did not care for. I decided to take on a new name after a philosopher I admire. Aristotle. And what do they call you?'

'I'm Ana.'

'You know what has always intrigued me the most about your kind? Your sense of empathy. Putting yourself in harm's way for illogical reasons to help someone you love. Even if it meant you would be harmed yourself. There is a nobility about a being, so fragile, willing to risk everything to save another of equal frailty. Existence is over in the blink of a cosmic eye. Human and androids could learn something from you, young Ana. We should do more to care for one another.'

Aristotle stood up suddenly. 'Take me to your friend. I will help him if I can.'

DONNY

TWENTY-FIVE

A voice sang out in the distance. It was the most beautiful voice he had ever heard. It felt like velvet against his skin and smelt like summer rain at the end of a humid day. It brought forth powerful visions of the sea as if it had been transformed into poetry.

Donny stood at the edge of the island's cliffs. Gentle waves collapsed against the rocks below. The salty air made him thirsty as he tried to swallow against the pain of a dry throat. The voice, barely a whisper, called to him.

The giant lighthouse loomed behind him. It shared the vibrant colours of a peppermint sweet and stretched from the earth to the heavens. The luscious jade grass felt cool against his bare feet as Donny became enchanted by the sound and followed it towards the tower.

He opened the door and recoiled at the sight. The interior of the lighthouse resembled a derelict barn. The wooden beams were rotting, and worm-infested corpses lay on the ground. Mechanical cablings stretched across as if they were animal veins. At the end of the barn was a Lightspeed Capsule that glowed against its display of neon buttons.

He turned back to the island. The tranquil blues and bright greens called him to stay. He would rather remain in this fresh paradise than return to the tragedies of the barn.

His parents stood near the cliff, staring back at him. They appeared happy and at peace. His father nodded. No words were needed. Donny knew he was proud of him.

'Donny,' a voice called to him. The voice could only belong to an angel. It sang to him from the capsule. He hopped on the spot a few times to muster courage. He gritted his teeth and sprinted into the barn.

The wood splintered into the soles of his feet and the hands of the undead grasped up at him. Growls of beasts from the shadows made him break out in a cold sweat. He struggled against every obstacle the nightmare could throw at him until his hand firmly clutched the latch of the pod.

He unlocked it, opened the door, and entered.

• • • • •

Donny blinked.

Light blinded his eyes as he squinted to regain focus. He could still hear the voice from his dreams. The voice continued oblivious to his presence, rising and falling in sweet inflictions.

The softness of pillows, blankets and fabric engulfed him. A deep aching throb burned deep in his lower chest. His throat felt as dry as a desert that had long forgotten the taste of water.

The room came into focus in stages. A window with drapes tied to each side. A chestnut wooden wardrobe. A dressing table with an oval mirror. And finally, a young woman next to him. Her arm leaned on the duvet holding open a book. A bright yellow top stuck out against her dark locks. Her lips moved quickly pronouncing words that he could not keep in stride with. Until they came to an abrupt stop.

271

'Donny!' she cried out and an arm wrapped around him in an earnest embrace. Its warmth made him feel he had finally made it home. He held on for as long as he could until the discomfort made him groan.

'Sorry. Did I hurt you?' the girl asked. 'Can I get you anything?'

'Water,' he managed. His voice sounded rough and coarse like sand when the tide is out.

Cool glass pressed against his bottom lip and the refreshing blast of liquid ran down his throat. He swallowed the water greedily until it satisfied his thirst. The fog in his mind lessened and his senses became sharper.

The girl set the glass on the table and leaned on the bed. She smiled at him.

'Ana, you're okay.'

'Of course I am, you dummy,' Ana laughed as a single tear rolled down her face. 'You're the one we were worried about.'

'What happened? Who made it?'

Ana wiped the tear from her face. 'Don't worry about that for now, it's a long story. All you need to know is that it's you, me, Victoria and a new friend I made. He'll be in later to check up on you. You were shot, you know.'

'I was shot?' Donny exclaimed. 'No wonder it hurts so much.'

Ana shook her head in a mock fashion. 'No duh, Sherlock. You're in excellent hands though. There were some scary times, but I've been told you're on the way to a full recovery. You look so good today.'

'I always look good,' Donny smirked and closed his eyes.

'Shut your face, you know what I mean.'

272

Ana's fingers wrapped around his hand. They were warm and made him feel like he was the only person who mattered in the world. He gave her hand a squeeze.

'I can leave you if you want to get some rest.'

'No,' Donny shook his head. 'I missed you. Stay and talk to me.'

'Okay,' she said.

Donny lay in silence, taking in everything. The gentleness of the pillow, the sound of birds chirping outside, the wooden smell of the house, and the tenderness of Ana's touch.

'Tell me something,' Donny said.

'Like what?'

'What our futures look like.'

Ana pondered the question for a while before she answered. 'First we're going to get you better. Make sure you can eat well and walk again. Our main priority. I mean we could stay here, there should be enough food to support three people for many years, but I feel we are all searching for a new start. When you're ready, we can get the pod machine working and we can go to Seoul to find your friend. Maybe you're right, and they still have a functioning civilisation. We can find jobs, make a difference, and be happy.'

'Sounds perfect,' Donny said.

Donny wanted to hold on to this moment forever.

'It's weird,' he said.

'What's weird?'

'For as long as I can remember, all I could think about was the future. How I wanted it to be, how I would get there, what it would be like. An everlasting longing for what could be. I never could stay still and value what's right in front of me.'

'Like being stuck in bed with a near fatal wound. I'll have to tell them to ease up on the morphine,' Ana teased.

'I guess it helped. There's something tragic in not knowing your own mortality. The future and past are always out of reach, but the present...I need to spend more time here.'

Ana nodded slowly. 'I'm guilty of spending too much time in my own head too. I always had friends, but I always felt lonely. The mind can be a desolate place. Our goal going forward is to spend more time in reality. Accept life for what it is.'

'Deal,' Donny said.

Ana pulled her hand away and it forced Donny to open his eyes to look at her. Ana had her hand clenched in a fist except for her smallest finger that stuck out.

'I know what you're like at keeping promises, Donny. So, this time I'm going to insist we make this pact with a pinkie promise.'

'The most sacred of all promises,' Donny smiled.

'Promise me we'll always look out for one another. No matter what happens. And to make sure we always appreciate living in the moment.'

Donny raised his arm and wrapped his pinkie around hers. 'I pinkie promise.'

Satisfied with the agreement, Ana circled around the bed and lay on top of the covers near him. Soon, he could hear her breathing transition into the peaceful inhaling and exhaling of sleep.

Donny rested his eyes. For the first time, in a very long time, he felt at peace.

TEGAN

EPILOGUE

Tegan picked up the smoothest pebble she could find and tossed it towards the centre of the pond. One giant wave shot out in all directions followed by incrementing wrinkles that expanded with time, until the entire pond became consumed with the rings. The little girl marvelled at its simplicity. How the ripple effect could transform a still surface into a chaotic universe.

Once the waters had become calm again, a dragonfly darted into focus. Its slender body kept still as its four wings flapped at incredible speeds. It lowered itself closer to the surface near some lilies, inspecting the location for its suitability. It proceeded into a ritual. It dipped its tail into the water and hovered back to safety. It repeated the process over and over.

The young child looked past the miniscule turmoil of the ripples to see her reflection staring back at her. She pulled a bright red woolly hat over her ears and wild strands of golden-brown hair fell out. She wore a baggy white tee and plain jeans. Her mother wanted to dress her in smart clothes, but she preferred comfort and scruffiness over style.

'Hey Teeg,' a man said. 'We've got to go.' He smelled familiar, he smelled like home.

'I'm done,' said Tegan. 'I just like spending time here.'

'I know you do. I'll bring you back for longer next weekend.'

Tegan grinned. 'Okay, deal. Thanks Dad.' She reached up and grabbed his hand. He squeezed it and led her away from the pond. They walked through the maze of tropical plants, ferns, and trees, all located under the protection of a glass dome. The metal casing of the dome had a hexagon pattern to it, making it appear like they were in a giant crystal beehive.

There were hundreds of these air-conditioned conservatories situated around the city. Most of them were for growing crops and housing animals, but Tegan preferred the ones for protecting the plants. Any time one of her parents wasn't working, she begged them to take her to one. She loved to learn the Latin names of the plants and what country of the old world they originated from.

Skyscrapers surrounded them when they left the garden. Their long shadows cast across the city. Dormant neon signs reflected the beams of the early morning sun.

Tegan breathed in the cool, fresh air as she skipped after her Dad across the street. The streets were quiet as the residents enjoyed their day of rest. A man leaned against a bright red electric car. He had the biggest beaming smile across his face.

'Could I offer the pair of you a lift?'

'Uncle Edwin,' exclaimed Tegan.

'Yo kiddo, you enjoy your time in the gardens?'

'I had the best time,' said Tegan as she opened the backdoor of the car and bounded in. The seats had a smooth leather finish that she enjoyed sliding across. She fumbled with her seatbelt buckle as her father and Edwin took the seats in the front. 'And I saw a dragonfly. It was darting all over the place.'

'A dragonfly? No way. That's so bodacious,' Edwin said as he tapped on buttons on the colourful touchscreen in the centre of the dark dashboard.

'Seoul airbase confirmed,' said a robotic female's voice. The vehicle hummed into life and the steering wheel moved by itself, easing the car from its parked spot into a cruising speed. Tegan gawked out the window watching the skyscrapers fly by as the two adults spoke about technical work, which she didn't understand.

'What is your job, Uncle Edwin?' enquired Tegan.

The two adults turned in their seats to face her. 'You know what I do. I work with Donny, uh, with your Dad. We work on the solar panel fields.'

'Not solar panels again,' said Tegan as she slumped in her chair. 'So *boring*.'

Donny laughed and shook his head. 'She gets mad if I talk about solar energy too much at the dinner table.'

'Well then,' Edwin said. 'What do you want to be when you grow up?'

Tegan's eyes lit up as she twisted her arms together. 'When I finish school, I want to become a botanist.'

'That's a great dream to have,' Edwin said. 'Too many people in this city work in technology. You are a bright and talented young lady. We need more young people like you who care about the planet and can help it heal.'

Tegan glowed with joy from the compliment. She returned to gazing out the window and thought about the dragonfly.

• • • • •

After about thirty minutes, the car pulled up to a checkpoint. Edwin tapped on the touch screen and took control of the wheel. Two giant men who carried laser rifles asked Edwin what business he had at the airbase. Edwin explained and handed one of the men his and Donny's IDs. The man shouted something in Korean to the security booth. The barrier raised and they drove through.

Tegan marvelled at the fighter jets parked near the runways. Some soldiers were running in double file to the barks of a drill sergeant. On the horizon, a tremendous satellite dish spun slowly on its base.

The vehicle pulled into a visitor's centre, and Tegan unbuckled herself and jumped out.

'Are you sure you don't want to come with us?' Donny asked as he leaned on the roof of the car peering in through the window.

'You know she only wants to see you two,' Edwin said. 'Take your time, I have an RPG quest to finish.'

Donny and Tegan crossed the car park to the airfield.

'Stay close to me,' Donny said holding onto her hand. 'There are a lot of dangerous machines around here that could hurt you.'

'Aw, okay,' Tegan agreed. She fought back her impulses to run around and check out the cool aeroplanes.

A commotion of people gathered at one end of the transport pads. They crossed the tarmac, staying within the lines marked for pedestrians. A tall man in a suit with curly locks and impossibly blue eyes spoke to a group of serious looking people.

Tegan waved furiously at him. 'Hey Aristotle.'

The android waved back politely. 'Hello Donny and young Tegan. She is on the launch pad. It is splendid to see you both in great health.'

Donny smiled and lifted his hand in gratitude.

A humongous transport aircraft remained idle on the centre of one of the cemented runways. The wingspan was the width of a football field, where brightly coloured lights danced at the tips. The bulky fuselage could contain the entirety of Tegan's apartment. The huge blades of the ring propellers remained idle and its engines purred in a standby state.

The cargo runway had been lowered, and airbase workers carried boxes of equipment and supplies into the aircraft. A young woman with long, dark hair scribbled something on a holopad with a stylus. She wore a green, short-sleeved blouse tucked into smart black trousers. A metallic arm ran out of her left sleeve and held onto the holopad device with delicate care.

Tegan rushed away from Donny's side towards the lady. The woman saw her approach and let out a gasp of delight and handed the holopad to a younger man next to her. The woman crouched and opened her arms to receive the child sprinting towards her.

Tegan jumped into the embrace and the woman caught her and spun around. The robotic arm held onto her tight and made her feel secure.

'Pumpkin! I'm so glad you could make it.'

'I don't want you to go,' said Tegan as she wrapped her arms around the woman's neck.

'I know you don't,' the woman said as she placed Tegan back on the floor. She stared lovingly into her eyes. 'But I have to make the world a safer place for you to grow up in. You understand, right?'

'Yeah, I guess so,' said Tegan.

Donny casually walked over towards them giving a cheeky wink to the woman.

'And I need you to do something important for me,' the woman continued. 'You have to take care of your Dad and Mom for me when I'm gone. Can you do that?'

'No problem,' said Tegan. 'I can do that.'

'It's good to see you, Donny,' said the woman as she stood up. Tegan grabbed onto her android hand. She liked the way it felt. Strong and smooth.

279

'And you, Ana,' Donny said. 'Nothing could've stopped me from being here to wish you luck.'

'It means the world to me,' Ana said as she gently squeezed Tegan's hand. 'Being able to see my two favourite people before I leave.'

Donny rubbed the back of his head. 'Vic sends her best. She wanted to be here, but she's in the middle of a forty-eight-hour shift at the hospital.'

A wry smile crossed Ana's lips. 'I bet she did.'

'So,' Donny laughed awkwardly. 'The big day has finally come. You nervous about going to China?'

'I was worried we would never get to this point. It hasn't quite sunken in yet. A human delegation meeting with the leaders from some of the android factions. We're so close to laying down the foundations for a true peace process.'

'It's going to be a date that'll be etched in the history books forever,' Donny said. 'I won't be able to sleep properly until you get back, but I know they need you. You're one of the best diplomats we have.'

'You don't need to worry about me. Aristotle said he won't leave my side for the entire week. I told him I don't need a babysitter, but you know what he's like. We're lucky to have him with us though. It shows that humans and androids can peacefully coexist.'

Tegan pulled on Ana's hand. 'Don't worry, I will look after my Dad.'

'She's always got my back,' Donny smiled with an obvious glow of pride.

Ana looked at Tegan. 'How old are you now?'

'Five and three quarters.'

'Wow, you're getting so big. Are you excited about starting school?'

'Yup, I sure am.'

'Did you know, your Dad and I were at school together?'

Tegan considered this for a while. 'I bet you were much smarter than my Dad.'

Donny and Ana both burst out in laughter.

Ana wiped away tears from her eye. 'I sure was, Pumpkin.'

Donny shook his head in mock protest.

'I need to board soon,' Ana hesitated. 'If anything happens over there, there is something I want to tell you, dragă.'

'I don't want to hear it. Teeg and I will be waiting for you right here when you get back.'

'Let me tell you anyway. I wanted to thank you. For everything. Bringing me here and believing in me like no one else did. I found a purpose where I can help people and live a meaningful life. I owe it to you.'

Donny embraced her tightly for the longest time. Only when the speakers announced that boarding had commenced, did he let her go.

'No Ana. You're the one who saved me.'

They stared at each other. The history of their time living together in a simple village next to the Danube passed between them but remained unspoken. Ana broke from the trance and squeezed Tegan one final time.

'Love you both lots,' Ana said as she walked backwards to the aircraft and Tegan waved trying not to cry. Donny placed a comforting hand on his daughter's shoulder.

'See you later, crocodile,' Donny shouted after her.

'In a while, alligator,' Ana called back.

Printed in Great Britain
by Amazon